Stamford
And The
Unknown Warrior

Garrett Pearson

Published by Morepork Publishing

Cover Design: More Visual Ltd

PB ISBN: 978-0-473-49331-8
K ISBN: 978-0-473-49334-9

For Graham
My friend and brother in all but name

Author's Note

1066 AD, the year of three major battles in England. Fulford, Stamford Bridge and Hastings, each one resulting in a victory for each of three different nations, Norwegian, Anglo Saxon and Norman.

Fulford, won by Harald Sigurdsson (Hardrada) King of Norway. Stamford Bridge, won by Harold Godwinson, King of England. Hastings or *Santlache Hill*, won by William Duke of Normandy, nominally known as William the Bastard but soon to be William the first of England and eventually, by the thirteenth century known as 'William The Conqueror'.

All three men vied for the throne of England, left vacant by the death of Edward the Confessor who died without leaving an heir or clearly nominating one. Neither of the three men had any real right to the throne by succession or strong blood ties.

Harald Sigurdsson claimed an interest through the former Scandinavian Kings of England: Cnut the Great and his sons, Harthacnut and Harold Harefoot. Harold Godwinson claimed and ascended the throne on the strength of a promise, supposedly given to him by King Edward the Confessor as he lay on his deathbed. William of Normandy claimed a similar promise; allegedly made much earlier to him, also by King Edward. He also claimed an oath of support was given to him, to back his claim for the English throne by Harold Godwinson, when he was a detainee or guest? At William's court in Normandy in 1064 AD.

The invasion by Harald Sigurdsson and his army of approximately nine thousand men was the last great invasion of England by the Viking and heralded the end of the 'Viking age'. The death of Harold Godwinson at Hastings ended the line of Saxon Kings and saw the steady decline of the Saxon people in positions of power in England.

The interesting questions and thoughts from this critical year are; if Harald Sigurdsson had been triumphant, would England have become Norse?

If Harold Godwinson had triumphed, our language and culture may never have changed.

If William of Normandy had not triumphed, the French words in our language and many of the 'noble' families we know today in England would never have been!

Into this momentous time comes my fictional characters: Bjarke and Hakon, foster sons of Eysteinn Orri (A real Norse *Jarl* or Earl and friend of King Harald Sigurdsson) who had no children that I can find evidence of, hence my creation.

Of King Harald's wars in Denmark, not much is known, so I have taken liberties with the places, times and outcomes. The other battles in this book, Fulford, Stamford and Hastings, I have left as history renders them to us, I have but added Bjarke and Hakon and a name or two when needed.

I ask the forbearance of the reader regarding the poem at the end of this tale. The Norse at this time were predominately Christian, the same as their Saxon enemies, so my mention of the old Norse Gods, Thor and Odin is a little whimsical. However, I do believe that in the outlying and more remote areas of Scandinavia and even Saxon England, where the priests and the Christian church did not reach, some worship of the ancient deities would have continued. No doubt, some folk would choose to 'hedge their bets' anyway and pray to both the old Gods and the relatively new Christian God.

I have used some 'old Norse' and Saxon words here and there to add flavour but explained their meaning in English so not to confuse.

I hope you enjoy the book for what it is; a look through ordinary men's eyes at what was an almost unbelievable bloody but short part of English history the outcome of which changed our language, culture and way of life forever.

Garrett Pearson 2019

Part One

The coming of the Bear

Chapter One

The village of Borg, kingdom of Norway, early winter 1043 AD

The night sky was dark as the grave, the clouds obscuring the stars and moon. The small farmhouse on the edge of the woods shuddered as the wind howled and moaned, rattling the wooden roof and driving snow in all directions, bending the trees to its forceful will. This unseasonable and early winter storm had surprised many, bringing snow and cold before the festival of *'Winternight'* or 'All Hallows Eve.'

A woman's cries carried on the wind, disappearing into the frost-hardened trees at the rear of the house. A strip of light showed from a gap in the window shutters, casting a faint yellow glow onto the snow. The door opened wide and a man stumbled out into the wind amidst raised voices, both female and male.

"Out! Out! … Away with you man! Away to the village and ale. This is woman's work; be gone from under my feet, Helka is not the first woman to be with child."

The man cursed beneath his breath, his muttered reply ignored as the door slammed shut behind him. Slipping and unsteady on the snow he shook his head in consternation, thinking to turn about and force the door to his house, instead he lifted his hood, drew his cloak about him and turned down the track towards the lights of the village in the distance.

Back in the house, the elder woman fussed over the younger, making her comfortable and feeling her belly.

"Not long now Helka, the child has turned, it wants to be born."

"My boy, Freyja! My boy wants to be born." Helka's panting became a groan then a scream as a contraction tightened her lower stomach. She closed her eyes in pain and didn't see the concern etched across Freyja's face, the baby was going to be huge.

Eysteinn looked up as the hall door opened, allowing a flurry of snow and the cold wind to blow in.

"Bjarke! Come away in man, you have news? Helka has calved?" He shouted while guffawing, then seeing the unhappiness on Bjarke's face, he probed further, frivolity replaced by concern. "Helka … Helka is fine? The child?"

"So far, Lord, aye. That woman though, Freyja, they should have named her Hel's daughter or Satan's sister."

Eysteinn's face creased in laughter. "So you suffered the old witch's wrath! You're not the first Bjarke and won't be the last, come man, you are better out of the way, enjoy a horn of ale with me, calving is best left to the women."

"Thank you Lord, I but worry, the birthing has been long already."

"God above, Bjarke! You never shrank from the shieldwall nor any fight that I've known you in, worry not about a calving, here, sit by me, drink."

Bjarke managed a smile and accepted the proffered ale horn, taking a chair beside his Lord and friend, Eysteinn Orri.

Helka panted as the contraction stole her breath again and forced more beads of sweat onto her brow.

"I see the crown! Push! Push Helka, the baby is coming." Freyja looked in amazement at the size of the head, visibly stunned, she was too slow to reach for the knife to cut Helka and the lower skin tore. Helka's gasp became a strangled cry as the baby's head forced out. Her lips mouthing a prayer, her eyes tight shut while Freyja encouraged her to push more.

As the baby's body quickly followed the head, Helka let out a long and piercing cry, almost a moan of despair.

Outside, back in the wintered trees, a pair of brown ears twitched.

Freyja just stared at the size of the infant before her. Snapping from her reverie, she pulled gently on the birth cord bringing the afterbirth out along with a copious amount of blood. Slicing the cord quickly, she hefted the baby onto Helka's breasts.

"Your boy Helka! Your boy!"

Helka sighed in relief and wrapped her arms over her baby, her eyes wide when she saw the size of her son.

Freyja worked quickly, hooking a finger into the baby's mouth and clearing away mucus then scooping the afterbirth into a bowl and trying to staunch the copious blood flow from between Helka's legs.

"He is whole?" Helka gasped. "No imperfections?"

"He is fine and well, now shush!"

Freyja felt the first fingers of fear in her spine as she looked at the blood soaked rags; the blood flow was not easing. Dashing back to the small kitchen and the bubbling water pot containing more clean cloths, she took the bowl containing the afterbirth with her. In her haste, some blood and mucus slopped from the overfilled bowl as she hurried to the door, she deposited it roughly by the outside step, thinking to burn it later.

In the trees, a black snout twitched then sniffed the wind.

Freyja returned with the cloths, exchanging them for the blood-sodden ones. The baby bawled as she wrapped him against the chill, silencing him only when he was offered to Helka's breast.

"He's hungry, Freyja." Helka's voice was already quieter.

"A good sign, now shush, save your strength."

With little sign of the blood flow slowing, Freyja began to panic. She wished she hadn't banished Bjarke to the village and neglected to bring her young slave girl with her. Calling on God to help, she rubbed the silver crucifix at her neck then kissed it; despite her Christian beliefs, she ran to her travelling bag and fished out an effigy of her namesake, the Goddess Freyja. Coming from a family of healers and originally from a remote village further north, where the 'old religion' still held some sway, they and many like her sought help from more than one deity.

"Freyja, Goddess! Help me save this …"

Suddenly the door burst open, banging hard against the wall and sagging onto one hinge. A rush of cold air and snow blew in as a brown bear pushed into the house, afterbirth and blood running from its mouth. Freyja screamed and the bear roared, rearing onto its hind legs and pushing further into the house. Freyja ran into the bedchamber urging Helka up. The bear followed, sniffing its way along the blood trail left from the spilling bowl. Seeing Helka was too slow to rise and less able to run, Freyja took flight and ran out of the back door screaming.

Weak from loss of blood but understanding the need to fight or flee, Helka slipped her baby to one side, snatched Freyja's knife from the bed and stood to face the bear.

A swipe from a huge paw felled her, snapping her neck like a twig, the claws opening her face to the bone. The bear roared; the baby cried in hunger and in the distance, Freyja's screams carried on the wind.

Freyja's screams were heard in the village long before anyone saw her. Anxious heads poked out of doors and someone ran to the hall seeking Eysteinn and his warriors. By the time Freyja arrived in the village, men were exiting the hall with axes, spears and swords. Eysteinn grasped Freyja by the shoulders.

"Christ God, woman! What is it? What have you seen?" He looked over her shoulder into the darkness but other than his people gathering about him, he could see nothing. His warriors looked about, hefting their weapons and expecting an attack but also saw and heard nothing except snow and wind. "Christ Almighty, Freya! What is it?" He shook her hard as she gabbled incoherently. He slapped her face and she seemed to return to sanity.

"A bear! A bear!"

"What? Where? Talk sense woman." He shook her again.

"A bear! A bear in the house!"

Bjarke set off at a run towards his house.

"Spears, javelins, torches now! To Bjarke's house." Eysteinn bawled then set off after Bjarke.

Breathless from the long run and combating snow and wind, the men arrived at the farmhouse. Eysteinn seized Bjarke by the shoulder holding him back from entering. Bjarke shook him loose but Eysteinn grabbed him again.

"Think man! Think! I know it's your woman but it won't help if you go in there and the bear kills you. Ask yourself; is she in there? Has she escaped? We'll hunt this bear down and find Helka but we will do it properly. Brynjar! Find us this bear."

Brynjar moved cautiously forward stepping around the paw marks and footprints in the snow; he lifted his torch high then squatted down looking closer.

"The bear has gone Lord, back towards the woods, it's taken …"

"What in Christ's name is a bear doing here, why is it not asleep in its cave?"

"The autumn has been dry and warm Lord, this snow as you know has come strangely early and sudden, the beast was not ready to sleep."

Bjarke pushed forward into the house, Eysteinn signalled for others to follow.

"The bear is injured Lord, see, it trails a front leg." Brynjar pointed to regular scrapes in the snow. "Methinks perhaps it cannot hunt well and is hungry, desperate even, maybe that is why it came to the house." He shook his head, his face grave as he looked up. "It's taken Helka, Lord, see how the prints deepen as they head away."

Bjarke exited the house carrying a hefty bundle in a blanket, his expression distraught. Eysteinn stepped closer and peered into the blanket. Amidst splashes of blood, a baby looked back at him.

"Take the child to the hall Bjarke, we will find Helka and this bear and kill it."

"No Lord, the beast has taken my woman, vengeance is mine by right."

"You're angry Bjarke, this is not the time, take the child!"

"Lord I beg you, it's taken my Helka."

"And if it kills you, your child is an orphan." Eysteinn looked at Bjarke and pretended not to see the tears. He sighed resignedly. "Very well! Elof, take the child back to the hall. Brynjar, lead on."

The tracks proved easy to follow despite the still falling snow, blood splashes and droplets marking the way. As they entered the forest however and the trees thickened, the snow faded slowing the tracking process, Brynjar casting the torch about seeking tracks or blood splashes amongst the leaves. Moving much slower now, thy followed the tracks for most of the night, losing then picking up the trail. Just as dawn paled the sky, they came to where the trees gave way to a rising, rocky bluff. Moss covered boulders of all sizes stood out from the ground, marching their way up the hill towards a small plateau, at the back of which the dark mouth of a cave led into the hillside.

"Brynjar, go see if our beast lies yonder, Bjarke, stay here … I command it!"

Brynjar began threading his way upwards through the rocks. He disappeared from view over the plateau lip then reappeared a moment later beckoning them on. The men moved silently upwards, Eysteinn forcibly pushing Bjarke behind him. On the plateau, the trees were small and stunted and the snow had filtered through, the paw prints once more clear, Brynjar pointed into the cave.

The men tentatively approached the cave mouth, a smell of dampness and decay assailed their nostrils.

"It's sheltering in there, Lord."

"It's den?"

"Perhaps Lord, though usually bears dens are dry, this cave is damp."

"Are you sure this is the right place?"

Brynjar turned Eysteinn away from Bjarke and opened his hand showing the remains of a broken amber-bead necklace. Eysteinn nodded.

The men slipped into the cave then cast torches deep into the blackness, the clatter echoing slightly and giving a weak light that flickered and danced on the walls. A long roar answered, echoing loud and terrible in the cavern, followed by the thumping of heavy feet on the earth floor. Men raised spears and braced themselves, holding torches aloft as the roaring and thumping tread came closer. Out of the darkness a huge brown bear appeared, lips curled back showing long yellow fangs. Seeing the flaring torches, it hesitated momentarily then reared onto its hind legs. Eysteinn was distracted trying to organise his men and Bjarke pushed past him, his spear lowered and roaring like a bull.

"Bjarke, get back!"

Bjarke was already in front of the bear, blocking any javelin throws from his fellow warriors and thrusting upwards with his spear. He ducked quickly as a huge paw swept towards his head. Eysteinn, taking his chance hurled a javelin over Bjarke's head striking the bear in the shoulder. As the bear stalled, Bjarke powered up, thrusting his spear into the bear's chest then stepped back pulling it clear. The animal roared in agony, its head turning quickly, saliva flying from its jaws, watching as the men tried to surround it. Eysteinn's javelin dropped from its shoulder, however the wounds from it and Bjarke's spear were deep and blood sloshed down the brown coat. The bear was badly hurt and began edging backwards, deeper into the cave, roaring and snarling as it retreated, the men pressing forward, their spears probing, torches illuminating the darkest reaches. It was then that Bjarke saw the pale, naked, half-devoured body of Helka.

Anger overflowing and reason gone, he screamed his challenge and charged the bear.

"Bjarke, no!" Eysteinn bellowed.

The spear drove blade deep into the bear's chest again, this time finding its heart. The bear seemed to shudder, emitting a low growl from its maw; Bjarke was still pushing on the shaft with hate-fuelled force and didn't see the massive paw that ripped his face away.

He was flung across the floor with the force, his body hitting the rock wall. The bear, already dying, staggered as four javelins thudded into its chest and it collapsed back onto all fours, snapping the wooden shafts and emitting a low growl, Eysteinn finished it with a chop to the neck with an axe.

"Bjarke! … Bjarke!" Eysteinn knelt alongside his friend. Bjarke moaned softly and lay still, one side of his head was caved in, grey-pink jelly oozing out. His jaw smashed loose from his skull, his cheek and eye socket a mangled red pulp.

****

Eysteinn sat in his chair, ale horn in hand, the other stroking his plaited beard, deep in thought.

"Inger! … Inger, bring me Helka's child and young, Hakon."

Inger appeared with the baby while shepherding a little boy Hakon, in front of her.

"Come Hakon; greet your new foster brother." Eysteinn pulled Inger and Hakon in close, ruffling the boy's hair in rough affection, then accepted the baby into his arms.

The baby was huge, over double the size of a normal child. He pushed his finger into the baby's hand and felt a grip, a strong grip. He smiled as the little one snuffled and looked back.

"So little one, how you are here and not bear food I don't know. A hard start for one not yet a day old and an orphan already. You are my friend's child; I mourn the loss of him and your mother, good folk both. Thus, little man." He smirked at the thought of little. "We will raise you; you will become our child, my second foster son. This is your mother, Inger". Inger pushed her long hair back from her face smiling at the babe. "And this is your older brother, Hakon."

"What will you name him, Lord?" Inger asked.

"I will name him for his father, Bjarke and for our family, he is Bjarke Orrifostersson."

Inger gave a small shiver, a grimace clouding her fine features. "Bjarke means bear, does it not?"

"Aye girl, it does, It's fitting don't you think? A bear has orphaned him but Christ God knows; he is going to be as big as a bear when he's grown."

Eysteinn reached into his pouch and pulled out a still bloodied bear claw and a long yellow fang then tucked both in the blanket alongside the baby.

"Welcome to the world and your family, Bjarke Orrifostersson. May the strength of the bear be yours throughout your life? Live long and prosper."

He produced another tooth and claw, each already cleaned, polished and threaded to a leather cord and slipped them into Hakon's hand.

Handing Bjarke to Inger, he pulled Hakon closer, having the boy lift his long brown hair from his shoulders while he fastened the cords about his neck.

"Hakon, son, you and Bjarke are brothers, brothers by tooth and claw." He smiled at Hakon. "My boys!"

Inger cleared her throat loudly. Eysteinn threw back his head and laughed loudly. "Christ on the cross woman! Our boys! Our boys!"

Chapter Two

The Forest, Borg 1053 AD

The small deer lifted its head and sniffed the breeze, then took off at a steady trot across the meadow slipping into the trees at the edge of the forest. The two boys laid in the long grass looked at one another.

"The winds changed, it's smelled us." Hakon grumbled and Bjarke smiled. "Come on, we need to move downwind from it."

"We will have a better chance in the forest anyway." Bjarke added.

"We will if you can be quiet, those big feet of yours are bound to step on something."

Bjarke pulled a face and punched Hakon playfully. The pair rose and moved position, heading towards the forest but well downwind from where the deer had entered.

Slipping into the gloom, Hakon seemed to glide quietly and effortlessly over the ground, Bjarke at pains to move quietly, the pair unslinging bows from their shoulders and laying arrows on the string as they went. Hakon signalled a halt and cupped his ear then pointed to his eyes, indicating they should listen and watch. All was quiet, with nothing to see in the distant trees. Hakon signalled Bjarke off to one side, he also swinging away in an arc. The forest was not too dense in these lower reaches, being populated with deciduous trees rather than the firs and pines of higher up, the shade and coolness however, drying the sweat on the boy's bodies. The breeze almost held at bay compared to the openness of the meadow.

Swinging in a wide circle and slipping noiselessly through the trees, the boys managed to keep eye contact with each other, Hakon ahead of Bjarke.

Coming to a wide clearing, Hakon saw the deer on the other side, pulling at some low hanging branches and munching leaves. He looked back at Bjarke and raised his hand above his head spreading his fingers like antlers, he signalled Bjarke to stay where he was.

Stepping back behind a beech trunk, he adjusted the grip on his bow then peered round it, easing the bowstring back to his lips, eyeing his target.

A twig snapped and the deer ceased its feeding. It looked around quickly, ears twitching and nose sniffing. Hakon slipped back behind the trunk and glared at Bjarke, who had stopped initially but moved since Hakon had stepped forward to take his shot.

"Stand still!" Hakon mouthed silently, his face flushed in anger and mouth twisted.

Bjarke nodded, looking remorseful.

The deer, hearing and smelling nothing further, returned to feeding but took only small nibbles, turning constantly to look around. Hakon watched and waited, wanting the deer to settle and turn flank side onto him.

Time passed and the deer seemed to relax more, the boys watching from behind the trunks. The deer walked a few paces to another tree and pulled again at the low hanging leaves. Hakon took the tension up on the bow, once more eyeing his target. Behind him, Bjarke readied his bow for a second shot should Hakon's miss. His bow creaked slightly as he took up the tension. The deer stretched its neck and raised its head, its ears turning trying to place the sound. Suddenly it bounded off into the trees. The boys eased the bows to rest and Bjarke made his way to Hakon, who glared at him, his face like a thundercloud.

"Christ God, Bjarke! Can you not be still? Not be quiet?"

"The bow creaked, it wasn't my doing." He beseeched.

"If you had a smaller bow instead of that great thing it would be better." Hakon slapped the horn reinforcing and glued binding on Bjarke's bow stave.

"But I broke my last two, father had this made for me, it works well."

"Aye! Very well, as a deer frightening tool."

Bjarke dropped his head. "I'm sorry!"

"Come on, I don't think it will have gone too far. It heard us but hasn't smelled us this time. Quietly though! If you know what that is." Hakon smiled, it was hard to be angry with his brother, Bjarke smiled back and fell in behind him as they pushed deeper into the forest.

It was well into the afternoon when the pair caught up with the deer again, it had moved higher up the hill, the climb punishing the boy's lungs and forcing sweat from their pores despite the coolness of the forest. As before, Hakon was ahead of Bjarke, the larger boy slower, at pains not to make more noise and suffer his brother's ire. The deer slipped from sight again and the boys climbed on hoping for a clear shot. Hakon suddenly stopped and turned back, his hand halting Bjarke but his face lit with excitement. Easing the bow down, he held both hands to his head splaying his fingers wide and mouthing. "Huge stag!"

Bjarke smiled and nodded back, this time staying where he was. Unable to see the stag, he watched Hakon as he lifted then lowered his bow, the stag obviously moving in and out of bowshot. After what seemed like an eternity, Hakon lifted the bow again, pulling the arrow to full length, the string touching his ear, a longer shot thought Bjarke. Hakon lowered the bow again, grimacing but still watching the stag. Bjarke was desperate to move, to come alongside his brother and see the huge beast. Hakon, as if sensing his brother's thoughts and without looking back, held up a halting hand. Bjarke could hardly breathe now he was so excited. Hakon lifted the bow again and stepped around the tree trunk. The bow came to full draw, quickly this time. The arrow flew with just a light twang from the bowstring followed by a whoosh of wind over feathers. There was a pained call from the trees and Hakon raised the bow crying, "Yes!"

A moment later, he was gone from the tree, his footsteps loud over the forest floor as twigs broke and old leaves rustled beneath his boots. Bjarke followed on, reaching the place Hakon had been, he saw his brother racing towards the stag as it staggered in a tight circle then sank to its front knees emitting a low, pained bellow.

Hakon drew his seax as he ran, eager to finish the stag and claim his prize, the animal on its belly now and panting, the arrow lodged deep in its side just behind the front shoulder. Bjarke was also closing quickly, his long legs eating the distance, his heart beating fast in excitement. Reaching the stag Hakon stood quite in awe looking at the size of its antlers and head, which had sunk to the earth, its eyes flickering then closing. He stepped in close, seizing the antlers and lifting the head up grunting with the effort, his seax in hand, stooping, he sought its throat. Suddenly, the stag twitched and struggled to its feet, its head coming up last, as if the weight of it was too much. The antlers pulled from Hakon's hand. Determined not to lose his prize he stepped closer trying to sink the seax into the animal's chest. Instead, the bottom point of the antlers hooked in Hakon's belt and it lifted him from his feet.

"Bjarke!" Hakon shouted in shock as the stag, as surprised as its human load, tried to run while shaking its head.

Hakon was thrown from side to side as the animal tossed its head but remained held fast by his belt. His seax flew from his hand after which he tried to hold onto the antlers with both hands.

"Bjarke! … Bjarke! Help me …"

Bjarke sprinted the last few paces, coming alongside the stag as it struggled along with its human cargo, the weight pulling its head down. He roared in shock and fear as he threw himself at the stag, his hands encircling the stag's neck. His added weight pulled the stag off balance and boys and animal hit the floor in a gout of leaves, dust, grunts and a bellow from the stag. Bjarke was winded as the stag's neck and forequarters came down on top of him. Hakon yelped as the upper antlers raked down his chest, then fell backwards clear of the stag's head as the antler point came clear of his belt. Bjarke was still hugging the animal's neck and grunting from the weight as the animal thrashed. Hakon struggled to his feet and grabbed for his seax, finding the empty sheath, he remembered he had dropped it when the stag had taken off with him. Running around the animal to

Bjarke, he tugged the seax from his brother's belt and stepped back to the animal's head, plunging the blade deep into the heavily maned throat, working it side to side in desperation to kill it. A moment later, it was over, the stag let out a long sigh as blood fountained from its neck and it ceased its thrashing. Hakon dropped the seax and seized Bjarke, whose head was still held in close to the stag's, his arms tight about its neck.

"Bjarke, Bjarke! Are you alright?" His voice unsteady with shock as he shook his brother.

Bjarke slowly let go of the stag's neck and rolled onto his back, coughing and gasping for breath.

"Yes … I think so." He managed between gasps.

Hakon flopped down alongside him holding his chest, the pair looking in wonder at each other and then at the stag.

"Thank you … thank you, brother! I thought that was the end of me." Hakon said as he rubbed his chest and winced in pain as his hand touched tender flesh.

Hakon removed his shirt, his chest and stomach scraped and cut with some purple bruising already showing but no sign of a piecing wound, Bjarke started to laugh. Hakon grinned and broke into laughter himself then laid down alongside his brother, the pair shaking with mirth and awe. They lay for some time, catching their breath and recovering from the shock of it all.

It was the buzzing flies that drew them from their apathy. Hakon pulled himself to his feet, groaning as his injuries made themselves known; he offered his hand to Bjarke, his brother taking it as he started to get up. As the weight come on, Hakon wrapped his other hand on Bjarke's arm and heaved. He groaned with the effort.

Hakon cut through the deer's neck muscle and between the pair of them, they managed to snap the spine and claim the head and antler rack, the boys counting the points and becoming excited again, when they numbered twelve. Collecting their bows and seaxs, they prepared to load themselves with the stag. The beast was huge, the size of a heifer and beyond even Bjarke's strength to carry more than the butchered hindquarters across his back. Hakon heaved the head up, piggybacking it and holding it by its antlers, the pair setting off for their long walk home.

The pair reached the village as the sun was setting, catching some appraising looks at the stag's head and meat-heavy hindquarters. Reaching the hall they saw Inger waiting at the top of the steps, her arms folded, she glared as they smiled and called a greeting.

"Now we're going to catch it." Hakon muttered. "She isn't happy."

The boys were half way up the steps when Inger's anger broke.

"Where in God's name have you been?"

"Hunting, mother." Hakon replied, a little too flippantly.

"Put the head down." Inger replied quietly, seeming affable. However, the moment the head touched the floor, she slapped Hakon about the head repeatedly.

"Do I look stupid?" She shouted. "Do I?" She had to stop as the effort of hitting Hakon stole her breath, her long blonde hair falling in disarray from its binding.

Hakon managed to slip out from the beating and bolted into the hall. She turned on Bjarke, he deigning not to put his load down. Undeterred, she slapped him about the head until he dropped the meat and ran, her calls ringing in their ears.

"What time of day do you call this? … I've been worried sick! You had better both be in one piece or I will give you such a hiding!"

Eventually both boys were inspected and any hurts sorted, Inger still giving the odd slap as she saw fit. At supper however, the boys were lauded for their prowess in bringing down the stag and some wonderment expressed at the load Bjarke had carried for a boy of only ten years. Inger sat back quietly thanking God for keeping her boys safe, her reckless, strong, brave boys. Eysteinn, in his element with the pride of it all.

Chapter Three

Borg 1055 AD

"Eysteinn! … Eysteinn, where are the boys?"

"They are long gone Inger, they left at first light."

"Hunting again?" Inger's voice rose in anger.

"Aye, I suppose. The dogs are gone."

"And you didn't try to stop them! Christ God, Eysteinn they are too young to be hunting alone!"

"Hush woman! We are raising men."

Inger's eyes flashed at the rebuke. "Those damned dogs, I wished you'd never bought them, they and the boys run wild!"

Eysteinn chuckled into his beard.

"You encourage them!"

"How so?" He held up his hands in a hapless gesture, feigning dismay.

"The dogs! Those antler handled seaxs you had made for each of them …"

"It was from the boys stag Inger, their prize, it was their idea! Nothing to do with me."

"And you just went along with it! Did as you were bidden, Eysteinn Orri, a Norse Lord and commander of men, I don't think so!"

Eysteinn turned away, hiding a smirk.

"They're reckless; the pair of them! Hakon is the worst."

"They'll be alright girl! Bjarke is big enough to look after Hakon, he will steady him."

The noise of a dish being picked up had Eysteinn duck, the dish flying over his head to smash against the wall.

"Bjarke is only twelve, in case you've forgotten! He does everything Hakon tells him to do." Inger bawled. "Send Elof and Brynjar to find our sons and bring them home … now!" Another dish crashed against the wall as Eysteinn slipped out the door closing it quickly behind him. Stepping into the street, he roared with laughter while bellowing for Elof and Brynjar. She was a fine wife Inger, a beautiful woman, a good woman and a good mother to their foster sons and fierce with it. How he loved her.

Deep in the forest, all was peaceful; an occasional creak came from a tree bough moving with its canopy in the breeze. Dust particles danced in the blades of sunlight while high above, some pigeons cooed softly from their roost. Hakon beckoned Bjarke forward and to bring the dogs on quietly. At sixteen, Hakon was thickening in the body and growing tall but dwarfed by his twelve-year-old sibling who stood a head taller, his arms and chest thicker and larger. Hakon held his finger over his lips then grimaced as Bjarke's foot snapped a twig. He looked to the boar that was rooting in the clearing; the boar was already looking up, its ears twitching and snout sniffing the air. The two elkhounds were also sniffing and straining at the leash, throwing their heads trying to escape the muzzles. Hakon grabbed for his dog's leash.

"Damn it Bjarke make more noise why don't you."
He hissed … "Quickly, un-muzzle Fenrir, the boar's
heard us and is going to run."

Bjarke fumbled with his dog's muzzle while Hakon
already had his dog, Garmr, un-muzzled and loose.
Garmr took off at a loping run that became full speed
after the boar, which had already exited the clearing.

"Come on! Come on! For the love of God man,
hurry!" Hakon chided. "That boar is huge! It needs both
dogs and us to bring it down!"

Bjarke fumbled on.

"Christ man! Give it here!" Hakon deftly unclipped
the buckles of the muzzle and slipped the leash. Fenrir
leapt forward, chasing after Garmr and the boar, the boys
erupting out of the undergrowth leaping over fallen
branches and running full speed after the animals,
howling like fiends with excitement.

The dogs were barking now some way ahead of the
pair and lost in the trees, the boys almost breathless as
they crashed through the undergrowth and old leaves,
following the noise of dogs and boar. The noise changed
to a sharp yelp then snarling and the sounds of fighting
but one dog barked on.

"Oh no! There's only one dog on the boar!" Hakon
managed between gasps. As the sounds of fighting mixed
with barks of frustration, the boys sought more speed.
One dog was lost!

Coming to another clearing, they saw Fenrir on the
other side barking and chasing a smaller and very agile
young boar in and out of the trees. The sounds of
fighting came from deeper within the forest.

"Fenrir! Heel, now!" Bjarke yelled.

The dog ignored him and carried on chasing the
young boar. Hakon ran on across the clearing and into

the forest again, towards the sound of the fight, Bjarke chased his dog, calling it back.

"Come on!" Hakon called, his voice echoing back from deep in the trees.

Fenrir nipped the young boar's hind leg, tripping it and the pig rolled in the dirt. It swung its head around to bite the dog but was too slow, Fenrir seizing it by the ear. Bjarke drew his seax as he ran. A moment later, he was alongside the wheeling, snarling animals; leaves, twigs and dirt flying. Seizing the pig by the other ear, he stabbed at it seeking its heart. The pig and the dog spun around as they fought and Bjarke's seax stuck in the thick, hide-shield covering the rear of the pig's head and shoulders and the blade glanced away. Stepping across for another try and almost tripping over the twisting animals, Bjarke managed to stab behind and below the front leg and the pig went down. Fenrir changed his grip from ear to throat and Bjarke stabbed again twice, the young boar gasped, twitched and then lay still, the dog still savaging it.

Bjarke seized Fenrir by the collar and pulled him away, the dog yelping from the force. He pulled it a few paces in the direction Hakon had gone, Fenrir seemed to understand and bounded off into the trees towards the sounds of fighting. Bjarke followed, leaping over the scrub, desperate to catch up with Hakon, the squeals snarls and barking sounding closer and closer.

Running as hard as he could, Bjarke didn't see the ground falling sharply away beneath the fern carpet and tumbled headlong down a steep bank, crashing and rolling through bracken, ferns and small trees. As he regained his feet, he saw the large boar and Garmr spinning around about, locked in a death struggle, the boar trying to gore and the dog trying to hold or bite,

Hakon was trying to intervene to stab. The boar was huge and Garmr was losing the fight, with just one dog on it, the pig was at bay but could move without fear of an attack from behind. Both pig and dog were bleeding copiously. Fenrir was still weaving his way down the bank to help when the boar lunged and caught Garmr in the chest with its tusk. The dog yelped horribly and backed off, the boar; full of battle rage followed and gored Garmr again, the tusk lodging deep in the flesh as the pig shook and savaged the dog.

"No ooo!" Hakon cried and pushed into stab the boar.

"Hakon, no!"

The boar flung Garmr to one side like a broken doll and slashed its massive head and tusks at Hakon. Hakon sidestepped and stabbed his blade into the boar's flank. The boar's head snapped back around and the tusk hooked into Hakon's calf, tearing muscle and skin and knocking him off his feet. Hakon yelped in pain and the boar turned, ready to gore and bite the fallen boy.

"Hakon!" Bjarke cried and hurled himself onto the boar's back, his seax stabbing repeatedly.

A moment later Fenrir joined the fight and took hold of the boar's ear, hanging on grimly as the boar shook its head.

Boy, boar and dog went down in a tangle of limbs, snapping teeth, grunts and snarls.

Bjarke stabbed again and again, bright blood spurting in gouts, the boar finally sinking onto its knees and gasping as its life force gave out.

Garmr whimpered and gasped then lay still. Hakon rolled on the ground, swearing and holding his leg; Fenrir panted and sniffed at Garmr and whined. Bjarke struggled to his feet, his face and shirt spotted and wet with pig blood, his hand and seax covered in it. Badly shaken, he stumbled and fell to one knee.

"Hakon! Hakon! …"

"My leg! My bloody leg! Christ God …"

"Let me see! Let me see!"

"Where were you? Where was bloody Fenrir! … Shit, it hurts!"

"Shush, let me see, let me see!"

Hakon moved his hand and a rush of blood, stark and red against the light brown of the fallen leaves ran out from a long, deep gash in his calf, his trousers already heavily stained.

Bjarke gasped at the sight and ripped the sleeve from his shirt, tying it tight around the leg closing the wound.

"Come on, we need to go home!"

"How in Christ's name am I supposed to do that, you idiot!"

Bjarke bent down and made to scoop Hakon up in his arms. "Put your arm around my neck."

Looking up, Hakon took fright at the blood splattered all over Bjarke's face and shirt and forgot his anger. "Christ! Bjarke, are you hurt?"

"No brother, don't worry it's the boar's blood not mine." Bjarke reached under Hakon's back and legs and lifted him, shuffling him to settle his grip.

Hakon was shocked at the ease in which Bjarke lifted him, he knew his brother was abnormally big but he hadn't realised how strong.

"You'll never carry me all that way, we are miles from home!"

Bjarke was already striding up the bank, Fenrir following at his heel, Garmr and the boar dead where they lay.

They were almost half way home and Bjarke's arms felt like lead. He had been forced to stop more than once to renew his grip on Hakon but had refused to rest or put him down; he kept on walking. As they cleared the forest's edge onto the meadow hill, Fenrir barked and sniffed the wind; Bjarke heard shouts in the distance and recognised his and Hakon's names being called.

"Over here! … Here!" He shouted. His head rang with the shouting, he was weary and his throat was parched. He turned towards the shouts and took off towards them at a steady ambling gait. He saw Elof and Brynjar before they saw him and he shouted again. The men looked up, seeing the body in Bjarke's arms they started towards him at the run. Panting from the uphill climb, the pair closed on the boys, questions and anger overflowing in a jumble of words.

Bjarke just sank to his knees, his brother still held close. The men ceased their questioning and took Hakon from him, Elof checking the wound and Brynjar checking Bjarke. Elof added a tourniquet above the bandage then the group turned for home, the men taking it in turns to carry Hakon. The blood flow had stopped but the wound was deep and going by the staining on his trousers and boots the boy had lost a fair amount of blood. With the men taking over, Bjarke began to shake, the shock of it all bringing tears.

"It's my fault, all my fault; I chased Fenrir instead of following Garmr and Hakon. Will Hakon be alright?"

"He'll be fine, lad. The wound needs stitching and care but he'll survive. How far have you carried him?"

"I don't know. Garmr and the boar are still back in the woods somewhere, at the bottom of a steep hill, that's where it happened."

Brynjar slipped his arm over Bjarke's shoulder. "You did well lad! The wound was bound tight … and to carry him … we don't know how you managed it?"

"He's my brother."

"You're a bloody idiot!" Hakon grumbled from Elof's arms.

"You should have waited!"

"You're too bloody slow!"

The men smiled, these two were brothers all right.

As the small group arrived back at the hall, hell broke loose. Inger rapping out commands to servants for more bandages, water and wound dressing materials while shooing the dog, fretting and haranguing the boys and snapping at Eysteinn and the two men.

"God's bones, woman! They're alright; they are not dead or dying!" Eysteinn grumbled as the door slammed shut to their private quarters.

"No thanks to you and those damned dogs."

Knowing he would lose the war of words, Eysteinn said nothing. After ensuring the boys were being treated and comfortable, he headed back into the hall and sought Elof and Brynjar.

"Where did you find them?"

"At the top of the hill at the far end of the hay meadow, Lord. They were just coming out of the forest."

"The other dog?"

"Back in the forest somewhere, dead, Lord. Bjarke said it and the boar they had killed were still in there, at the bottom of a steep hill."

"Do you know the place?"

Brynjar scratched at his beard. "Aye Lord, there is a steep hill on the other side of the forest but it's a long way from where we found the boys."

"The pair of you, saddle two horses and go and take a look now. Bury the dog and bring the boar home if it is decent.

"Yes Lord."

"Don't bring it in sight of Inger." He winked at both men.

"No Lord."

In the hall, Inger and two serving women began treating the boys who were now busy arguing and shouting at one another.

"It's your fault Bjarke; you're too slow … aye and too damn clumsy!"

"You should have waited, it wasn't my fault Fenrir chased the young boar!"

"That's enough!" Inger snapped. The boys however were in full flow of anger and carried on.

"Garmr is dead now; he's dead because you're slow and Fenrir is stupid!"

"I'm sorry about Garmr, Hakon but it isn't my fault, I will give you Fenrir to make it up!"

"Fenrir is bloody stupid!"

"Don't say that! …"

"You're bloody stupid!"

Inger slapped both boys hard across their faces stopping the argument. "Enough!" She growled before hugging each in turn.

"You're home and safe, it's enough!"

Inger had pulled off Hakon's boots and cut away his trousers, and was washing the wound. Hakon flinched as the hot water touched raw flesh and looked as if he was ready to complain when the servant produced a bone needle and gut thread but was silenced by a steely look from Inger. The other servant hauled Bjarke's shirt over his head, his chest was covered in small cuts and a plethora of bruises and he too winced but remained silent as the wounds were washed.

It took Hakon a while to recover from the gash in his calf; initially he'd blamed Bjarke for it, more so when he had to wait for it to heal as it curtailed hunting and slowed his entrance to warrior training, Bjarke having to amuse himself. However, when Bjarke appeared a few days after the accident with the boar's tusks, drilled and polished, ready to add to their necklaces, Hakon soon forgot his anger.

"How did you get those?" He asked, his eyes lighting up as he rubbed the large, curved hook of smooth ivory.

"From Brynjar, he and Elof brought our boar home. Father had the tusks polished and drilled but isn't admitting to it, if mother finds out there will be a swearing all round." He smirked.

"That tusk is the one that hurt you; Brynjar says that by us killing the animal and taking the tusks we inherit the beast's strength and spirit."

Hakon looked bemused. "What?"

"Brynjar says its hunting lore from the old religion Hakon, from Ullr, the God of hunting."

"Christ God, Bjarke, don't mention that to mother, you know how pious she is about God and us being Christians. Hide it for me, there in my wooden chest, until I am up and about and can wear it under my shirt."

With only one dog, boar hunting was not possible and Bjarke was confined to hare coursing and deer stalking but missing his brother he had taken little pleasure from it. When Hakon did recover, they hunted a few times together but without the same fervour of before,

Hakon's thoughts and energies being channelled into warrior training, weapon skills and practice for battle.

Chapter Four

Borg, midsummer 1057 AD

"No Bjarke, It's not that I don't want to hunt. I cannot. I have weapons training again, more sword work."

"Come on! They won't miss you; father is at court seeing the King. We can be away before they know you are gone!"

"If Sigurd sees I'm missing he'll kick my arse! Then, he'll tell father and I'll get another thumping. Anyway, if father is seeing the King, it means trouble in the wind, probably more fighting with Denmark. King Harald is determined to have the Danish throne as well as the Norwegian one."

"So?"

"Which means I will have to fight if it comes to that."

"So?" Bjarke looked questioningly at his brother.

"Christ God, brother! I am eighteen years old, well of an age to fight and if I have to fight warriors of Sigurd's experience I need all the practice I can get. The Danes are not milksops you know!"

Bjarke looked uninterested and downcast. "We haven't hunted together for a long time, Hakon."

"I know! I'm sorry but I think our hunting trips will

be fewer now, I am no longer a child, time is not my own anymore, I have responsibilities."

"You're still angry with me over Garmr and your leg, you blame me!"

"No brother, I'm not angry and I don't blame you. That was a long time ago and yes, I was angry at the time, as it stopped our hunting and prevented me starting my warrior training but I have thought on it, much since then. You probably saved my life, that boar would have killed me without doubt. It wasn't your fault that Fenrir took off after the young boar. You jumped into that fight without pause or thought for yourself and the boar could just as easily gored you as well."

"You're my brother Hakon; you would do the same for me."

"I would try Bjarke, but your strength made the difference then, and when that stag tried to take off with me."

Hakon lifted his necklaces from his shirt, the bear tooth and claw looped alongside the boar tusk and a wooden crucifix.

"What is it father says; brothers by tooth and claw … and now tusk!" Hakon grinned.

"And antler!" Bjarke laughed and slid his antler-handled seax halfway from its sheath.

The pair hugged one another.

"I have to go, Bjarke. Sigurd will be seeking me."

Bjarke went with Hakon down to the practice meadow and watched for a while as the young warriors were put through weapons exercises but becoming bored, he wandered off. It was too late in the day for hunting so he decided on a walk. Passing by the hall on his way out of the village, he whistled shrilly and Fenrir appeared at the door. Seeing his master, he bounded onto the road, tail wagging and jumping up to playfully bite at Bjarke's arm. With a beautiful afternoon and long summer evening to come, Bjarke opted for a lengthy walk. Exiting the village, he wandered past the hay meadow and the small farmlets but instead of turning into the forest as they usually did when hunting; he pushed on further up the valley. At the valley head, it widened and flattened, the fields were already full of crops but the farmhouse at the end of the clearing was in disrepair. It wasn't an area he and Hakon had frequented, as it was off their hunting trails. Though he had noticed the house in the past, he wondered at it standing derelict but surrounded by fields of crops. It was a well-positioned house, facing south it caught the sun most of the day and the valley was wide enough here for the sides not to place it into shadow too early, even in the wintertime.

Whistling Fenrir back, he cut across the fields towards the house. As he approached, he could see it was well built of logs with a wooden and turf roof. The windows were shuttered and closed but the door hung ajar at an angle on one hinge. The path to the door was overgrown and the winch above the small well in the yard no longer had a bucket hanging from it, the rope blowing gently in the breeze. Walking to the door he hesitated and decided to walk right around the house first, it seemed deserted but on the other hand, it was a well-made and good-sized building, why would no one live there. Pacing around the rear, he found the vegetable garden and the remains of a wooden rack for hanging beast to butcher after the winter slaughter. Weeds and small bushes had reclaimed the vegetable garden; only the weathered remains of some bean frames hinted at its former use. The back door was wide open and also sagging on its hinges, leaves dirt and small branches had blown in from the forest, just a bow shot away.

Fenrir padded in through the door and sniffed the floor then disappeared into the gloom. Bjarke stepped in behind, loosening his seax in its sheath, however with no noise from the dog, he doubted anything or anyone was inside. Stepping through the leaves, he pushed the shutters open letting the light in, the fresh air combating the musty smell of the place. In the main room, there was no furniture other than a broken chair, the central fire pit, outlined by its metal fenders and a hooked chain from the ceiling for hanging a cooking pot over the centre of it, was now full of leaves and rubbish. A smaller room off to the side still contained a bed. The straw filled mattress was mildewed and rotten, a large dark stain remained in the middle, the pillows were scattered on the bed and the floor, they too were dark stained and grey-green with mould, the wall too showed dark splatter stains. Fenrir appeared from the other room and went to cock his leg against the doorway, Bjarke seized him by the collar and pushed him out of the door, he wasn't sure why he did it, other than he didn't think it right the dog messing in the house, derelict or not.

He pushed more shutters open and the sunlight flooded in, lighting the corners, the smell of mould and decay however remained. Why would no one live here? It was a very serviceable house, why had it been left to decay? Looking closely at the structure he could see it was solidly built, strong roof beams, stout walls, a wooden floor, the shuttered windows; much good work had been done when it was built, why was it empty? His people were not wasteful, they used what they could again, why would no one live here, a good house, fresh water, a garden, fields and all not too far from the village? Stepping back out the house and looking to the forest he saw a small stream tumbled out of the trees providing running water and irrigation for the fields if needed, bemused he turned for home and decided to ask his father about it.

The following morning he and Hakon were awoken by the clanging bell announcing ships heading up the fjord.

"Father! It has to be father returning from court." Hakon cried as he leapt out of bed, hauled his trousers on, and strapped his seax on. "Come on Bjarke! Let's get down to the wharf."

The boys pushed their way through the crowds gathered on the wharf already watching the approaching ships. With little wind, the sails were furled, the ships instead beating down the fjord at speed in an impressive display of flashing oars and sea spray. From the topmast, Orri's pennon trailed lazily, his warriors' shields fastened along the side strakes showing his colours of black and red on their faces. The ships prows were naked of their serpent and dragon head decorations, these being stowed as the vessels were in home waters. Orri stood by the sharply upswept prow, its foremost timber carved in a filigree of twisting, interlocking snake-like shapes, he magnificently dressed in a red coloured cap with beaver trim and wolf pelted cloak, his arm, covered in gold, warrior rings lifting to wave when he saw his sons. As the ships neared the wharf, they lowered the oars in deep, slowing the vessel while mooring ropes were hurled and the ship began manoeuvring to dock. Orri jumped onto the wharf before the ropes were tied off, the boys coming alongside eager to greet their father.

Orri's *Hearth-weru* or house troops stepped off next.

These however waiting for the gangplanks dropping as all were dressed in mail hauberks to their knees and heavily armed with swords, seaxs and hand axes, helmets however had been left off, the martial show being more of prestige for Orri rather than a war footing. The sun shimmered on their mail like salmon skin as they walked, the warriors' hair bound into ponytails, their beards pulled into plaits, moustaches drooping to their chins. The oarsmen shipped their sweeps and took up their sea chests, stepping onto the wharf to greet their families.

"What news father? How was court? Did you see the King?"

"Is it war with Denmark, father?"

"Whoa, steady boys! One at a time eh!"

"Firstly, how is your mother, is she well?"

"Yes father, she is well."

"Has she slapped you both about the head lately?"

"Aye father, just yesterday. Fenrir puked the remains of a dead rat up in the house. Mother hit us both and chased Fenrir with a spit."

"All's well then!" Eysteinn broke into laughter and hugged both boys close.

"Your training is progressing well, Hakon? Not too many thumping's from Sigurd?"

"No father, I'm learning."

"Good, good! It won't be long till you're training Bjarke, you too are almost a man grown."

Bjarke just smiled but said nothing, his head full of the log house and thoughts of hunting.

The evening saw Eysteinn's Captains and leading warriors seated at the long tables in the hall. When all had been fed and ale horns replenished, Eysteinn rose to his feet raising his arms for silence.

"Captains, warriors, you will all be anxious to know what our King has to say and what he commands of us."

Men placed ale horns back on the table, their attention acute.

"Sweyn Estridsson, the pretender to the Danish throne refuses to bow the knee to our King Harald, thus it is war again with the Danes."

There was some cheering but not the usual euphoria that greeted news of war or a raid, for the war with Denmark had been a long running, hit and miss affair with no great gains for Hardrada or his people. The Danes had proved worthy and hard adversaries and with the Norwegian ships being intercepted more often than not before they could land, the fighting had yielded little in the way of gold or valuables. Hakon however was excited at the prospect of his first battle. Eysteinn continued.

"We sail to meet with the King when the moon is next full. We will need provisions and supplies for a month at least, as the King plans numerous raids along the coast, we will take a thousand men, twenty ships."

Bjarke waited patiently for his chance to talk to his father about the farmhouse. Three days passed, Eysteinn's time eaten up with preparations for war. Finally, with only the family at the dinner table his chance came.

"Father, I have a question to ask."

"Ask away lad, as long as it's fit for your mother's ears." He laughed into his ale horn. "I trust it's not about girls, not yet!" He winked at Bjarke who had blushed and Hakon sniggered. Inger gave all a disparaging look.

"No father, no. It's about the farmhouse …"

"Farmhouse? … Which, where?" He interrupted.

"The one at the end of the valley father, just before the forest. It's well-built of logs with a wooden roof but deserted, why would no one live there?"

Inger stopped eating and cast an anxious look at Eysteinn. He noted the look and stopped his voracious assault on a goose leg, looking thoughtful as if considering his words.

Bjarke looked at Eysteinn then Inger. Seeing the apprehensive, concerned faces, he spoke quickly.

"Have I said something to upset you? If I have …"

"No lad … no …" Eysteinn seemed lost for words.

Inger went to speak but hesitated and though her lips formed words, nothing came out. Both boys looked unsure, their father always had answers, always seemed sure of himself, always in command. What had unsettled him?

Inger reached across and squeezed Eysteinn's arm. He cleared his throat and wiped grease from his mouth. He looked at Inger. "He needs to know Inger, he has the right. Let's have it all out and be done." He said very quietly.

Inger said nothing, her eyes widening, her face flushing.

"You both know you are my, our foster sons … Hakon, you are my stepbrother's son and you know your real father died from his battle wounds, his health not recovering after we came home from Sicily. He and I served in the Varangian guard along with King Harald, though he was then just Harald Sigurdsson, our Captain."

Hakon nodded. "Yes father."

"Bjarke, your real father was my very good friend. He too was a warrior and brave, a good man, you are named for him but you also carry my name as I, we …" He corrected himself and smiled at Inger. "We too claim you, claim you both. Sons or foster sons, it matters not, you have Inger's love and mine. Hakon, as you already know you too are named for your father and also for me, family is everything. Both of you are growing into fine men and honour your real fathers' as you honour Inger and me."

Both boys were surprised, shocked even by Eysteinn's words, though they knew they were cared for and loved it was strange to hear their foster father say it. He, very much the Norse Lord, a leader of men, a famous warrior and ruthless when he had to be, though he had a very gentle side where his boys and his woman were concerned.

"Your father and mother both lived in the farmhouse you mention. You were born there."

Bjarke just stared. Inger now looked distressed; Hakon glanced at each person around the table.

"Yours's was a difficult birth, you being so big …"

"Did I kill my …"

"No lad, you didn't … no. The night you were born the snows came early, it was an early winter storm …"

"Please Eysteinn, must we go through this part now." Inger pleaded.

"I think we should Inger, the lad has asked and he has a right to know where he came from."

A tear rolled down Inger's cheek and she shivered involuntarily.

Bjarke was torn between seeing his mother upset and wanting to know more, he was about to close the conversation when Eysteinn continued.

"I'll spare the grim details lad, in short, the winter storms came very early that year and a bear came with them. It broke into the house and killed your mother just as you were born but for some reason did not kill you. We tracked the bear and your father slew it, the bear slaying your father as it died. You have a claw and tooth from it about your neck, as do you Hakon, brothers by tooth and claw! The farmhouse ... well, the reason it is uninhabited is because of superstition and fear ..."

"Eysteinn, please must you?" Inger fingered the crucifix at her neck.

"It's alright Inger, let's have it all out now, better from us than someone else."

Inger nodded but looked unconvinced.

"Folk fear the farmhouse because of the bear and it killing your mother, they think it cursed, thus no one will live there. I thought to pull it down but it is too good a building to destroy, I hoped that over time folk would forget and someone would wish to move into it."

"Could Hakon and I have it, father? It would make a good hunting lodge for us; it's at the right end of the valley for the forest ..."

"No Bjarke!" Inger snapped, and then moderated her tone. "No son, you belong here, at home, where you both belong."

"Just for hunting mother, it would save us a long walk ..."

"No, I would rather you didn't." Inger was becoming upset again and seeing it, Bjarke conceded."

"Very well mother, I will not hurt you over this, it's not important."

Looking relieved, Inger gathered herself. She lifted her head proudly though her blue eyes sparkled with tears; she smiled at her boys and sought her words. "You may repair it, clean it and make it habitable but I want you both home when the hunting is done, long walk or not."

The time for the fleet's departure came quickly. Bjarke watched solemnly as Hakon's hair was combed out and bound back into a heavy plait that reached to the bottom of his shoulder blades. Inger and a servant hefted his mail hauberk over his head and helped him into it. He sagged a little under the weight as it settled across his shoulders, it hanging to just above his knees. His quilted trousers beneath tucked into his boots, with long strips of leather puttees bound over the boot tops and his shins and reaching to his knees. A leather belt hugged his waist and helped take some of the weight of the mail shirt, his seax, slung parallel to the belt at the small of his back. A baldric held his sword and a loop on his belt at the right hip held a hand axe. Laced, leather bracers covered his forearms; a pair of kid leather palmed, gloves with bull hide backs completed his attire. Inger reached for a cone shaped helmet with a wide nasal guard. She looked him up and down and nodded to herself as if satisfied. Holding the helmet in one hand, she ran her other hand down his face gently, approvingly and then slapped him hard. Hakon was shocked and looked suddenly angry.

"That's so you remember to do as you are told! … I have two sons; make sure it remains that way!" She said fiercely, then hugged him close and kissed him on both cheeks. She tried to hide the tears but they slipped from beneath her eyelids to course down her cheeks. She cuffed them sharply away. "Your father will be waiting, go!"

Hakon stepped a pace or two away then turned back to kiss Inger quickly. "I'll be back, I promise!"

"Go! Make your father proud! Make me proud, Hakon Orrifostersson!"

Bjarke picked up Hakon's shield and escorted him out of the door and down to the wharf, Fenrir following at his heel.

The wharf was crowded with warriors, women and children, the atmosphere tense as farewells were said, wives were hugged, small children lifted into armoured embraces and kissed, sons and fathers shook hands, the ships slowly filling with warriors. Eysteinn saw his sons; he waved them on towards his ship, the largest of the fleet, and moored at the very end of the wharf pointing seawards. The boys and Fenrir made their way over. Stopping at the bows, Bjarke handed Hakon his shield then crushed him in a bear hug and shook his hand; his face strained with concern, he had no words.

Hakon, making a show of bravado gave a forced laugh and punched Bjarke in the shoulder in rough affection.

"Don't worry little brother, I will be back. Someone has to give you hunting lessons!"

He stooped to pat and stroke Fenrir who licked him and whined. Hakon stood, turned and climbed aboard the longship.

"Next time, Bjarke!" Eysteinn called. "Take care of your mother for me, lad."

Bjarke nodded and raised a hand to wave as the ship pushed off from the wharf, floating aimlessly into the current. A clatter of wood saw oars pushed through the oar ports followed by a command to row. The blades dipped and the ship seemed to become stationary for a moment, then as the second stoke of the oars came it began to move, slowly gathering speed as it nosed out into the centre of the fjord. The air filled with shouts as other vessels pushed off and turned in the lee of Eysteinn's ship, oars dipping rhythmically, the grunts of the rowers drifting back to the watchers. Sea spray combined with air and sunlight, sending myriad flashes of light as the oars lifted, flexed and dipped again, the ships gathering speed.

Fenrir whined soulfully and sat at Bjarke's feet, Bjarke's hand falling to ruffle his ears, boy and dog staring seaward until the ships disappeared from sight, only then did the pair turn for home.

Chapter Five

Borg, autumn and winter 1057-58 AD

With Eysteinn and Hakon both gone, Bjarke became the eldest male of the household and Inger had kept him around and involved with the day-to-day work of managing the estate and village, despite the abundance of able servants and slaves. Thus, Bjarke's time for repairing and cleaning the farmhouse had been limited.

Orri and Hakon returned home along with the fleet much later than expected, the planned month's campaign stretching to almost two and taking the time into early autumn. With time of the essence, everyone had been summoned, the boys included, to help bring the late harvest in before the autumn frosts.

Bjarke had noticed a change in his brother since he returned home; he was more serious than before, moody at times and occasionally sought to be alone. He also had other interests than hunting, in particular was a blonde haired girl, Asta, she being as beautiful as her name proclaimed. Hakon taking any chance to talk with her, more so if they could find a quiet part of the hall to be alone.

Initially Bjarke had badgered Hakon to tell of the war and his adventures, Hakon explaining that though the

King had called for war against the Danes it had really been no more than a large *strandhewing* or series of raids around the northern peninsular of Denmark and a seizing of wealth, women and able bodied youths for the slave market. A demonstration to show that King Sweyn could not defend his people. As Bjarke pressed for details of the fighting, Hakon had been sketchy and passed it off as nothing much. Steering Bjarke away from further details he had presented him with a beautifully made, yet very practical, fighting, hand axe.

"It's well balanced Bjarke, it will handle well."

Bjarke grinned as he hefted it in his right fist, liking the feel of it, his muscled arm handling the weight easily. He tried a few swipes in the air, Hakon noticing that the axe moved quickly and without effort.

'All Hallows Eve' passed and midwinter had come and gone and Yuletide along with it. Hogmanay had seen the old year die and the new year of our Lord, 1058 born. The celebrations in Orri's hall and the village had been riotous with much merriment, drinking and eating, Orri being noted for his hospitality to his retainers and his people, ensuring all had something in their bellies for the festive season. The hall had rung with laughter, it being visited over the season by tumblers, acrobats, magicians and famed *skalds* - the singers of songs and reciters of poems. With the festival ending, folk waited for the first signs of spring, Easter and better weather. The winter snows lingered however and were deep, keeping folk indoors and around the hearth, thus Hakon and Bjarke had been restricted to indoor pursuits. Much of their time was taking up with playing *Tafl* or planning hunting trips and servicing their weapons ready for the first signs of spring, and in Hakon's case, playing court to Asta.

The small lake at the end of the valley froze and on better days gave the chance for ice skating, Bjarke abstaining from it when the animal bones used as skate blades were not large enough nor strong enough to sustain his weight, much less the ice. He, secretly happy enough to watch his brother taking Asta by the hand and leading her around the frozen surface from the comfort and warmth of his bearskin cloak. He was disturbed from his apathy by a tap on the back and turned to find a young woman offering him a beaker of heated wine.

"Bjarke, some wine to keep out the cold? … It's just fruit wine but it's hot, with some spices to give it flavour."

Bjarke looked down at the girl, she too swathed in a cloak and matching hat made of silver-grey wolf skin, her blond hair hanging loose beneath. Her large, doe like eyes, as blue as sea ice sparkling in the sunlight.

Surprised by the intrusion and quite awed by the beauty of the girl before him, he only just managed a, thank you. He smiled as he took the beaker, his huge hand encompassing it and fleetingly touching the girl's wrist above her glove. He also noted that Fenrir had not barked at the intrusion but was busy pushing his body against the girl and wagging his tail, seeking a stroke or a pat. The girl smiled up at him.

"Are you not skating?"

He smiled and blushed slightly. "My size on ice! I think not is wisest."

She giggled and hid her face in her cup.

"What about you? Do you not skate?"

She giggled again. "I do, I did, until yesterday …" She looked around and lowered her voice. "Until I fell on my arse and now it's bruised and sore!" She giggled again, making Bjarke laugh.

"How do you know my name?" He asked.

"My cousin, Asta is becoming close to your brother, I heard from her."

"And your name ..."

"Eerika ... Eerika Andersdotter. My father is a warrior with your father's *Hearth-weru*. Shall we walk; take the dog? It's better than standing here in the cold and it's a nice afternoon, no more snow yet."

"Yes, why not."

"I have to be home before dark or my father growls but I think I will be safe with you and ..." she pointed to the dog.

"Fenrir."

"Fenrir." She ruffled his ears. "Named after the wolf of the old Gods?"

"Yes, much to my mother's disgust."

Eerika giggled again. "Come Bjarke, come Fenrir." She walked off, the snow crunching beneath her boots, Bjarke catching up with her in a couple of strides, Fenrir, strangely walking alongside her.

Winter finally gave way to spring and the land was released from the grip of ice and snow. Bjarke had seen Eerika a few times since their first meeting but each time she was with her family or her father. Managing a respectful greeting, he had passed on but noted a demure look and a warm smile from Eerika.

He was keen to return to the farmhouse and continue with the repairs and refurbishments and desperate to be out hunting again, Hakon it seemed was also keen and thus they set off just before dawn on their first trip of the season. Entering the forest, they had quickly picked up fresh deer tracks in the soft earth and followed them through the stands of beech and oak, the past autumn's leaves freshly disturbed from the deer's passing. The forest was full of light, as the trees were just turning from buds to leaves, making vision and bow work easier. They caught up with a young buck early in the day, it nibbling on the fresh new grass shoots in a clearing. Sensing danger, it took flight and ran across the clearing seeking safety in the trees on the other side, Bjarke bringing it down with an arrow through the neck, a very good shot considering the distance and the animal moving at speed. With no marvellous head and antler rack for a trophy but good, fresh meat for the table they gralloched it, feeding Fenrir the heart and sweetmeats, while deciding to carry as much meat as possible away, rather than just the choice cuts they usually took later in the season. With a long walk ahead of them and fully loaded they decided to head back to the farmhouse as a break in the journey, also taking the chance to do some more work there before returning home with their prize. With the head removed and the guts out, Bjarke carried the buck on his back, Hakon taking the bows, quivers, the water skins and food bags.

Arriving at the farmhouse, they found a suitable tree that would remain shaded and hauled the animal up high into it, well above the range of most flies and insects. There was still work to do to the house but Bjarke had swept it clean, refitted the doors so they closed and burned the old bedframe, mattress and pillows. Opening the shutters let the light and fresh air in again and removed the musty smell of closed, dark spaces. The old smell of decay and mould was gone, the building now being sound and dry. Bjarke had dragged three tree stumps into the main room, two serving as seats and the largest as a 'make do' table.

"What do you think, Hakon? It will make a good

hunting lodge for us methinks?"

"It's good Bjarke, very good. I can see why you were keen to have it."

"Yes, have it for us Hakon, for you and me, our lodge."

"But it's yours, yours by right, it was …"

"Yes, I know. Now it's ours. You're my brother and what I have is yours as well."

"Same here Bjarke, what I have I will share, like we have always done." He punched Bjarke playfully in the ribs. "All except Asta, I am keeping her for myself!" The pair laughed. "Mind you, the last I saw, you were doing alright with Eerika."

Bjarke blushed. "We're just friends is all, I have caught a couple of side glances from Anders, her father, and he doesn't look that friendly."

"Don't worry Bjarke; it's just a father and daughter thing." Bjarke looked confused. "A bit like mothers and sons, think in reverse, you know how mother is with us? What is it father says when she isn't listening, a she wolf with her cubs!"

Their laughter was disturbed by a bark from Fenrir. The dog stood up from its position at the door, ears pricked and nose sniffing, then barked again before stepping out into the sunlight, the boys following to see what the disturbance was. Coming across the meadow were half a dozen boys, all much the same age as Hakon. Fenrir barked repeatedly until Bjarke came alongside and settled him.

Hakon shielded his eyes from the sun as he looked, then groaned. "It's Ingvar Halvorsen …"

"Asta's brother?"

"Yes, one of many!" He sighed. "That's Kettil with him; he's younger, not so bad really. The others with him

I don't know, other than Sten, he's no relation, all of them went with us to Denmark." Hakon's voice was full of disdain. "Ingvar has a big mouth; he thinks he's a great warrior already. You've seen him, hanging around with the older men, ingratiating himself, talking his way up to fame."

"He can fight then?"

"I suppose so, he did alright last summer in Denmark I heard. He's just full of himself."

Shortly the arriving party were close to the house and Fenrir was again barking, Bjarke having to pull him back by his collar.

"Christ God, boy! Can't you settle your dog, who's the master?" Ingvar shouted; this drew some guffaws from the group.

"See what I mean." Hakon muttered beneath his breath. Bjarke said nothing. He tapped Fenrir lightly on the snout with his finger settling him.

"What do you want, Ingvar?"

"Nothing, we are just passing through, on our way home from the hunt."

Hakon glanced at the group, seeking animals. "You've had no luck then?" He sounded amiable but couldn't resist a smirk.

"There's nothing about."

"We managed."

"Managed what?"

"Well, the boy here." He winked at Bjarke and smirked, then turned to Ingvar, his voice full of sarcasm. "The boy put an arrow through a buck on the run at fifty paces early this morning, like you say though, there's nothing much about. Well, at midmorning anyway!" He looked up at the sun.

Ingvar cast Hakon a dirty look. "So where is this

buck?"

"Gralloched and hung, all ready for home and the table." He pointed at the carcase high up in the tree. "Along with us after we've had a drink and a bite."

"You can share some of that with us then, I'm parched and hungry."

"I don't think so; we only have enough for us."

"Well, if you have brought food for him." He pointed to Bjarke. "There'll be enough for us all."

"And I say no!" Hakon's voice hardened and the sniggers that had started up from the group stopped abruptly.

Ingvar puffed his chest out and stepped forward, his arms hanging loose at his sides. Fenrir raised his top lip baring his teeth, a low growl in his throat.

"Control your dog, boy!"

Hakon turned side on to Ingvar, his eyes narrowing. "It's our land, the dog has every right to growl and my brother's name is Bjarke, not boy!" He spat.

"My apologies, Bjarke." He quipped sarcastically, then. "Control your dog, you great lummox!"

"You steaming goat turd!" Hakon snarled and went to step forward, his fists rising. Bjarke lifted his arm across his brother's chest holding him back from Ingvar, his other hand holding Fenrir back.

Ingvar's fists bunched. "I'll make you eat turd, Hakon Orrifostersson!"

Kettil and Sten grabbed for Ingvar, holding his arms and forcing him back, he struggling wildly, wanting to be at Hakon. Fenrir was now rearing on his hind legs, barking and snarling, Bjarke holding him tightly by the collar.

"And keep away from my sister, you arse-wipe! Or by Christ, I'll knock you senseless!"

"Anytime, Ingvar … anytime!"

As the diatribe grew more vociferous and bitter, the other boys tried to calm things, Ingvar and Hakon still struggling to be at one another.

"Anytime is it Hakon? Is that anytime you stop puking your guts up! Call yourself a warrior, you couldn't handle the sailing, never mind the fighting, you stinking pig turd!"

Hakon snarled and struggled hard to be loose from Bjarke, Fenrir also pulling ready to attack the group, the impetus of brother and dog dragging Bjarke forward, though he never let go of either of his charges. Ingvar and the group backed quickly away from Fenrir as he strained to be free, all taking fright from the big elkhound's vicious snarls and barking.

Hakon laughed. "Chicken shit! … Call yourself a warrior." He spat in disgust.

Ingvar finally forced himself from Sten and Kettil's grip and stooping to pick up a fist-size stone from the path, hurled it hard at Fenrir. The dog yelped loudly as the stone hit its chest. Bjarke, snarled and hauled Hakon back hard, rocking him on his feet.

"Stand there!" He growled; the first words he had spoken since the exchange began.

Shocked by the uncharacteristic aggressive tone, Hakon did as he was bidden. Fenrir was barking again, clearly hurt and agitated, Bjarke stooped to settle and examine him, trying to calm him. Seeing blood on the dog's coat, he snarled and looked at Hakon. "Hold Fenrir!"

Standing to his full height, he glared at Ingvar, his finger pointing.

"Don't ever, throw stones at my dog!"

"Or what, oaf? What …? Are you going to growl at

me instead?"

There was no laughter this time from anyone. Ingvar's friends were again trying to pull him away. He shook them off harshly and stepped towards Bjarke.

"Or what? You big lump of pig shit!"

Bjarke threw a huge punch at Ingvar's head. Ingvar ducked quickly beneath it and stepped in close, thumping Bjarke in the stomach. Bjarke gasped as the wind came out of him and folded slightly, Ingvar was already to the side of him and punched him twice in the kidneys. Bjarke stumbled and Ingvar stood back watching for the counter attack.

"Boy? … Oaf was the better word! Go home oaf, and take your puking brother and mangy hound with you! … And you!" He pointed at Hakon. "Keep away from Asta!"

Hakon was also beside himself with anger and went to slip Fenrir's collar. Seeing it, Ingvar unsheathed his seax.

"If you loose the dog, I'll kill it!"

Bjarke, still gasping for breath held up a halting hand to Hakon. Kettil and the others again struggling with and pulling Ingvar away.

Bjarke stepped towards the group again. "You hurt my dog."

"You want some more, Oaf! Christ God, you are as stupid as you look!" He brandished the seax as Bjarke stepped closer.

"Ingvar, drop the seax! Now!" Kettil shouted. "It's a fight not blood feud!"

Ingvar slowly sheathed the seax and beckoned Bjarke forward. "Come on then oaf, it seems you are a slow learner!"

Bjarke stepped towards Ingvar, watching Ingvar's

eyes and his body for the first sign of movement. Ingvar stepped lightly to the side and Bjarke counter moved, he feinted a punch and Bjarke moved again.

"Hah! You're learning, oaf!"

Bjarke stepped in quickly, his fist raised but his guard open. Ingvar stopped him with a short, hard jab to the face bursting his lips, he hit him again fast but this time Bjarke twisted his head to one side, the blow glancing off his cheekbone. Bjarke seemed to ignore the pain and snatched Ingvar by the jerkin, dragging him off his feet toward him, his forehead smashing into Ingvar's face. Blood sprayed as Ingvar's nose collapsed and his lips burst. Bjarke powering his other fist into Ingvar's stomach, the force lifting him off his feet and sending him sprawling backwards, landing in a heap at his friends' feet.

Bjarke stepped after him and punched Kettil in the side of the head as he tried to help Ingvar up. Kettil went down senseless. Sten, bewildered at the speed of the destruction was too late to move or defend himself and he too was knocked out as Bjarke hit him with a roundhouse punch. The rest of the group backed quickly away as Bjarke came on like an avenging angel, all reason gone and his temper broken. The other boys held up halting hands.

"Enough, enough! For God's sake enough!"

Hakon's voice stopped further destruction. "Bjarke! Fenrir needs you … come on, enough!"

At the mention of Fenrir, Bjarke stopped but pointed to the remaining boys and an almost senseless Ingvar. Blood dripped from his chin and sprayed from his mouth as he spoke.

"No one maligns my brother or hurts my dog … understood!"

He looked around at the devastation. Ingvar lay on his side holding his head, blood dripping through his fingers and pooling on the path. Kettil and Sten were both unconscious on the grass.

He walked over to Ingvar who held up his hand for peace.

"One other thing, Ingvar Halvorsen … If Hakon wants to court Asta, he will."

Ingvar raised his open hand again and managed a nod. Bjarke walked back to Hakon and Fenrir. Hakon tried to look at Bjarke's face but was pushed gently away as he bent to see to his dog. Fenrir was alright, the stone had cut the dog's chest and there was some blood but the cut was not deep and Fenrir did not seem perturbed by it. Bjarke ruffled his ears, pushing his head gently against the dog's face then walked back to Ingvar.

Ingvar was still on his side.

"Enough Bjarke! Christ God, enough! … I'm sorry about the dog."

Bjarke stooped, offering his hand. "Can you get up?"

Ingvar looked at the hand, unsure, thinking he was to be tricked and beaten further. Bjarke instead squatted down and hefted Ingvar slowly to his feet.

"Come on, let's get cleaned up." He helped a still half-senseless Ingvar towards the farmhouse. "Hakon, can you fetch some water?" He laid Ingvar inside the door, propping him against the wall. He went back to where the boys were standing around Kettil trying to help him up.

Bjarke picked the still unconscious Sten up. "Bring Kettil." He said to the boys.

Soon the three were laid inside the farmhouse, Hakon and the boys offering wet cloths and drinks of water. Bjarke sat on one of the stumps, catching his breath and stroking Fenrir's head, which rested contentedly in his lap. The dog quite peaceful now the shouting and fighting was over.

Bjarke looked at Kettil and Sten. "I'm sorry I hit you, you did nothing to my brother, my dog or me."

The pair just stared back, hands raised in acknowledgement, Kettil still groggy from the punch.

Hakon spoke up. "We had better have our stories straight before we go home, I don't fancy a thumping from my father over this."

"Agreed." Ingvar muttered. "I suggest we all go home together, that way it looks less like there has been trouble, what do you think, Bjarke?"

All noticed the new respect in Ingvar's voice.

"Agreed, Ingvar."

Hakon looked thoughtful. "How's this sound? We were all hunting together, chasing the buck." He pointed outside to the tree. "It went over a steep edge in the forest, we went after it, running full pelt. Ingvar, you fell and split your face on a stump, Bjarke, you were hit in the face by a branch coming back at you as we ran through the forest. Kettil, Sten, you two fell down the hill banging your heads."

Ingvar started to laugh then held his head as the movement hurt it. "Christ God! What a mess, all these injuries, four of us for one buck. Do you think they will believe us?"

Hakon shrugged. "I can't think of anything better. If we all sing the same song though, who's to say different?" He glanced around the room and received nods and mumbles of agreement. "A hunting accident it was then."

By the time the group arrived in the village, all the blood had been washed away excepting the stains on their clothes. Ingvar's broken face and Bjarke's lips were swelling, Kettil and Sten nursing blue-black bruising on their faces. Bjarke carrying the buck on his back.

"A good day, boys?" Brynjar called from behind them.

"Yes, a good day." Hakon managed genially as he turned to speak.

Brynjar caught up with them, he also carrying a buck across his shoulders. "A lot of injuries there lads, for a buck! Did he put up a fight?" He chuckled, raising his eyebrows.

Hakon relayed the rehearsed tale, it all sounding plausible. Brynjar smiled and nodded, looking at each boy in turn, as he was mentioned in the tale, then ran his fingers over the buck on Bjarke's back.

"So, the buck and three of you fell and Bjarke stopped a branch? It strikes me as strange though, that there is no bruising on the buck. Did he fall outside the farmhouse I wonder? Just there is an awful lot of blood on the grass down there."

Hakon paled and the boys looked anxious. Brynjar just smiled knowingly. "You're all alright? Everything is settled?"

A chorus of yes's came back at him.

"All's good then."

"Brynjar! ..." Hakon began.

Brynjar was already walking on, he stopped and turned then pinched his lips with his fingers, laughed and walked off.

Chapter Six

Borg 1059 AD

Bjarke pulled the bone comb through his hair teasing out the cots and tangles; he stared blankly, deep in thought. His hair, long and blonde reached half way down his back; he had always worn it loose, else held by a single leather cord in a simple ponytail. Today it was to be plaited and tied, for today he would begin his warrior training, formally. Like all boys, he had tried his hand with weapons but other than the javelin, hunting bow and his beloved seax, all of which he was highly proficient with, he had shown little interest and even less skill in regards to the sword.

He was a giant of a young man, standing six feet seven inches tall, his shoulders wide, his arms thick with muscle and his chest broad, his outdoor life and love of hunting having helped strengthen and shape his body. However, he struggled with his size and co-ordination of his hands and feet, still growing, he was clumsy at times and drew the ire of his brother for it. Hakon, now twenty, had gradually drifted away from his brother, having married Asta, and finding the pleasures of married life, ale and the company of other budding young warriors more to his liking than hunting and his younger sibling.

"Are you ready for me, Lord?" The slave girl asked as she entered the room, a basket of combs, scissors, ties and leather bindings in her hands.

Bjarke just nodded his mind elsewhere, his thoughts drifting back over the last while as the girl ran a comb through his hair again then trimmed his fringe above his eyes. Pulling the rest back over his shoulders, she separated it into three long strands. After much twisting and binding, the girl finished his hair. It pulled now into a thick, tight plait and strengthened every hand span or so with a stiff leather tube binding, weighting it and keeping it in place despite any movement he was likely to make.

Walking out into the village he made his way to the open ground where crowds of warriors and youths gathered, some already engaged in mock fights, others taking instruction as to weapon position, shield use and their stance. His father stood to one side quietly observing.

Receiving no special treatment for his rank, he joined the groups waiting for their first instruction. Given a round shield and armed with a fighting spear, he was then pushed into a line of other young men.

"Shields up!" Gunnar called and there was a rattle of wood. "Lock shields!" The rank shuffled and shield edges overlapped. "Spears front!"

The two trainers, Sigurd and Gunnar walked the line, adjusting a shield here and there, closing up or widening the gap between boys as required. Bjarke's shield was higher than anyone else's, his height forcing him to stoop when his shield was pulled lower. Gunnar ordered the first rank onto one knee, calling a second rank into place behind, the shields coming over the top to overlap, Bjarke's height again causing difficulties, this time for the warrior behind. Swapping Bjarke to the rear rank allayed the issue somewhat though with little enthusiasm on Bjarke's part. Sigurd walked the line again, stopping every so often to barrel bodily into the shields or kick them hard with the flat of his foot. When it showed signs of buckling, Gunnar rearranged the boys, sorting their stance and balance. The disassembly and reassembly of the shieldwall continued for some time interspersed with running and stopping on command, the efforts to make and break the wall becoming faster as the youths learned what was required of them. Bjarke was strong and fit enough from his constant hunting trips so the running while encumbered with weapons and heavy shield brought no difficulty, however his size and height left him awkward in his stance and forced him to stoop when making the sheildwall.

Using the small javelin at the targets brought no difficulty for him, having used it extensively when hunting but when combined with a shield in his other hand it seemed to throw him off balance. His throws were powerful and the range long but as he threw he opened up his shield arm too far, exposing his chest, Gunnar quick to point out the weakness with a sharp rap to the chest with his stick. He fared little better with the sword. Again, his strokes were fearsome and some of his opponents backed away as he swung the blunted weapon in huge arcs, knocking shields out of hands else breaking them. However, the opponents who stood their ground; quickly closed under his guard and battered him in the chest where his shield should have been in defence. At the rest period, Eysteinn caught up with his son, moving him to one side.

"It's not all about strength, Bjarke. That is important of course, as is your endurance but first you must master the basics; your balance, your stance, your guard … especially your guard."

"It just feels awkward father, the shield, I don't like it."

Eysteinn cupped his chin, deep in thought. "In time you could learn to fight with two weapons I suppose but you must master the art of defence first. As you have seen, some men will shy away from you out of fear of your strength but those with the balls to stand went under your guard. Without your guard in place, son, either from a shield or from your weapons, you are a dead man."

Bjarke shrugged. "Maybe I am not meant to be a warrior father? I'm a hunter, would that not suffice?"

"No lad … no, it won't. You're my son, the son of a Lord and when I'm gone, you and Hakon will have to lead our men and fight alongside them. You're an able lad, good with the bow and javelin; the other weapons just take time is all."

"The sword feels awkward in my hand, father and I'm too big to work in the shieldwall."

"But being a Lord's son, the men will expect you fight with a sword, I will have one made for you, one that suits your size and hand, which will make a difference."

Bjarke shrugged again.

"If I have the sword made for you and you master it, you could leave out the shield and use the hand axe Hakon gave you instead of it, as long as you cover yourself when you fight, two weapons can work well."

Bjarke continued to look downcast, watching as the other boys manoeuvred in the shieldwall, others engaging in sword and shield work. Many of them seemed to be settling into the exercises and becoming more dextrous, their balance and movement improving.

"I'm too big father, too slow and clumsy."

"No lad, I won't have that. If you can hunt, and God knows you do that well enough, you can learn to use other weapons. Just time lad; time and practice is all and bear in mind, the King himself is about the same height as you and no one doubts his ability with sword, spear or long-axe."

"But the King is a great warrior!"

"Aye he is, through training and practice, he wasn't born with all those skills you know!" He laughed and punched Bjarke playfully.

Bjarke lowered his head and his voice. "Father, I think … I also think …"

"What lad? … What's eating you? I know it's not fear of a fight. Don't think I don't know about the hunting escapades when you've protected your brother or the fight with Ingvar, Kettil, Sten and the rest of them." He chuckled when he saw Bjarke's look of astonishment. "Your mother may not hear of everything but I have men, loyal men, who tell me what happens in my own village. So what is it, lad?"

"It's … I think I lack the will to hurt someone who hasn't hurt me …"

"But that's war, lad. The way it is. People will be hurt or killed that you don't know and maybe they don't want to fight you either but at some time you will have to fight, be it for land, riches, reputation or family or even your life."

"I understand family, father. I wouldn't let anyone hurt you, mother or Hakon. That's different."

Eysteinn looked thoughtful and was about to speak when their discussion was interrupted. Hearing a greeting called they looked up and saw Hakon wave as he and some older warriors walked onto the practice field and picked up shields and practice swords. Eysteinn waved back and grinned at Bjarke, then slapped him on the back.

"You'll do alright lad believe me, you'll see!"

Eysteinn walked onto the practice field hailing Sigurd and Gunnar to one side. The young warriors being given a moment to rest, while the three men talked and pointed, gesturing to different points on the field and the different warrior groups. Eventually the three broke apart, Sigurd and Gunnar quickly sorting everyone into groups but mixing them with experienced and novice warriors. As Bjarke walked reluctantly back onto the field, he was directed into the same group as Hakon. Hakon grinned at him.

"Come on little brother, here, beside Ingvar and me."

Since the fight at the farmhouse and the subsequent marriage to Asta, Hakon and Ingvar had become not just 'good brothers' but firm friends. Gunnar came alongside each group adjusting warriors as he saw fit, changing some positions while pushing Bjarke between Hakon and Ingvar and changing his sword for a bearded but blunted hand-axe. Sigurd looked at the eight groups then shouted a number to each.

"Right, groups one and two, fight. Groups three and four fight, five and six fight and seven fights eight. The winners will move to the next round and so on. We are watching for teamwork, guarding your comrade as well as aggressive but sensible attack. Groups one and two you will start."

Placed in group two, Bjarke, Hakon and Ingvar were in the front rank and they closed together tightly as they sought to clash with group one.

"Stay tight little brother, shield down a bit, watch my right side for me. Guard me and yourself, Ingvar will look out for you, when you can, hook their shields out the way and I will deal to them." Hakon winked. Bjarke smiled and nodded, happy to be alongside his brother and ready to do as he was bidden.

The two sides clashed with a crack of wood and a loud grunt. When Bjarke's opponents closed, they couldn't push him, his reverse shove pushing them back in disarray and of which Hakon quickly took advantage. A determined attack against Hakon saw Bjarke smash shield and warrior over with the axe, Ingvar stepping in to guard Bjarke's right side. Hakon stepped into the new gap, Bjarke and Ingvar following. With Bjarke's huge strength the three began pushing ahead of their line, the associated warriors to either side of them following and by accident forming slanting lines like an arrowhead. Within moments, the opposing group's sheildwall was shattered as the apex of Bjarke, Hakon and Ingvar broke through it, all cohesion and solid defence gone. With the wall broken, Bjarke's group scattered the other group like chaff.

A horn blew to stop the fight and Sigurd and Gunnar came across the field, waving the other groups in close.

"Did you all see what happened there?"

"A *'svinfylking'* formed, Sigurd. A swine-head." One of the older warriors offered.

"Yes, albeit by accident." Sigurd and Gunnar chuckled. "Bjarke pushed through with Hakon and Ingvar on either side, the rest of the line trailing at an angle from either side of them." Sigurd made an arrow shape with his hands. "A swine-head smashes the *'skjaldborg'* or shieldwall and scatters warriors, leaving them vulnerable. We haven't practised that yet, as it takes discipline to do it but you will have to learn it. Well done group two! Next!"

The mock fighting continued throughout the day and it was found that, those who hunted regularly or had trained their bodies survived the best. The fighting slowed as warriors tired, the shields becoming heavy and the push and shove wearing men down.

"Keep working!" Gunnar shouted. "Tired men die easy! Don't think every fight is going to be over quickly, it can come down to who is the fittest and strongest, who has the endurance and the balls to keep fighting!"

"And he and Sigurd fought for a day and half, not even stopping to shit." Hakon chuckled from behind his shield and Ingvar and Bjarke laughed.

The final fight was between Bjarke's group and group eight. Both sides were battered and weary as they formed into their respective shieldwall. Eysteinn stepped between them and lifted a bag of silver warrior rings up.

"For the winning group, a ring apiece!"

Both sides cheered loudly, tiredness forgotten, weapons raised in the air. Ingvar stepped forward clashing his sword on his shield. "Two, two, two!" He shouted, the rest of the group taking up the chant.

In response, group eight closed their shields tight as a warrior called time. The warriors coming on a pace at a time with a loud grunt at every step. Ingvar eased back into line and bellowed.

"Shields locked! Let them come!"

Sweat wet, hands tightened on weapon hilts. Heads shook sweat away that had leaked from under helmets onto faces and into the sparse beards of the youths.

"That's stirred them up, Lord." Gunnar chuckled as he watched the lines approaching.

"Aye, silver does that to men." Eysteinn laughed and folded his arms watching intently as the two sides closed.

"It does Lord." Sigurd agreed. "But putting brother alongside brother does it too. Have you noticed; Bjarke defends Hakon at all times? Not just because he is shield side of him and that's what he needs to do but you will have seen the difference since we paired them and put them beside Ingvar."

"Yes and I like what I see. Bjarke just needs discipline and practice yet but that will come. I also have another idea about how he will be most useful."

"The long-axe, Lord?"

"Aye, if we use Hakon and Ingvar to either side of him to guard him, I think that would be a deadly configuration, what think you both?"

Sigurd and Gunnar nodded. Gunnar, the oldest of all three ventured his thoughts.

"If we give Bjarke the long-axe and place Hakon to his right, Hakon's shield will help protect him, on the other side we place Ingvar who is left handed, so Bjarke has protection from two shields while he fights with both hands."

Eysteinn nodded approvingly.

"And." Gunnar added. "Let him use the hand-axe as a second weapon instead of the sword, just in case the long-axe is lost or broken. Give him one of those kite-shaped shields the Saxon *Huscarls* use, to sling on his back, it will be out of the way more so than a round shield but will be there should he need it."

"I would have liked him to have a sword, as befits his rank but as I have seen today, I think my son is an axeman and if it keeps him alive and he's comfortable with it, who am I to say different?"

"His father and Lord!" Gunnar put in with a smile.

"Aye but a father first and keeping my boys alive is the priority. A sword can wait, and heaven and Christ

God forbid that I ever have to tell Inger that her boys are injured."

Sigurd and Gunnar laughed.

Back on the field, the two groups were battling it out. There was only noise from the clash of weapons now, men saving their wind for the fight rather than shouting. Finally, with a last, great push from Bjarke's group the opposing shieldwall collapsed and warriors went down exhausted, hands raised for quarter. Ingvar turned towards the three watching men and raised shield and sword in victory, while a weary shout came from his warriors.

Eysteinn stepped onto the field again to congratulate the group and award the silver arm rings. As he handed out the rings personally to each warrior, a servant came alongside him, handing another bag to him. Eysteinn summoned the defeated group.

"Well fought by all, methinks!" He shouted. "Though victory lies with group two, I think the defence and resilience of group eight also deserves reward. Step up lads, warriors all, you've earned your silver."

Chapter Seven

Borg 1060 AD

"Come on Bjarke, come!" Hakon badgered as the pair walked across the meadow.

"I'm sorry Hakon; I promised mother I would take supper with her. Father is with the king again as you know and with war coming again, he is away at court more than he is here and I think she gets lonely when he's gone."

"Oh, come on Bjarke! Asta has roasted a goose and made that sweet, fruit pie you like and she will be pleased to see you."

"I'm sorry Hakon, I …"

"I'm asking so nicely brother." Hakon flashed an exaggerated grin.

"It's not that Hakon; you have Asta and your own house to run, I still live at home, I'm responsible for it and the care of mother when father is away."

Hakon sighed resignedly. "I know; I know … you are a better son than I … You give her my love then, little brother. Tell her I will be around to see her."

"Do that brother, she misses you, misses the family."

"I promise. You will come for supper one night though? … For I miss you!"

"I promise."

"Bring Eerika too." He called as he turned away towards his house.

Bjarke smiled and hitched the buck further up his back. It was a good size animal and a good catch this late in the year, possibly the last taste of venison they would enjoy before winter. Soon the autumn culling of the domestic animals would begin; the best animals being kept for breeding, the poorer conditioned ones slaughtered and the meat salted or stored in the icehouses to feed people through the winter.

He thought of Eerika as he walked towards home, his heart warming. Their courting was finally official, Bjarke having sought permission from Anders, Eerika's father. The gruff old warrior seemingly none too pleased, had finally consented but only after laying down strict rules and threats of retribution if his commands where not followed to the letter. Inger had also been hostile in her own way, having lost one son to marriage she did not want to lose the second so quickly. Eysteinn had said nothing but was quietly enjoying the discomfort of the over protective father and the doting, somewhat possessive mother, of a son who seemed to have lost his wits and reason to a beautiful girl.

Bjarke was within a mile of home and passing the first of the cottages and huts on the outskirts of the village when he heard his name called.

"Bjarke! … Bjarke Orrifostersson!" The voice was old and husky and already fading as he turned towards it. He turned to see an ancient looking woman standing in the doorway of one of the huts. Her grey-white hair bound back behind her head showing a much weathered and lined face, her skin sallow and stretched tight over her prominent cheekbones. Her eyes however, were bright and sharp and as green as those of a cat.

"What is it old mother?" He asked kindly.

"That's a fine buck you have there and so late in the year."

"The hunting was good, old mother."

"I see, I see!" She cackled. "Ullr has been good and granted you a prize."

Bjarke looked surprised at the mention of the old Gods. Seeing his surprise, she fished in the neckline of her dress and produced a number of necklaces all bearing differing symbols and small effigies of the old Gods along with a crucifix. Seeing his confusion, she laughed.

"At my age, Bjarke Orrifostersson, I cannot afford to take chances! Is my afterlife with the Christ God or the old Gods? Who knows?" She laughed again and beckoned him closer to the door. As he drew closer, he noticed Fenrir had not followed him but remained sitting where he had stopped when called.

"Fenrir! Heel!"

The dog gave a low whimper and walked slowly across to join him.

"Would you have a leg of that buck you could spare for an old woman? In exchange for advice."

"Of course, old mother. Here, I will cut you a piece."

"Hah! Every bit as kind as your foster father, our Lord, Orri. Bring it away in lad, here to the table." She swung the door wide and pointed to a long wooden table.

Bjarke had to duck low to pass through the doorway; stepping across the stone floor, he deposited the buck on the table. He turned to see where Fenrir was and saw the dog still sat outside the door. Before he could say anything Fenrir let out a low whimper and laid down on the doorstep, ears back and head between his front paws watching, when Bjarke summoned him in, he didn't move. The old woman cackled.

"He'll not venture further lad, I'm not a lover of dogs and they know it, he will be fine out there."

Bjarke unsheathed his seax and turned to the buck.

"I'll give you a hindquarter old mother, some of the best, most tender meat is at the rear, would that suffice?"

"More than, you are most kind."

Bjarke smiled and set about a hind leg, carefully separating it from the body.

"If you give me a pot I'll skin the leg and bone it, then you just have to cook it."

The old woman grinned; showing a few stumpy yellow teeth, all that remained in her mouth.

"You are kind Bjarke Orrifostersson, with a heart as big as you are tall. Watch that others don't take advantage of that, not all will come to you with openness and sincerity."

Bjarke just smiled back as he worked while the old woman disappeared to find a pot. Taking a moment, he looked around the room. It smelled sweetly of dried herbs and flowers that hung in bunches from the low ceiling. Shelves, of which there were many, were filled with pots and dishes of all sizes. Animal bones; bleached white and crisscrossed and strung on long cords hung from the ceiling, with others arranged in careful piles on shelves with the skull sitting atop them. In the centre of the room, a small fire burned with the chain and hook for hanging the cooking pot suspended over the centre of it. He was just bringing his gaze back to the buck when he looked past a bunch of dried lavender and saw a large, tabby cat watching him. It startled him a little, it however never moved, it just stared fixedly at him from large yellow eyes. Hearing the old woman returning he turned his attention back to the buck. By the time she arrived with the pot he had the skin peeled back and the meat off the carcase, boning it, he dropped it carefully into the pot, her arms lowering at the weight of the meat.

"So kind! So very kind."

"It's nothing old mother, you should just ask when you see me and if I have meat, I will share."

She laid the pot down and threw a cloth over the top then reached for a jug and two horn cups.

"Ale for the hunter? You have given now I must give." Before he could accept or decline, she was pouring the drink and ushering him to a stool by the fire. "Will you talk with me, Bjarke Orrifostersson? I don't have many visitors these days, my age and the Christ religion has rendered me less needed than I was." She groaned a little as she settled her ancient bones on a stool next to his.

"It was not always so." She mused, looking blankly into space. "Once over, folk sought my council, my knowledge and my abilities, now they come for healing remedies, potions and salves and little else. If you wish it, I can offer you more, much more."

"There is nothing I need old mother, I am grateful of the ale and am happy to talk with you while I drink it, though I only have tales of hunting to tell."

"You don't need to tell me anything, Bjarke Orrifostersson, I know all about you. Since the day you were born, when my daughter, Freya, helped bring you into the world, I have watched you grow. I know of the bear that took Helka, your birth mother and which slew your father as he slew it. The beast killed more than your birth parents that day though, my daughter never recovered from the shock of the attack, it turned her mind. You were the last child she helped into the world."

The old woman's gaze turned to the fire and she looked suddenly sad.

"She still lives? Your daughter?"

"No … no, she went to the Gods almost ten winters ago, there is just me now, me and my cat. My husband was already long since gone. He never came home from Constantinople and the wars there."

Bjarke looked at the cat which was still watching him intently, it hadn't moved since he saw it last.

"As you know, they call me, 'old mother." She sighed softly. "I was mother to all before the Christ God religion loomed large and strong … my name, my real name is Runa, Runa Thorfinsdotter and I have the sight, some still seek me for that."

"The sight?"

"Yes, the sight. I see things that are yet to be, I can warn of ill things to come but also of good things. Would you like to know Bjarke Orrifostersson, what life is bringing for you?"

Bjarke just stared then looked unsure.

"Inger, your foster mother used to visit me when she was young, plaguing me for what I could tell her, wanting to know what the *Nornir,* had decided for her."

"The *Nornir*?"

"Yes, the Fates, the three sisters; *Urðr, Verðandi* and *Skuld* that sit at the roots of *Yggdrasil*, the tree of life, they weave the threads of our lives onto the great tapestry, else cut them short with a snip of their shears." She cackled then looked sad again. "Now, with the Christ God religion strong in your mother's mind, she only visits me for healing remedies. It was my salves and potions that have healed you and your brother's injuries over all these years." She cackled again. "Inger told me much of you and Hakon … good boys, her boys! Now, do you wish to know more? I would pay you in words for your kindness."

Runa picked up the jug and poured more ale for herself then gestured to Bjarke. He drained his cup and held it up for a refill. Runa smiled.

"So, you would know what life will bring, Bjarke Orrifostersson?"

Bjarke just smiled and shrugged.

Runa drank her ale then poured water into the cup. Placing it on the table, she lifted down three of the jars and spooned some of their contents into it, stirring and swirling the cup she sipped it. Grimacing at the taste, she gulped the rest, letting out a loud burp as she finished, making Bjarke chuckle. She pulled her stool close and directly opposite Bjarke's and held out her hands gesturing for his. Unsure, he offered his, she folding her small hands tightly over his closed fingers, his whole hand too large to hold. Runa looked intently at Bjarke, he smiled but she remained impassive, gradually her eyes glazed over, her lips moved but no sound came out. Suddenly her eyes rolled back, leaving only the whites on show, Bjarke was alarmed and tried to pull away but was shocked at the strength of Runa's grip, holding him where he was. Without moving or her eyes changing, she uttered a gentle shushing sound, settling him again. They sat for some time before Runa's lips began moving again, slowly forming into silent words punctuated with small groans. She muttered some words Bjarke didn't comprehend then slowly changed into the Norse he could understand, though the words came out in disjointed sentences that made no sense.

"Beauty is short lived and passing and the flower will die before it blooms. ... Reputations will be made but glory is fleeting soon to

be lost. … A great harvest is coming that is not of wheat but of souls. … Kings and Jarls will lie down with men. … Both Angels and the Valkyrie will fly, gathering the brave. … Brother will fight brother but the raven, the dragon and the fighting man will give way to the leopard of gold. … Bifröst, the burning rainbow bridge will choke with those seeking the Gods. … The bear that heeds the hunter will not fall but the bear that doesn't, will into the river fall. …The bridge, the bridge, linger not on the bridge.

Runa's voice faded to a whisper then to nothing, her lips moving then slowly stopping. Suddenly her eyes rolled back, once more showing their vivid green, her pupils huge and dilated, she shook her head gently then seemed to awake from wherever her mind had been. The cat jumped up, arched its back, hissed loudly and disappeared from the room at the run, outside Fenrir howled mournfully like a wolf then went silent again. Runa let go of Bjarke's hands, he looking at her bemused.

"What does it all mean, old mother? I don't understand any of it, it means nothing to me."

"I'm sorry, Bjarke Orrifostersson, I am only the bearer of the message I don't understand any more than you do. You must decipher it for yourself."

"What bridge could the message be referring to? What is *Bifröst?*"

"That much I can explain, *Bifröst* is the burning rainbow bridge of the old Gods, it connects *Midgard* or *Middle Earth*, here, to *Asgard,* the home of *Odin, Thor, Loki, Freya* and all the Gods of our forefathers."

"What would that have to do with me?"

"As I said Bjarke, I cannot always tell, you must think on it and see what it means to you. Now you must go, I am weary; the messages take much of my energy these days."

Runa rose unsteadily to her feet, Bjarke standing to aid her as she sought her balance.

"Go now, Bjarke Orrifostersson, I thank you for your kindness … I hope the message will become useful in time. Give my regards to your mother."

Bjarke hefted the buck from the table and made for the door, Fenrir jumping up, walking ahead the moment Bjarke's foot crossed the threshold.

He was somewhat troubled on the way home, trying to make sense of the message but after hanging the meat, taking a wash and feeding Fenrir, he was no clearer in his mind so decided to put the riddle, for that is what it seemed, to his mother.

Inger was busy overseeing the preparation for the evening meal and carried on with what she was doing as he spoke, until he mentioned Runa. She stopped her work immediately.

"Where did you say you have been?" She asked tersely while ushering him quickly out of the kitchen and through into the private living quarters.

He explained Runa asking for the meat, the ale and then the message she had given him. Inger had him repeat the message twice, and then shook her head.

"I don't mind you giving Runa meat but don't ask her advice; she is strange, stuck in the old ways, she still worships the old Gods."

"She said you visited her much when you were young, for her advice."

Inger looked flustered. "That was a long time ago; I was young then and foolish."

"What's the harm, mother? She was kind to me and I think she is just old and lonely, she sent you her regards."

"There is nothing wrong with Runa, Bjarke, she is a good woman, just don't listen to her messages, it's not

Christian. When the priest visits, he warns against such, beware of false prophets, he says."

"Is that what she is, a prophet, a seer?"

"No Bjarke." Inger seemed to recover some of her resolve. "Runa is just an old woman and lonely like you said, worry not about what she has told you, it's all nonsense really."

"Did she tell you nonsense?"

"I don't remember, as I said I was very young." Inger almost snapped. "Now, do as I bid you and listen to her no more, be kind, by all means but that's it. Do you understand me?" Inger looked serious again.

"Very well mother, I was confused was all?"

Inger hugged him, her head only reaching to his chest, his massive arms enveloping her, almost hiding her from sight, her look of concern hidden.

"Have you seen Hakon?" She asked into his chest, changing the subject.

Garrett Pearson

Chapter Eight

The wharf, Borg, spring 1061 AD

The wharf was full of people, warriors, women and children, all crammed onto the long, thin wooden space that stretched out into the fjord as the ships loaded with provisions and men, ready for yet another war or assault on Denmark. Inger was dressed in her finest, a long dress of sea-green suede, her neck and wrists adorned in gold chains, her blonde hair gathered into a regal pile on top of her head and held in place with gold combs. Today was the day her whole family went to war.

Eysteinn was also well dressed, a noble, a Warlord. A brown bearskin cloak draped from his shoulders, his mail hauberk polished with river sand, shimmered as he walked up and down the wharf issuing orders. His warrior arm rings were of silver and gold, the huge silver buckle of his *Jarl's* belt which held his sword was twisted into shapes of writhing dragons, the small jade stones used for their eyes and the silver of their bodies all catching the sunlight and sparkling.

Hakon was already aboard the largest ship, helping load provisions and weapons, he waved as he caught sight of his mother and brother then clambered back onto the wharf heading towards them.

"Come little brother, up here with Ingvar and me, we've saved you a place."

Inger grabbed Bjarke by the arm holding him back, her other hand tightening on Fenrir's leash. "Hakon, a word … if you please." She said, more sternly than she intended.

Hakon grinned and pushed through the crowd closer to his mother and brother.

"You're not going to slap me again mother, are you?" He joked. "It's Bjarke's turn for that." Both boys chuckled, Inger said nothing, her eyes however were moist and full and she was struggling to find words.

"I'm sorry mother, I was but jesting!"

Inger waved away the comment and managed a smile. "Listen; listen to me, both of you."

Both boys turned to face their mother. She pulled herself up proudly and bit at her lip, taking a moment to find her words.

"Do as your father tells you. Hakon, you are older and have been to war before, look out for your younger brother, and keep him out of trouble, no heroics. The sagas are full of heroes, dead ones! I don't want you two or your father adding to them; am I understood?"

"Yes, mother."

"We'll both be careful mother and look out for father." Bjarke added.

Inger nodded, she swallowed quickly then cleared her throat. "Hakon Orrifostersson, you're my eldest, I love you and want you home, as does Asta." She gestured towards a beautiful young woman waiting further back along the wharf; she also dressed in her finest. "Go with God; remember your prayers and we will all feast when you return home. Here!" She held out a necklace with a finely crafted silver crucifix on it, gesturing for him to lower his head so she could fasten it. She tucked it into his mail shirt then kissed him on both cheeks, then pushed him towards Asta.

"Don't worry mother." He said quietly, as he gave her a sad smile and bowed his head respectfully then walked towards his wife.

Inger turned to Bjarke. "Bjarke Orrifostersson, you are my youngest, the strongest and also the kindest, the most gentle. Kindness and war don't always mix; don't let your heart put you in danger. Do as your father bids you, stay with Hakon and Ingvar and come home son, come home, do you hear me?"

"Yes mother."

She gestured for him to stoop and lower his head; then fastened an identical silver crucifix about his neck. As he stood back up, Inger looked up at him, her eyes full, and then suddenly slapped him, her face stern. "As I told your brother the last time, do as you are told, I only have two sons and I wish to continue having two sons, do you understand? Now go, Bjarke Orrifostersson! Make me proud, make your father proud!"

She beckoned him down to her again and kissed him gently on both cheeks; Bjarke smiled, kissed her forehead and hugged her. He squatted and ruffled Fenrir's neck; the dog lowered his ears, let out a low whine then laid down. Inger drew herself up proudly, cuffed her tears quickly then clicked her tongue and Fenrir jumped up as she turned away making her way towards her Lord. Fenrir looked back expectantly at Bjarke then howled mournfully as Inger led him away.

Eysteinn saw her coming and turned to meet her.

"You've seen the boys Inger? Did you …"

"Yes, I've seen the boys and warned both. Now it is you I wish to speak to." She said tersely.

Eysteinn smirked and went to interrupt but Inger talked over him, at pains to say her piece.

"You're my man, my Lord, my husband. You and the boys are my family, all my family, all I ever wanted, make sure you come home."

Tears rolled down Inger's cheeks again, which she angrily brushed away.

"It'll be alright girl, I'll see to the boys …"

"I've talked to the boys, now I'm talking to you!" she snapped. "I love you Eysteinn Orri, I love you so very much, so you come home, I'll be waiting."

He felt the dampness on her cheeks as she kissed him on the cheeks and the lips. "I'll be waiting." She said, as she turned and pushed her way through the crowds, passing a sobbing Asta, entwined around Hakon.

Bjarke was about to go aboard when Eerika caught his arm.

"Did you think I had forgotten you?" She said as she jumped up to kiss him. "I had to see my father off first … he takes priority as we are not yet betrothed or married!" She giggled wickedly as he looked down at her and laughed lightly.

"I also ask you to be careful but think your mother has issued enough warnings to you about coming home. I saw her slap you, did it hurt?" She giggled again.

"No … no, it's my mother's way is all, she hides behind being fierce but really she cares deeply, loves us."

"I guess so. Perhaps I should slap you then, Bjarke Orrifostersson, would you learn from that?"

A moment later, Bjarke reasoned the words and his face lit up, a huge grin and a chuckle coming out as he lifted Eerika up off her feet and kissed her full in the mouth.

"I … I love you too, Eerika." He whispered into her ear as he hugged her then gently lowered her to the ground again. "I will see you when I get home, I promise. Then I will go and see your father, we will have things to discuss."

Eerika beamed at him and hugged him tightly. "You come home Bjarke Orrifostersson, I will be waiting."

With the ships full of warriors and provisions, they cast off and rowed out into the middle of the fjord. Catching the tide and morning breeze, they dropped sail, shipped oars and headed seaward. Exiting the fjord, they caught a strong northerly wind. As the ships' turned southwards in front of it the sails cracked loudly as they filled with the blow and the ships took on a new speed, the hulls lifting in the water as they sped across a wind-flattened sea.

The men were in good spirits, with spring newly arrived it was a good time for war. The weather was improving; the longer days coming and the planting and animal management could be left to the older men and boys who'd remain behind in Borg. Also, this northerly blow saved their arms and backs from the oars and seemed to bode well for their venture, was God smiling on them?

Many of the warriors were Christian, the old, Norse religion replaced by the new Romish faith. Some however, still wore a Thor's hammer as well as a crucifix about their necks, deigning perhaps like Runa that having a foot in both God's camps would ensure salvation no matter what. Some warriors, those from the very remote farmsteads and crofts, where the priests and the new religion had not reached, still held to their old beliefs and wore their Thor's hammer necklaces or a bracelet with the hammer effigy hanging off it. Eysteinn however, didn't care what his men believed; especially men asked to fight and die if necessary for their Lord and his King. Surely, they had a right to worship who and how they chose. Though the priests and Inger would disagree, their Christian God being the only God in their eyes, Eysteinn had seen enough dying and death to know that a man will call upon whomever he chooses when the end was nigh. Valhalla, Odin, Heaven, Christ God, did it really matter?

Taking a hand at the steering oar of his flagship, Muninn, while he thought, he smiled inwardly, thinking of how appalled Inger and the priest would be at his reason.

The ships pushed on down the coast driven on the wind, passing small fishing craft working closer to the shore and the odd merchant vessel heading into land from deep sea. As it sailed south to meet the King and his ships at Oslo, Orri's fleet was joined by other warships that slipped from out of fjords and river mouths into the ocean. As the tide turned against the wind, white caps began appearing on top of the swell as the water and wind fought. Eysteinn felt the steering oar shudder and vibrate as the ship surged against the tide, it becoming almost a living thing as it flexed beneath the waves. Whistling sharply to catch his sons' attention, he beckoned them back from the bows.

"We're making good time, lads. This wind at our backs is driving us south at a great speed, here Bjarke, take the rudder, feel the ship."

Bjarke grasped the long rudder handle and felt the quiver along the stem, some salt spray spattering over the low strakes and wetting his face, he grinned as he felt the power of the ship and the sea.

"Watch ahead and watch the sail; keep an eye on the swell, adjust the rudder to suit, small movements just, give her time to respond. We have the land to our left so no need to worry about navigation so much but keep us well off lad, too close and we run the risk of shoals and rocks. Hakon, take over from your brother as he tires, fighting the wind and tide is hard work."

The fleet continued to grow in numbers as it headed south, the weather remaining kind with the sun slipping in and out of the clouds and the wind not ceasing its blow, filling the sails and saving men's backs.

Early evening saw the wind drop away. Men took to the oars as the ships sought shelter in a fjord away from the openness of the ocean. The boys took their turn at the oar bench, each being carefully allotted a place alongside a seasoned oarsman, the differing strengths of the pair seeing them separated and placed where the shipmaster thought best. Finding a wide bay not too far inland, Eysteinn called a 'heave to' and the ships began positioning and dropping anchor for the night. Fritjof, a huge man, stepped up to the bows towards the anchor.

"Bjarke! Here lad, help me with this."

Bjarke shipped his oar and stepped up to the large stone anchor. The stone was wedged between a 'y' shaped or wishbone like, tree limb, with another piece of timber running beneath it and fastened to either side of the wishbone limb, forming a stirrup shape for the stone to sit in. Both men grunted as they hefted the huge anchor and hurled it overboard.

"Stand clear lad!" Fritjof pushed Bjarke back a step as the looped, sealskin, anchor rope played out quickly as the stone sank to the bottom of the fjord. Fritjof tying it off as the rope went slack once more. After lighting a lantern and placing it atop the mast, the men settled down to eat and rest.

"Another day's sailing like today and we will be in Oslo by tomorrow afternoon." Eysteinn said between mouthfuls of bread and cheese as he pushed in alongside Bjarke and Hakon. He swilled the food down with ale. "A good day lads, don't you think? Perhaps God is smiling on our endeavours?" He lifted his crucifix to his lips and kissed it. "Or perhaps Rán, the Goddess of the sea and her nine daughters have been kind and granted us safe passage?" He winked and poured a drop of ale overboard and bowed his head. "I'm hedging my bets boys, don't tell your mother!" He laughed then coughed, spraying cheese and ale.

The following morning dawned windless and chilly, the shadow of the towering cliffs hiding the sun and holding back the light and warmth. Men pissed or squatted over the strakes then took a quick, meagre breakfast, keen to be at their oars and able to warm themselves with some work. Anchors were hauled up amidst grunts and gasps from the men, then oars dipped, the ships once more turning seaward, the chant at the oars began to give timing for the strokes followed by bawdy songs as the ships gathered speed. Nosing out into the ocean again found the same northerly blow as before but much reduced in power from yesterday, the sails were dropped but did not belly as before, the men staying at their oars to help drive the ships southward.

As the sun climbed and midmorning approached, the wind gathered in speed and once more, allowed the oars to be shipped as the sails filled and the boats speed increased. Having caught the tide before it turned against the wind, the ships seemed to glide across the water, riding the large but gentle swell and thrilling the men with the speed.

"Greyhounds of the sea, boys! Don't you think?" Eysteinn shouted above the noise of the ocean and wind, the boys nodded and grinned as the ship rode the swell. "Here, feel!" He offered the rudder arm again. "She's as smooth as silk today; we are not fighting the tide see." The boys each took a hold of the rudder in turn. "Our speed is the greater and the ship is lifting with the blow, we are skimming the water. Our draft at worst is just over a sword length, at the moment it will be half that, less resistance, more speed!"

Late afternoon saw the fleet turn back northwards once more, out of the ocean and into the long sea inlet and approach to Oslo, as the wind died away the oars came out again, the ships making steady progress up the sheltered fjord. As evening approached and twilight came, Eysteinn's fleet was already in the narrows approaching the harbour at Oslo. As the narrows opened again into the huge natural harbour, Eysteinn called for speed and the men responded with gusto, the ship surging through the water as the oars rose, dipped and fell, each pull accompanied with a loud grunt as men worked the sweeps hard. The ships increased speed and beat proudly towards the already assembled ships tied up at the wharfs, the men at pains to put on a good show for the gathered crowds on the harbour wall and beach. Just before the Muninn came into dock, the oars dug deep, slowing and turning the vessel broadside on to the land, the oars lifting then held above and parallel to the water.

"Now Lord?" Fritjof asked, making for the stern.

"Aye Fritjof, show them what northern lads can do!"

The big man clambered nimbly over the stern strakes onto the rearmost oar. Setting his balance, he stepped, almost hopped onto the next and the next, heading towards the bows. He began to sing as he went, the oarsmen chanting back in chorus. For a huge man he was surprisingly agile and reached the bows of the ship without a slip or a stumble. A huge cheer erupted as he reached the foremost oar at which he jumped in the air, twisted and landed, facing the stern again. The ship's crew cheered loudly, the two boys dazzled by the display of agility and bravery, the crowds on the wharf joining in, cheering and clapping. Fritjof made greater display on his way back, stepping backwards and forwards on the oars and punctuating his movements in time to the song. Reaching the stern, again without a stumble, Eysteinn himself helped him back over the strakes, congratulating him and slapping him on his back, the crew wild with delight.

"That'll let the King know we are here!" He shouted to his men.

Laughter and roars of approval came back at him.

"Take us in lads, food and ale and a warmer place to sleep than last night awaits."

The oars dipped again and the Muninn glided into dock, Eysteinn leaping onto the wooden staging before the mooring lines were thrown.

"Eysteinn Orri! Christ God man, can you not arrive without a show!" A giant of a man roared, as he laughed and stepped out of the crowd, his arms open wide in welcome.

"Lord King!" Eysteinn bowed low.

"Up man! Up! We were sword brothers long before I was a King. God in heaven, it's good to see you!" The two men came together amidst much backslapping and hand shaking. "Inger, Inger is well? And where are these pups of yours? You've brought both, yes?"

"Aye Lord, both, and the youngest is almost big enough to give you a thumping!"

"A real man then!" Harald roared. "I know, I know, you breed them well up north! Come, come, tell me of your journey, and I will tell you my plans to thrash Sweyn."

Chapter Nine

The Court of King Harald Sigurdsson (Hardrada) at Oslo

Oslo was full to bursting point with ships, warriors, merchants, whores and the populace, young and old. A sense of excitement in the air along with some trepidation as to what was coming.

The King's hall was full to overflowing and the taverns, houses, stables and barns all crammed with men seeking a place to sleep before the fleet sailed for Denmark. Eysteinn and the boys were allotted a place to sleep in the rear of the great hall, he being a Lord in his own right and a friend of the King since their days of service in the Varangian Guard. The hall tables were placed around a great central fire pit and laden with platters of venison, pork, fish, cheese, bread and ale, the men squashed onto benches amidst their gear, eating their fill, talking and shouting in the chaos. Torches lined the walls, some spluttering and flaring as the draughts caught them, the oil-black smoke creeping upwards, caressing the already dark stained roof beams to filter out through the roof thatch. Candles, thick as a man's forearm and bunched together onto metal stands, lined the tables. Greyhounds and elkhounds laid apathetically near the fire, panting with the heat else lingered near the tables, hopeful of a morsel or two.

On a raised dais at the end of the hall the King sat at the table on a large, high backed chair, Eysteinn and the other *Jarls* seated to his right and left, they too as loud and raucous as the men on the tables below. Bjarke and Hakon found themselves on a bench close to the high table along with the King's, *Hearth-weru*. Most of the men seated on the bench were middle aged, the same as Eysteinn and the King, with a handful perhaps still in their early thirties. The boys caught a few cursory glances at them and the odd nod of a head, their placing at the table denoting them as folk of rank, despite their tender years.

The pair sat quietly, quite in awe of the men with which they sat. All were seasoned warriors, most bore scars of some description across their faces or forearms; some had tattoos of intricate, swirling patterns across their cheeks or foreheads in blue or black ink. Their hair was long and pulled back into ponytails or plaits; some had their heads shaved with just a ponytail springing from the back of their heads, others wore their hair from a centre parting with the other side shaved, showing a tattoo across the bare side of their head. Beards and moustaches were plaited and weighted at the end with small silver or gold tubes. Their arms heavy with gold and silver warrior rings. These men were the greatest of the King's warriors, and amongst the best in Christendom, earning their place as his personal guard through bravery and prowess alone, a mighty company in which to sit.

Despite the war footing, a sense of carnival prevailed and the feasting was interspersed with entertainments.

A pair of jugglers appeared first, each throwing small leather balls in the air, the brightly coloured spheres going higher and higher until they almost reached the rafters before throwing them to each other whilst juggling the ones that came back to them. The watching men's interest was brief and they turned again to the food until the jugglers changed the balls for three, hand axes each. The elder of the pair threw an apple in the air while turning an axe, blade side up, letting an apple fall onto it, the apple slicing cleanly into two, the men at the tables turned again to watch, nudging comrades to also turn and see. Again, the pair began by juggling individually, then, as before, threw the axes to each other before juggling them and throwing back. The crowd began to cheer and slam the tables in appreciation. Another man appeared with three more axes and threw them one at a time to the two men. Suddenly each man had three axes to juggle with the other three spinning through the air to the other. The bright metal heads shimmered in the torchlight as the axes somersaulted through the air, the audience now wild with delight. One of the jugglers positioned himself beneath a roof beam and as the axes spun back to him, he launched each upwards, the blades lodging into the timber, forming a row of nine. The men at the tables cheered and rose to their feet, clapping or hammering the tables in appreciation, the two boys looking on in wonder.

They had seen jugglers before but never with sharpened war axes. The jugglers bowed their heads to their audience then tuned to the King and bowed low, he throwing three bags of coins to the eldest man who caught them and juggled them briefly before throwing a bag each to his comrades. As the jugglers disappeared to the back of the hall, the men turned back to the food and talk.

A gradual hush came over the room again as a man walked into the open space in front of the tables. His head bound around and around with cloth forming a huge headdress, his trousers wide and flapping as he walked, and his feet encased in small, pointy-toed, leather boots. His eyes were shaded black on their lids, his skin brown as tanned leather. A pointed black beard and moustache hid most of his face, his ears weighted with numerous gold rings. Under his arm, he had a wicker basket and in his hand a reed flute.

Hakon nudged Bjarke and whispered. "He must be of the east, I've heard father mention their strange dress."

Bjarke nodded while watching the man intently. The man placed the basket on the floor and sat cross-legged in front of it. Taking the flute, he began to play, blowing a slow, wailing tune. Shortly, the basket began to move and the lid to lift slightly, the audience gasped as the basket lid lifted higher and a snake's head appeared beneath it. The snake rose slowly, the lid balanced on its head for a moment until its body began to sway in time to the flute's tune. The audience stared and murmured in wonder, Hakon and Bjarke just gawped, men at the back of the hall began climbing onto tables to see what was happening. Hakon did notice that his father, the King and some of the older warriors were smiling knowingly while the rest of the hall looked on enraptured. The snake swayed slowly on as the man played. As he angled the flute upwards, the snake rose higher, its tongue flicking in and out, tasting the air. The man gradually lowered the flute again, changing the tune to a very slow drone and the snake began lowering itself back into its basket, then disappeared from sight, the man putting the lid in place. Loud cheers and clapping came from the hall, the man standing to bow.

As the applause eased, an assistant appeared with another basket. The flute player took it and cautiously, teasingly, lifted the lid. The audience gasped as he eased his hand in tentatively. He yelped, grimaced, and pulled it out, trailing a thick piece of rope and the audience laughed while some booed in disappointment. He smiled and held up a hand for peace and placed his finger over his lips. Carefully, he formed the rope into a circle, just larger than a warrior's shield. Then, taking the first basket with the snake in it, tipped it upside down and the snake fell into the middle of the circle, he jumping back and away. The snake hissed and reared at the rough handling, flaring its hood wide behind its head and the audience gasped again. The man capered around the circle, slowly waving his arms downwards as if trying to settle the snake, it watching and following his every move. He turned to the King and bowed low, one hand still moving slowly keeping the snake's attention. Harald threw a bag of coins to him, which he deftly caught then bowed again.

Turning to the snake, he opened the bag and took out the coins, throwing them one at a time into the circle beside the snake. The snake hissed as each landed, the audience murmuring in appreciation when they saw the coins were gold. The man took a stick and banged the floor within the circle, the snake reacting with a hiss and a strike each time the stick struck. The hall was totally silent now, so quiet the snake's hiss could be heard. The man knelt in front of the snake, just outside of the circle. Holding the stick up and towards the snake, he readied his other hand, flexing his fingers. He wiggled the stick and the snake struck at it, at the same time his other hand snatched a coin from the circle. The audience responded with a buzz of appreciation and then clapping as the man continued to take coins while distracting the snake's attention with the stick. The snake coiled and uncoiled as it followed the man as he moved around the circle, it becoming more agitated while the clapping grew louder.

Eventually there were only two coins left, both in front of the snake. The man signalled to the audience for quiet then reached into his pouch and pulled out a live mouse, holding it by the tail he held it up for the audience to see. Putting his stick down he showed the mouse to the snake, the snake's tongue flicked repeatedly, tasting the air and mouse. Suddenly, the man threw the mouse into the circle. The snake struck like lightning, seizing the mouse in its jaws before it could clear the circle, at the same time the man snatched both coins, one in each hand. The audience went wild with appreciation, whoops, cheers and thumps on the tables resonating in the hall. The man bowed graciously to the king and his audience, while his assistants captured the snake using forked sticks, carefully placing it back in its basket.

A troop of dwarves appeared next, all dressed as warriors but carrying wooden weapons. They ran into the centre of the room, capering and blowing war horns; their small shields bore the colours of King Harald, raising cheers and laughter from the tables. Another troop appeared from the other side of the hall, similarly dressed but their shields bore the colours of Sweyn of Denmark, amongst this group was one wearing a brass coloured crown around his helmet and leading a very portly, woman dwarf by the hand. The king roared with laughter when he saw the parody.

"Christ God, Eysteinn, its Sweyn and his Queen!"

The audience all hooting and cheering as the two sides lined up as if readying for battle. The side bearing King Harald's colours turned their backs to the, would be Danes and bared their arse's, one or two managing to fart loudly for affect, the audience now beside themselves with laughter. After a mock battle play and more capering, all the Danes except the Queen lay on the floor as if dead, while the Norse contingent raised their wooden swords and cheered. The Danish Queen waved her arms and made beseeching cries for help, the crowd hooting in laughter. One dwarf from the Norse side snatched the brass crown, holding it aloft in the direction of King Harald while the strongest one in the group seized the wailing Queen and hurled her over his shoulder. Pushing her dress up with his sword, he ran around the room slapping her bare backside with it, reducing the audience to fits of laughter. Another horn blew and the little people presented themselves in front of the King, bowed low and ran out to loud applause.

A pause in the entertainment saw the audience settle once more and their attention return to the food. As the buzz of conversation began again, slaves appeared pulling small carts laden with different size rocks followed by a giant of a man. The men at the tables began turning around to see what was coming next. After the rocks were tipped off the carts onto the floor, the big man raised his arms, hushing the audience. He turned around as he spoke, ensuring all in the hall could hear.

"Warriors! I challenge any man here to a game of stones, any that you can lift and place on the cart, I will lift the next largest until I am challenged no more or beaten."

The men at the tables looked at the rocks, those at the back of the hall again climbing onto the tables to see and knocking dishes onto the floor as ale befuddled movement. The rocks ranged in size from what would be a hefty one man lift to an almost impossible two man lift, the shapes changing from round boulders to long, lozenge like stones. The big man waited until the hubbub died down before speaking again.

"I will wager this silver." He held aloft a small bag of coins. "Against similar or something else of worth … do I have a challenger?"

He turned slowly, looking around the room, his arms outstretched and the bag held high. Men looked along the tables to see if anyone ventured the challenge.

"Here! Here, strongman! I'll take your money." Fritjof got to his feet.

There was sudden interest from the room before Fritjof's friends began pulling him back to his seat.

"Christ God, Fritjof! You're soused with ale man."

The strongman looked on hopefully, only to be disappointed when Fritjof's friends finally settled him back at the table, albeit amidst drunken grumbles and curses. The man looked around the room again. There was much talk and some of the larger men in the room seemed to be considering an attempt, however the high wager was a lot to lose should they fail. Hardrada rose to his feet.

"Is there not one among you who will take the challenge?" He laughed loudly. "It's only silver! Must your King teach this rock-lifter who is the strongest?" He pulled his shirt over his head revealing a heavy muscled frame swathed in blue tattoos.

"Lord King! … By your leave."

One of Hardrada's *Hearth-weru* rose from the table and pulled off his shirt, his body also tattooed and heavily scarred; his arms and chest thick with muscle. The men cheered and banged the table in applause. Hardrada smiled and gestured acceptance.

"Very well, I'll match the strongman's purse if you beat him, Master Ulf."

The crowd roared and banged the tables again; hands slapped Ulf's back as he made his way to the floor. The two men eyed each other, taking in size and age, the strongman graciously acknowledging Ulf's size and applauding that he had taken the challenge then gestured to the rocks.

"I offer you first lift, Master Ulf. Choose and I will lift the next largest."

Ulf studied the rocks, looking at their differing shapes and sizes. The crowd began calling encouragement as he pondered. Selecting one he stepped up to it, then stepped again to the next largest, the men at the tables cheering and whooping. Ulf spat on his hands, grimaced then squatted to the rock wrapping his arms round about it; the crowd went silent as he took the strain. Growling in his throat, he heaved and the rock left the floor, the crowd once again yelling and cheering. Hefting it to his waist, he hugged it close as he steadied his legs. Setting his balance, he stepped slowly, a pace at a time to the cart depositing his load with a thump onto the cart floor. The strongman smiled and nodded, holding his hands up and clapping Ulf's effort. The crowd went silent as the strongman stepped to the next largest rock; he pointed to it and to himself then looked at Ulf as if seeking confirmation of his choice. Ulf nodded and the strongman squatted to hug the rock, the crowd went silent. He made to lift then growled and gurned his face as if it was all too much, the rock lifted a little and his arms shook, the crowd went wild as he struggled, Ulf looked on, a smile forming. The strongman looked as if he was about to drop the rock then suddenly powered upwards, the room falling silent as he walked to the cart and laid the rock gently down, the cart sagged beneath the weight and the crowd's excitement with it. He turned to the room, raising his hands inviting applause. Hardrada banged the table.

"Well done, big man! Well done!"

The crowd joined in with a somewhat muted applause.

"Will you venture again, master Ulf?"

Ulf looked at the larger rocks then shook his head and reached for his purse, his face twisted and bitter at his defeat. He took out a handful of silver coins and gave them to the strongman. The man bowed graciously and raised Ulf's other hand turning him to the crowd.

"A brave effort! A brave effort." He called, the crowd applauding. "Is there another? … Is there another who will match me stone for stone?"

He gestured for the rocks to be returned to the floor while some of the younger, big men at the benches were jostled and harangued by the crowd, being urged to wager their silver and try their strength. One man rose halfway to his feet but was pulled back to his seat by his friends.

"You could beat the big man, Bjarke." Hakon said as he nudged his brother.

Bjarke looked down at the table then shushed Hakon when he badgered him again.

"Is there another?" The strongman shouted again.

"Go on! … Go on!" Hakon shoved Bjarke.

Close by, others noticed the harassment and joined in, coercing and urging Bjarke up and to take the challenge. One warrior slapped some silver on the table while calling for his friends to add to it to make the wager, as the pile grew the men's shouts and yells rose, calling to the strongman that they had a challenger. Bjarke was jostled and pushed to his feet, the warriors whooping in delight when they saw the size of him. The strongman also applauded and invited Bjarke forward to the rocks, gesturing that he remove his shirt.

"God's bones, Eysteinn! You do breed them big in the north!" Hardrada slapped Eysteinn's shoulder in delight. "The lad might just see him off and win the silver … Bjarke! … Bjarke Orrifostersson, again I offer to match the purse if you beat the Rock God, there!"

The audience roared in delight, those who had fallen to ale induced sleep were shook awake.

The strongman bowed his head to Bjarke, applauded then gestured to the stones.

"I offer you first lift, young Orrifostersson."

Bjarke studied the stones then picked the same one Ulf had chosen. Bending to lift he hefted it and walked easily to the cart, depositing it gently onto the cart floor, the watching men slapping the tables in approval. The strongman nodded approval and applauded, he turned to the same rock he'd lifted before and this time lifted it cleanly without mummery. The watching men were excited now, a real trial of strength looked to be on and individual wagers were being laid between them.

"Will you back your boy, Eysteinn? A wager between us? Bjarke's a strong looking lad but methinks he will lose to the big man, age and technique will triumph, my silver is safe."

"I'll take the wager Lord King, what kind of father would I be not to back my boy."

Back on the floor, Bjarke had selected his next stone and was readying to lift; it was larger than the last and the watching men fell silent. With just a slight growl he lifted the stone and walked to the cart, as the room erupted into cheers he noticed the strongman no longer looked as comfortable and was readying to lift a larger rock and perhaps steal the audience back. The man hefted the larger rock, the weight forcing a loud grunt from him and making him plod towards the cart. More silver was quickly placed on the table as the audience raised their bets on their favourite.

The big man just gestured to the rocks this time, saving his breath and showmanship for his next lift. Bjarke rubbed his chest where the stone had bruised and cut it, then walked to the second largest rock.

"Christ on the cross! He'll never lift that!" Hardrada nudged Eysteinn, who was looking concerned.

The strongman smiled grimly, the boy was hurting and seeking a quick finish, he was overstretching himself. Bjarke rubbed his sweat-slicked hands on the dirt floor and then together, then squatted to hug the rock. He moved position, seeking a better grip, then lifted quickly, forcing his legs under him to support the massive load. The watching men roared approval, it growing louder as he stepped slowly across to the cart. As the cart bellied with the weight the hall exploded into cheers and groans as men considered their wagers. The strongman was quiet and serious looking as he approached the largest of all the stones; it had been some years since he'd last had to lift it. Wiping his hands on his trousers, he squatted and sought the best hold. Silence fell without request. The man heaved and growled loudly as the rock came off the floor, his face reddening with the effort, still crouching, he shuffled the rock onto his thighs then powered upright. Men cheered as he staggered towards the cart. Suddenly his grip loosened and the rock slipped, the watching men gasped. He tried to hold it and step faster towards the cart but it slipped from his grip and thumped to the floor. The hall rafters seemed to shake with the noise from the crowd, hands sought winnings and Hakon jumped up from the bench to congratulate his brother.

Bjarke gently pushed him away and walked over to the rock the strongman had dropped. As he squatted to embrace it, the hall began falling silent, arguments over wagers ceased as all turned to watch. The strongman looked on while shaking his head. Bjarke tested his grip on the rock then seized it and with a loud growl powered to his feet. The hall went wild with excitement as he began stepping toward the cart. He stopped halfway and hefted the rock, seeking a better grip, the watchers gasping in amazement at his strength. Dropping it on the cart men cheered and the strongman bowed, placing the bag of silver in Bjarke's hand. The King and all at the top table were on their feet applauding, Eysteinn cheering loudly. Hardrada banged on the table with a dish seeking quiet. As the hall quietened, he spoke.

"It seems even a King must pay his dues!"

He laughed and pushed some gold coins to Eysteinn and threw a bag of silver to Bjarke who caught it and bowed low. Bjarke walked back to the table but paused alongside Ulf.

"Master Ulf! You were the bravest of us all. The first to take the challenge."

Bjarke pushed a bag of silver into his hand. Ulf was taken by surprise then snarled and thrust it back.

"Keep your damned silver boy, I don't need it!" He growled bitterly.

Bjarke was shocked and even Ulf's comrades uttered their disapproval at his response. Ulf barked them to silence, he seemingly of some rank.

"You can go boy." He grunted while turning away, dismissing Bjarke like a servant.

A jubilant Hakon embraced Bjarke before he reached his seat, Ingvar and Kettil also crowding in to offer their praise. Seating him, they filled his ale horn and raised theirs in toast. Bjarke pushed one bag of silver into his purse, the second he tipped on the table and halved, giving one-half to Hakon and splitting the remaining half between Ingvar and Kettil.

Chapter Ten

The Norse sea near the Danish city of Ribe

"Sails! ... Sails to the south, Lord!" Fritjof pointed forward from the bows while shouting to Eysteinn.

Eysteinn growled under his breath as he stepped up to the bows to see square sails dotting the skyline. "Aye, too far south! That's Ribe port there, methinks." He pointed landward. "And we're too long getting here; the bastards are ready for us."

"What was that Lord?"

"Nothing, nothing Fritjof. How long before we clash?"

Fritjof looked to the sun, the rowing men and the taught sails in the distance.

"I reckon before midday Lord, they have the wind at their backs and will be making good speed."

"Aye, I think you're right. Not enough time to land and take the town before they will be on our backs. It wouldn't do to be caught fighting the town's folk with Sweyn's army boxing us in, in the harbour. Look to the King's ship for a signal, he will have seen them also ... I think we have a fight at sea coming."

"Aye, Lord."

Moments later, a huge pennon bearing a black raven on a white filed unfurled from the mast of Hardrada's ship.

"The Land-waster's banner, Lord!" Fritjof pointed to the pennon stretching taught in the wind. Eysteinn waved his hand in acknowledgement then walked the rower's benches addressing his men.

"Sweyn is here lads!" He pointed over the bows. "We will fight at sea, look to your weapons and mail." He lowered his voice after. "Bjarke! Hakon! … Here!" Eysteinn shepherded the pair to the stern. "There will be battle before midday. Leave your hauberks off and stay back, helmets weapons and shields only, at least that way you have a chance if you end up in the sea. There will be little room to move so this is going to be fast and vicious, not ideal for new warriors. Fight you must, but do as I command and stay back near the steering oar and guard Fritjof, I'll send Ingvar, Sten and Kettil back as well, this, is work for my *Hearth-weru*."

The King was already signalling his ships into line and easing the pace slightly, saving his men's energy for the coming fight. The men took turns to leave the oars and ready themselves for battle. Mail shirts were quickly pulled over their heads, helmets fitted and short swords and hand axes placed in belts. From the bows, Hakon squinted into the distance and threw an arm around Bjarke.

"This is it brother, we stay together, you watch my back …"

Bjarke nodded and hugged Hakon fiercely; an apprehensive and worried look on his face. He leaned to one side and spewed. Ingvar gave a nervous laugh and shouted.

"Are you feeding the fish, big man?"

Bjarke wiped his mouth on his sleeve and gave a wan smile while Kettil opened his trousers and pissed over the strakes.

"It'll be alright, I promise you!" Ingvar tried to sound reassuring. "We stay together eh!"

The distance between the fleets closed quickly, the stiff wind driving the Danish fleet before it. Hardrada formed his ships from line to arrowhead, with his ship at the apex, the Danes still coming on, line abreast.

"Archers! Javelins! To the bows. Boys, back to the stern and cover Fritjof. Every second oarsman, ship oars, shields ready!" Eysteinn bellowed.

Sten, Ingvar, Kettil and the two brothers watched from the stern, shields up and swords drawn. Bjarke holding his hand axe, his sweat-wet fingers flexing and closing around the shaft, his heart thumping in his chest, his mouth sticky and his throat dry. The taste of vomit sour on his tongue. The first arrows began to fall, most fell short into the sea, only one or two lodging in the wood of the upraised bows.

"Hold lads, they have the wind behind them, we need to be closer." Eysteinn was at the bows with his missile men, shield up, his *Hearth-weru* bunched tightly behind him, the sunlight flashing off mail and weapons, light sea spray dousing them as the bows ploughed then rose on the swell. More arrows fell, this time the range found shields and men lifted them high.

"Hold lads, another ship's length then loose, feather the Danish bastards!"

War cries were starting up on both sides as the ships surged on, the distance narrowing fast.

"Archers, loose! … Loose! Javelins, hold…! "Eysteinn roared above the wind and the shouts of men.

The arrows flew almost straight now, rattling off shields and raising the odd scream as they slipped through the wooden wall, wounding or dropping a warrior to the deck. Moments later, javelins joined the missile storm, knocking some men off their feet as the impact and the surging ship took them off balance.

"Run us alongside Fritjof!" Eysteinn shouted back to the huge man on the rudder, while pointing with his sword.

"Stand clear, lads." Fritjof yelled to the boys as he heaved on the rudder and slewed the boat starboard. Ropes with grapnels flew from both ships, men heaving and straining to pull them alongside so the warriors could engage. With the range less now than half a ship's length, arrows and javelins were finding their mark, lodging deeply and men went down, some tumbling into the sea, others collapsing amidst their comrades making obstacles on the deck. Just before the ships came alongside two Danes leapt from the bows, one with a two handed long-axe, the second with shield and hand axe. The first was hit in the chest by two javelins, stalling him mid-air with the force, his body falling into the sea, his mail coat dragging him down, sinking like a stone. The second man landed on the bows, his shield and axe smashing into the Norse shieldwall, his impetus driving men back. A long-seax struck up beneath his shield finding his groin and the man stalled, the axe falling from his hand. He moaned like a beast at the winter slaughter as Eysteinn's men pushed forward again, toppling him into the sea.

The ships collided with a grating and splintering of timber, an oar, too late to lift, snapped like matchwood, throwing the rower backwards. There was a loud roar as warriors engaged across the bows and strakes, axes smashing shields down else hooking them away, short swords and seaxs' finding flesh. The ships listed slightly as warriors surged to the sides, men struggling for balance, others stumbling or tripping over the dead and wounded; the deck boards becoming slippery with blood. Eysteinn was in the midst of his *Hearth-weru's* shieldwall, his sword stabbing over shield rims, he bellowing encouragement to his men.

Back at the bows, an arrow thumped into Bjarke's shield. He peered slightly above it to see where the shot came from.

"Top mast, Bjarke!" Fritjof yelled. "Two of them! Get your shield up higher lad! He's going for another go! Close up lads!" The other four boys squashed together, shields overlapping, protecting themselves and Fritjof while he held on to the rudder. Another arrow lodged in Bjarke's shield, lower down.

"Watch him! Watch him!" Fritjof called.

A third arrow thumped into Hakon's shield and a javelin thumped into the deck narrowly missing Kettil's boot. As the two Danes sought new missiles, Bjarke stooped and wrenched the javelin from the deck boards, hefted it and hurled it up at the Danish mast. It took the archer in the chest, the force flinging him from the mast top, he knocking the javelin man off at the same time, their bodies crashing into the men below and breaking a hole in their shieldwall.

"Christ God, Bjarke!" Fritjof shouted, the other boys looking on in amazement at the power of the throw.

With the sudden disarray in the Danish shieldwall, Eysteinn's *Hearth-weru* forced the Danes back, the Norsemen stepping over the strakes now onto the Danish ship's deck, opening the gap in the wall wider.

There was a sudden crack and Sten stumbled and fell onto his knees, his helmet askew, and a broken arrow on the deck. Ingvar spun around seeking the source of the shot.

"Mother of God!"

The others looked to see a Danish ship coming up on their stern. It having slipped through the arrowhead of Norse ships and turned. The bows were crammed with warriors, bright painted shield faces and shining steel. Bjarke hauled a dazed Sten to his feet and pushed him behind him, the boys turning to face the new threat and locking shields once more. Javelins flew overhead, else stuck in shields and the deck. Fritjof quickly tied a rope loop over the rudder and seized his own shield while urging the group forward to the stern post.

"Don't let them get a foothold!" He growled.

Danes leapt for the Munnin's stern before the ships collided and Fritjof and the boys had formed up properly. Fritjof and his small group being forced back by sheer weight of men, wood and steel as the Danes filled the stern. A huge Dane stepped out of the second rank, elbowing his comrades to one side and hefting a long-axe in a tight circle. The axe smashed down into Bjarke's upturned shield, breaking it, numbing his arm, and driving him and the Norse wall back again. The Dane's stepped closer and Ingvar's long-seax blade struck like a serpent over his shield rim but missed the huge Dane's throat by a hairsbreadth. It struck the warrior behind in the face, the sword glancing off the helmet nasal bar to enter the man's eye. He screamed and blood sprayed. The two sides clashed shield-to-shield, the men close as lovers. Warriors heaved, grunted and strained with the effort of holding back else pushing forward, the desire to kill spurred on by fear and the need to survive. The axeman was limited for space now as his comrades pushed behind him, he unable to swing the long-shafted axe. Over the shields, faces, crammed beneath helmets were frighteningly close; tattoos, scars, mouths twisted in anger and hate just inches away. The small walls seethed as men struggled, weapons coming over shield rims else aimed low seeking thighs, knees or groins. A long-seax flashed past Bjarke's face. He felt hot blood spatter like summer rain on the back of his neck and Sten crumpling into his shoulder, then slide past his arm, the blood pumping fountain like from a blade-ravaged throat.

"Sten! … No!" Ingvar screamed.

"Stay tight!" Fritjof yelled as he felt the tiny wall begin to crumble.

Sten hit the deck hard, falling between Bjarke and Ingvar's legs.

Bjarke roared in anger and pushed hard making a small space. He swung his broken shield backhanded at the oncoming Danes, the force knocking some backwards and making a small gap. Sten struggled to his knees, one hand holding his throat, the blood oozing quickly between his fingers, his other hand trying to push himself up, back onto his feet. The big axeman, pushing into the space, swung at Bjarke. The long-axe missed him, cleaving Sten in the shoulder, smashing his collarbone and top ribs to ruin and lodging there. Bjarke roared in both fear and anger and stepped forward, chopping his hand axe hard into the big Dane's shoulder. The massive force buckled then ruptured the man's hauberk, cutting through the padded leather shirt beneath and hitting bone. Ingvar and the others stepped after him trying to close the gap. Bjarke threw his wrecked shield to the deck and hit the dying Dane again with his axe. This time the axe hacked through the mail coif to the man's neck, chopping through flesh and muscle to the spine. The man collapsed, letting go of his long-axe. Bjarke seized it. Sten's broken body being dragged a pace or so along the deck before the axe released from his flesh and splintered bones. Bjarke swung it in a fluid move into the Danish wall, the force smashing shields and weapons aside, men spinning from the impact else crumpling onto the deck. He roaring in a berserk fury. The axe hummed in the air, the gap growing wider as the long-shafted axe tore into the Danes like a scythe through summer wheat. Men edged back and away. Bjarke following after like an avenging angel, leaving bodies, limbs, shields and weapons in his wake.

The Danes edged back to their ship's bows, while two tried to stand and fend Bjarke away, shields braced. The axe smashed into the first man, splintering his shield to ruin and chopping into his arm, the force pushing him into his comrade and sending both spinning off the deck. Bjarke stepped right up to the stern post, cutting down the last Dane to reach the bows of his own ship, the man tumbling into the sea. Looking as if he was about to board the Danish vessel, he was held off by probing war spears as the Danes hacked through the grapnel lines and the ships parted. Fritjof put a restraining hand on Bjarke's shoulder.

"Let them go lad! Stay safe."

Bjarke shrugged Fritjof loose and dropped the long-axe. Reaching to the deck, he snatched up a fallen hand axe, sending it spinning across the widening gap, hitting a spearman in the shoulder. He roared like a wounded animal at the departing Danes. They looking back, quite in awe of the destruction wrought on them.

At the Munnin's bows, Eysteinn and his *Hearth-weru* had cleared the deck of Danes, the Danish ship pulling away from the mauling, curses and the odd missile still flying from ship to ship as the vessels parted. The Munnin's bows were thick with the dead, the deck boards hidden by bodies, shields and weapons. Men lay twisted in death or heaped atop one another, some crawled from out of the pile calling to comrades for help. Any surviving Danes calling for quarter being quickly dispatched with axe blows to the head or neck or their throats slashed.

With his decks clear of the enemy, Eysteinn looked about him and saw ships disengaging, the Danes backing away and turning for Ribe port.

"Do we follow them, Lord?" Anders growled.

"See what signal we get from the King, we'll know soon enough." Eysteinn pointed to Hardrada's ship, which had dropped oars and was pulling across the front of the Norse fleet, the King assessing his damage and losses. "See to the wounded, Master Anders. Strip the Danish filth of weapons and anything of value then heave them over the side." He turned for the stern seeking the boys.

Seeing another mangled mess of bodies littering the stern deck, he quickened his steps, his heart beginning to race as he sought recognition of his boys. Fritjof was unlooping the rudder when he saw Eysteinn and recognised the concern.

"Young Sten is down Lord, the rest of us are whole methinks, flesh wounds only. They came from behind, I don't know how they broke through the arrowhead but they did."

Eysteinn looked at the bloodied deck and saw Bjarke gently lifting Sten's body from the carnage, his throat slashed open and his head lolling like a dead fish. Ingvar was helping Hakon and Kettil, sitting them to one side, Kettil retching then throwing up but only his food not blood.

"They hit us hard, Lord." Eysteinn nodded slowly as he looked at the carnage. "Sten went down and Bjarke went berserk, he took up that long-axe and smashed them to Hell, they ran for their ship."

Eysteinn stepped over to Sten's body. His right shoulder and top ribs were all mangled, broken and bloodied under his leather shirt. His throat still oozed blood but slowly now, the heart no longer pumping, his eyes stared, wide and fish like. Eysteinn stroked them closed with his fingers.

"It could have been much worse, Lord."

"Aye …" He shook his head slowly. Remembering the others, he moved towards them. Bjarke was shaking, his face white, Hakon was pissing over the strakes but missing the sea and splattering his boots and the deck, Kettil still retched but had nothing left to vomit up. Ingvar stood quietly but managed a respectful nod to his Lord.

"Lord! … Lord!" Ander's shout broke Eysteinn's apathy and he turned to the call from the bows. "The King is signalling a turn for home, he has sent a dozen ships to chase the Danes into Ribe port; at least we can claim a victory!"

"Aye, victory is ours!" Eysteinn shouted to his warriors, who cheered and raised weapons and shields aloft. 'But victory for what?' he wondered to himself.

Chapter Eleven

Borg, midsummer 1063 AD

Way off in the distance hunting horns blared and the barking and yelping of dogs could be heard. Fenrir stood up, his ears pricked, listening. Growling in his throat he was about to bark when Bjarke shushed him, tapping his nose gently. Fenrir gave a faint whine and settled back down, face between his paws, ears still up and eyes watching his master.

"It's all on!" Hakon said and winked at his brother. "We'll fill the larder for your wedding, Bjarke. Venison this week, food from the sea next week, plenty of oysters, eh brother? Keep you strong so you can hump Eerika all night and keep her a happy woman." He laughed then grunted when Bjarke punched him playfully in the ribs.

"A little respect around my woman, brother." He said sternly, pointing a finger at Hakon, and Ingvar and Kettil who were also chuckling, then he grinned. "I'm already strong enough … and don't count your deer till they are gralloched and hung!" He smiled and peered over the wicker screen, looking up the valley towards the sounds of horns and dogs, both coming slowly closer. Bjarke, with his small group and other hunters were all hidden behind wicker hurdles, half a war spear in height and which had been placed across the valley mouth in a staggered vee shape. The screens placed to funnel the driven deer inwards allowing the men quick and easy killing, this hunt being purely for meat rather than pleasure, the coming wedding feast requiring much food as the whole village was to be fed at Eysteinn's expense.

The barking was closer now and the men gathered up their javelins, each having at least half a dozen, they laid some in easy reach, others were stuck in the ground ready to be snatched up at a moment's notice. Further back, a handful of archers waited, ready for any animals that the waiting men might miss with the javelins. Fenrir's nose twitched and he stood again, his head turning from side to side. Bjarke grasped a javelin and peered over the screen, watching as a young stag came out of the trees into the open ground. It saw the hurdles blocking any side exits and the clear run through the middle of them; and it ran straight down the centre. It thundered past Bjarke's screen, he stood, tracked his target, then hurled the javelin, hitting it just behind and above the front foreleg, the force of the throw burying the javelin head to the shaft and knocking the animal sideways, it collapsing onto its side with a bellow. Bjarke was already running towards it, his seax drawn, the animal however was already dead, the javelin having burst its heart. Seizing it by the antlers, he dragged it out of sight behind the screens.

The noises in the trees were louder now, the sounds of breaking bracken, men, dogs and hunting horns announcing the arrival of a mob of deer. Deer of all sizes spilled into the clearing, along with two sows, a boar and a handful of piglets and like the stag before them, they saw the open ground and the hurdles funnelling down to what appeared to be a way out. They ran for the exit, their numbers forcing them to bunch as they passed through the staggered hurdles, making for easier targets for the waiting men.

The men stood now, the deer in their panic, just surged past, desperate to make the exit in front of them. The pigs were ignored for the moment as men killed the deer first, the piglets and sows squealing and running around the hurdles, desperate to escape. The boar stopped and looked back to the forest, seeing nothing, it was about to head back into the trees when the first of the dogs broke cover. The boar turned again and raced past the hurdles seeking the exit. He was big, frightened and very strong, his head dropped low as he took his run to full speed, barrelling through the milling, confused deer, knocking some over in his rush to be through the chaos and away from the death.

Bjarke saw the boar as it broke clear and he slipped Fenrir's leash. Fenrir surged forward, accelerating to full speed within yards, his large body going to full stretch, Bjarke racing after him. The boar was now intent only on the distant exit and running straight, Fenrir came up behind him and nipped his hind leg, sending the boar tumbling over and over, the dog trying to stop and seize it before it could rise. The boar however was fast and already up, albeit at a stumble and facing Fenrir off.

"Fenrir! Off! … Away!" Bjarke bellowed as he ran. "Away! … Away!"

Fenrir backed off, barking furiously but the boar was ready to fight and went for the dog.

With memories of Garmr flashing in his mind, Bjarke slowed and hurled a javelin at the boar. At that moment, the boar dropped his head to charge Fenrir and the javelin only creased his skin as it hurtled past. The boar squealed in pain giving it pause as it looked for the source of attack.

Fenrir and Bjarke were now either side of the animal and it grunted loudly, swinging its head from man to dog and back again, Fenrir barking non-stop while stepping this way and that. Bjarke stepped closer, drawing his seax. The boar saw the knife and the big man and deciding the dog was the weaker, dropped its head and turned for it. Bjarke sprinted after the boar but slipped on the grass and dropped his seax, not stopping; he threw himself at the animal's hindquarters. Man and boar went down hard, Fenrir dashing in to seize the boar's ear, biting hard then backing away with a jump as the boar swung its head, tusks seeking flesh. Bjarke jumped up, weapon-less. He grabbed the boar's hind legs and hefted them up, holding them high as the animal stumbled on its front trotters. Holding the boar's hind legs it couldn't turn on him to gore him but when the dog came close to bite or hold, it ran the risk of the tusks and had to back off. Suddenly, man and boar were locked in a dance, neither capable of killing the other as long as they stayed together, the dog barking and snarling adding to the chaos.

Hakon had ran after Bjarke but hadn't been able to keep pace with his long strides, now he came alongside, breathless and shouting his brother's name. Seeing the spectacle in front of him, man and pig capering and the dog's barking accompanying them, he burst into laughter.

"God's bones, Bjarke! That's an ugly partner for a dance!"

"Kill it, Hakon! Christ above, blade it!"

Hakon was joined by Ingvar, who'd also came at the run and who was also laughing. "Shall we fetch a harp, Bjarke?"

"Kill the bloody thing!" Bjarke growled.

Hakon and Ingvar were beside themselves with laughing, each leaning onto the other as Bjarke continued to caper with the animal, the boar grunting and squealing but slowing now as it tired.

"Kill the bloody boar!" Bjarke shouted.

Hakon walked over to Fenrir and called him to heel, urging Ingvar to hold his collar.

"Very well, brother." He said graciously and slowly walked up to the boar, slipping his seax from its sheath as he came. He stopped and yawned. "The things I do for you brother!"

"Kill the damned boar!" Bjarke growled.

"What do you think, Ingvar? Should I kill it? … Surely, it will spoil the dance!"

"Kill it!" Bjarke shouted.

Hakon stepped closer then deftly stabbed the pig in its throat. "Your wish is my command, brother." He said before sheathing the seax and backing well away, Ingvar doing the same as the boar slumped into a heap, snorting and breathing heavy as its lifeblood flowed out.

Bjarke dropped the hind legs. Snarling and cursing, he stepped after Hakon and Ingvar, fists rising. The pair ran, still laughing. Bjarke, weary from the struggle and with adrenalin slowing, stopped and resting his hands on his knees stated to laugh himself. Fenrir coming alongside to nuzzle and lick his face.

"Are you calm, brother?" Hakon called from a good distance.

Bjarke, sat down heavily and laughed, waving his brother and Ingvar to him.

The hunt resulted in much venison and additional wild pork for the wedding feast, it being butchered and stored in the icehouse ready for roasting on the day.

Midsummer's day dawned cloudless with the promise of a windless, sunny day. Inger was up at dawn, rousing the house, slaves and servants, organising. The village church had been decked the previous day with bunches of summer flowers from the meadows and tree branches heavy in leaf. These, cut and woven into shapes representing fertility, bringing some life and colour to the stark, whitewashed church interior. The couple had wished a service in the open air but had been overruled by the priest's insistence that it was heathen-like to be married alongside the beasts of the field. Fenrir had also been banned from accompanying Bjarke into the church, the priest claiming an animal had no place in God's house. However, and much to the priests disgust but Eysteinn's insistence, two corn dollies, one a man, the other a woman and both with exaggerated anatomy had been placed near the altar, a hint and blessing from the old religion.

Bjarke had bathed the night before in the stream before joining his friends, father and Eerika's father for his *steggr* night celebration. His only preparation now being a shave and the combing and dressing of his hair and beard. A slave appeared bearing combs and shears, asking if he was ready for her. With a head still fuddled with ale and weary from lack of sleep, he grunted his consent. Perched on a stool he struggled to hold his head up as the ivory comb pulled through his locks. His hair was long and thick, the colour of ripened wheat and hanging half way down his back. The slave girl teased out the tangles and trimmed the ends with shears then bound it all into a ponytail as thick as a woman's arm. She shaved his jaw and neck clean, leaving his moustache and beard long on his chin, which she also plaited.

Eysteinn strode into the room, the slave quickly gathering up her shears and combs, bowing and exiting through a side door.

"How's the head, lad? Still full of ale?" He laughed as Bjarke grimaced and reached for the water jug. "You downed enough last night to fell a horse. I imagine Hakon will still be unconscious." He laughed again. "Come on! Breakfast is ready, eat up, that will sort you out."

As the pair entered the room, Inger looked up from the table and scowled.

"Christ on the cross! I'm surprised that either of you are on your feet!" She snapped. "And you, Eysteinn! You, were supposed to look after him and supervise; instead I had to send servants to find …"

"Peace, Inger … peace! For God's sake."

Inger's face clouded and she looked about for something to hurl. Eysteinn recognised the look and hid behind Bjarke, laughing hard.

"If you miss me and hit the boy you'll bruise him and his bride will be none too pleased!" He chuckled.

Inger moved to one side a dish in her hand, Eysteinn pulled Bjarke around for cover, he still too soused with ale to realise what was happening. As Inger moved, so did Eysteinn, until eventually both burst out laughing and Inger put the dish down. Eysteinn stepping over to hug her close.

"Get off me, oaf! You stink of ale! … Come eat! You too Bjarke. Soak up some of that ale."

The church bell rung, calling all to the service. The crowds gathered, lining the lane to the church and filling the small churchyard, the notables already within the church waiting. Eysteinn and Bjarke were dressed in their finest; Eysteinn in a tunic of black and silver trim, his Jarl's belt buckle polished bright, his sword strapped on as a mark of his rank, the priest warned not to insist to his Lord, on no weapons in the church. Bjarke was attired in a dark blue wool tunic, the trousers tucked into calve length, doeskin boots, the pair waiting for Inger before walking to the church.

Inger duly appeared, her blonde hair piled up and held with combs, a dress of cornflower blue from neck to ankle, her wrists and neck adorned with gold. Eysteinn gazed at her, his head shaking slightly, he quite in awe of her beauty. He stepped toward her, offering his arm.

"Shall we see our son to the church?"

Inger smiled and nodded; her eyes full.

As they walked through the crowds, Eysteinn acknowledged his people, exchanging greetings here and there, Fenrir walking alongside Bjarke, to the church door at least. Hakon and Asta joined them, the family entering together to stand by the altar. The priest fussed over who was to stand where until a sharp rebuke from Eysteinn stopped his bustle.

The church had no pews, the congregation expected to stand for all services. To announce the bride, horns blew, the notes rising, lilting and causing the congregation to turn towards the door. Four little girls appeared first, each bearing a wicker basket, the congregation easing apart allowing them clear passage to the altar. Smiling, almost giggling they scattered flower petals as they walked down the aisle all the way to the altar where they stopped and waited. The crowd turned back now, looking toward the door, seeking the bride.

Eerika and her father, Anders, entered. Anders dressed in his finery, warrior rings about his wrist and a heavy silver chain about his neck, denoting his rank of, Head of Eysteinn's *Hearth-weru*. Eerika wore a long white dress that trailed the ground, her waist belted with a wide, intricately plaited girdle of brown suede. Her long, blonde hair hung past her shoulders, lustrous and cut in layers, a headband full of daisies, cornflowers and bright green ash leaves holding the hair back from her face. Shy and demure, she looked down as she walked until seeing Bjarke waiting at the altar, her face lit up and she beamed. The priest called the congregation to order then droned on without pause, advocating the merits of marriage under God, Eysteinn eventually growling at the man to 'get on with it' and receiving a whispered rebuke from Inger for his anger.

Eventually, with formalities complete, the couple were married, the bell ringing continuously as all exited the church to the meadow where slaves and servants were heaping benches with platters of venison, pork, fish, oysters, scallops and baskets of bread loaves. Whole cattle beasts and lambs roasted on spits while horses and carts arrived, bringing huge barrels of ale and mead, enough for all and jars of wine for the family and honoured guests.

The festivities continued all day, the couple allowed no peace as people came to wish them well, Bjarke's friends at pains to kiss the bride. By the time dusk came; ale and frivolity had claimed many. Those with the energy still danced and capered while others slipped away to the shadows, the warm evening encouraging thoughts of love making, which the ale and mead had started.

The new couple were finally allowed their excuses and made to leave, making their way to a small house on the edge of the village, gifted from Eysteinn and Inger.

The briefly departed sun was already casting a new, faint light in the east, the moon beginning to fade. With torchlight no longer needed, Bjarke stamped it out and bent to scoop a weary Eerika up in his arms, she nestling her head into his chest as they neared their new home. Fenrir walked alongside the couple, the big hunting dog looking strangely at odds with the meadow flowers twisted into his collar.

In the shadows of the trees and unseen, an old woman watched. Holding Thor's hammer out from her chest, she mumbled words in Old Norse before raising a crucifix and whispered for Christ's blessing and protection on the newlyweds. Watching until she saw them enter their house, she finally turned away, her eyes wet with tears.

Chapter Twelve

Borg, late autumn 1065 AD

With 'All Hallows Eve' fast approaching and almost time for the winter slaughter of the poorer quality or older farm animals, it was also time for Orri's people to pay their taxes to him for the land, which they farmed or grazed. With Eysteinn and Hakon both at court again, it fell to Bjarke to act as overseer of the proceedings. Eysteinn, not trusting the priest to do the work honestly on his own, he likening it to leaving a fox in charge of a hen house warned Bjarke to watch him. When Bjarke had looked somewhat disbelievingly at his father, Eysteinn had just laughed and asked when he had last seen a skinny priest.

The autumn sun was bright but low in the sky leaving the air cold and Bjarke pulled his bearskin cloak tighter about his shoulders. Sitting at a rough wooden table placed outside in the marketplace he enjoyed a horn of ale and a plate of oatcakes, Fenrir sitting at his feet. All around him, the marketplace was a bustling chaos of people, noisy animals and differing piles of goods.

Some folk payed in copper or silver coin but most payed in goods, be it animal skins, firewood, crops, foodstuffs, barrels of ale or even live animals, all were accepted and accounted for, the priest acting as a scribe and entering the details onto a freshly scraped lambskin, all under Bjarke's watchful eye.

Eysteinn was not hard on his tenants, his service in the Varangian Guard and the wars in Eastern Europe had seen him come home a wealthy man, the recurring raids on Denmark helping top up his income from the plunder. Thus, in the event of tenant's genuine hardship or a poor crop yield, saw the matters taken into consideration and folk allowed time to pay. Despite the cold and the somewhat humdrum affair of accounting the rents, Bjarke was happy. Always of an amiable disposition, he was pleased to be left in charge of the revenue collecting; he felt he was helping his father. He was also in charge of sorting the animals for the winter slaughter and hunting to fill the icehouse, then organising the dry-docking of the ships so their hulls could be scraped and their planking caulked and sealed ready for the spring.

He and Eerika had settled into married life, enjoying their log house and each other's company, their contentment complete when Eerika announced she was with child. The news had delighted his father and mother and given Eysteinn further reason to leave Bjarke at home where he knew him to be happiest. Of his two sons, he knew Hakon to be worldly, interested in politics and the larger picture of what was happening at home and abroad, Bjarke to be home loving, content to manage domestic affairs and care for the people.

The priest, father Gudmund, was clearly not happy with Bjarke's presence and though grudgingly respectful had little to say to him, his brief words and interactions saved for the tenants as they came to pay. Ingratiating himself with those who were of some standing and paid easily, he grumbled or snapped at folk who couldn't pay or were behind in their dues, stamping his authority as if he was a Lord, then closing the discussion with a benediction, its sincerity depending upon who was receiving it. Bjarke had let the first few transgressions pass but eventually felt the need to intercede.

"Father, a little more civility and patience if you will. Not all have had a good year, not all have a good income and the wars with Denmark have left their mark and some households no longer have a provider." The rebuke was mild and given with a slight smile.

The bullet headed priest looked up, his pugnacious jaw pushing out, small, pig-like eyes peering from over a large hooked nose.

"Master Bjarke, I'm doing your father's work and his will, I ask you not to hinder me!"

"Agreed father and I seek not to hinder you but a little charity and understanding would not go amiss. These are my father's people, our people, and your flock as you like to term them." Again, Bjarke spoke quietly, amiably.

"You're new to this Master Bjarke, you don't see the wool being pulled over your eyes, you only hear the clever words designed to mislead and cajole you to leniency." Father Gudmund's words rapped out, like a teacher to his pupil.

"Father, I'm neither blind nor stupid, don't make the mistake of presuming so." This time Bjarke's tone was flat and without a smile.

The priest was startled by the sudden change in tone; he said nothing but managed a token nod of the head.

The proceedings continued with Gudmund a little more respectful in his dealings, until Runa stepped up to the table, he glowered at her, his lip curling in distaste.

"I trust you have all the money this time woman, you still owe half for last year!"

Bjarke looked up quickly from feeding Fenrir an oatcake. "Runa! Old mother, it's good to see you."

"It's good to be seen, Bjarke Orrifostersson." She smiled, ignoring the priest's tirade.

"Well woman, can you pay?" Gudmund snapped, bringing Runa's attention back to business.

Runa slipped some small coins from her purse onto the table. The priest eyed the pile and snapped.

"It's not enough!"

"It's all I have."

"You must have more than that! Those potions and salves you pedal bring coin do they not? Where is it?"

Bjarke placed his hand over the pile and spread the coins as if to count, while deftly slipping a silver coin on top.

"There, father!" He said pointing to the silver. "Old mother, you must have misplaced that, now there is too much." He collected up the small coins and slipped them back into Runa's hand, winking and smiling at her as he did so.

The priest glared at Bjarke, the big man just smiled. "I think that will cover Runa's costs for last year, this and next." His smile faded and he tapped the lambskin "Get it writ!" The priest looked as if he was about to argue but Bjarke's look hardened and he tapped the lambskin again. "Write it or I will!" He growled.

The priest took fright and made a noise as if he was choking then scribbled frantically. Bjarke looked at Runa and winked again. He couldn't read or write but the priest did not know that and was now too scared to call his bluff. Bjarke stood quickly, frightening the priest again with the sudden movement and walked around the table to hug Runa.

"Stay warm and well, old mother."

Runa whispered a quiet thank you into his chest; he kissed her head and turned back to his seat. Runa had turned to go.

"Aha! The benediction father, in all the excitement you forgot the benediction."

"She's gone now, no matter."

"But it does matter father, she has paid and my father has paid you, now you must pay … with a benediction." He smiled again. "Runa … Runa, a moment if you will."

"She's a heathen!" The priest hissed.

"All the more reason to bless then, surely." Bjarke chuckled, clearly enjoying the man's discomfort.

Runa came back to the table.

"Our pardon, old mother, we neglected your blessing." He turned to the priest. The man's lip gurned and his face twisted as if he had swallowed something distasteful. "Thank you for reminding me father, the blessing if you please."

The priest's face coloured with temper and his lips remained shut. Bjarke slid his hand onto the priest's waist at the small of his back and took hold of the cord tying his robe shut; wrapping his hand in the cord, he twisted it hard, tightening the cord and making the man wince and gasp.

"The blessing father." He said amiably while tightening his grip further.

"The grace of our Lord Jesus Christ and the love of God be with you, sister." He managed quickly.

Runa smiled. "Amen father."

Bjarke smiled and released his grip. "Time for food and ale methinks, father." He gestured to the inn and took the lambskin from the table causing the priest further alarm, he wondering if Bjarke could read. Bjarke put his arm around Runa and steered her towards the inn. The pair found a table and Bjarke ordered ale, bread and cheese. When the food arrived, Runa opened her purse to pay and fished through a pile of strange looking silver coins, seeking coppers. Bjarke frowned quizzically but placed a hand over hers and gave the innkeeper coins from his purse.

"Thank you again, Bjarke Orrifostersson, you are most kind. I have coin, enough to pay for our food and ale but I didn't have enough to pay all my rent. These coins look grand but are worthless." She fished out a pile of sliver with strange writing on it to show him.

Bjarke stared at the handful. "Worthless! I don't think so, who told you that?"

"Father Gudmund, when I tried to pay my rent with one of them last year. He told me it was foreign rubbish and worthless, he pushed it to one side and marked me as being in arrears."

"He didn't return it to you?"

"No, I left it on the table; I was too embarrassed at not being able to pay."

"Runa, these are Arab Dirhams, they're as good a silver as our own, perhaps more so; my father has some. Where did you get them?"

"From my husband, when he returned from the eastern wars the first time, the time before he was killed."

"But he must have known their worth?"

Runa shrugged. "He just used to laugh and call it Arab siller! I never thought to ask, material things didn't interest me."

"Well, now you know and I wager that damned priest knew. Keep the rest safe, Runa."

Making his way back to the table, Bjarke found the priest already seated and waiting. Bjarke's narrowed eye stare prevented any quips regarding lateness and the man looked down at the table. Bjarke stepped over the bench in order to sit while placing his hand on the priests shoulder as if for balance. Sinking strong fingers into the flesh, he squeezed hard, forcing a yelp from the man.

"Sorry father, I lost my balance." The priest grimaced and rubbed at his shoulder, Bjarke sat down hard on the bench his weight rocking the priest. "Steady father!" Bjarke's hand was on the priest's thigh now and again he squeezed hard wringing another cry from him. "My apologies again father, that was clumsy of me." Bjarke leant in close speaking low. "You cheat anymore of my father's people; priest and I will squeeze your throat as hard as I'm squeezing your leg." He squeezed harder and the man squirmed and groaned in pain. "Am I understood?"

"Yes, yes! Christ God, yes!"

"Good man!" Bjarke released his grip and slapped him hard on the back. "Good man!"

The priest recovered slightly, his face twisting into a snarl, he becoming brave as he saw people watching.

"You cannot manhandle a brother of the church so, Bjarke Orrifostersson! I'll report you to the Bishop."

Bjarke took a gamble. "By all means, father Gudmund but let's take the whole matter before my father first shall we? We can check the accounts line by line and speak to the tenants; we'll start with Runa and the silver Dirham you cheated her of. Then we can talk to my mother about her patronage of your church."

Father Gudmund seemed to shrink on his seat, outmanoeuvred and in fear of the giant next to him; he turned back to his list and quietly asked for the next tenant to come forward.

Part Two

The Leopard, The Raven and The Dragon

Chapter Thirteen

Rouen, capital of William of Normandy's Duchy, January 1066 AD

The servants outside of the Duke's chamber cringed as the sounds of breaking furniture, pottery and the cursing and growling of a man drifted through the walls and door. The door opened and a pale faced man, a messenger by his garb, was pushed stumbling into the corridor.

"Out! … Out! I've heard enough! God's bones, the low born …" The words became muted then incoherent as the door slammed shut rattling the frame.

The messenger found his balance and hurried off down the corridor, ignoring the servants, keen to be on his way. Exiting the corridor, he almost ran into two men coming the other way.

"My Lords! Your pardon … I crave your pardon."

The younger of the two scowled, the elder however steadied the messenger by the arm.

"No harm done but why the rush?"

"The Duke is not best pleased by my news, my Lord, I …"

"What news, man? Spit it out." The younger growled.

The messenger was now even more frightened; his nerves already on the raw from the Duke's anger. The older man respectfully quietened the younger while holding onto the messenger and speaking quietly.

"What news would that be? We are to meet with the Duke anyway, forewarned would be forearmed as they say. If the Duke is not best pleased we would tread the right side of his temper, if you take my meaning." He smiled genially.

The messenger stared at the pair, his mouth forming words though no sound came out. The elder man smiled again and raised his eyebrows encouraging the man to speak.

"My Lords! You are well come." The Duke's voice boomed from the opening door. Looking at the messenger, he clicked his fingers and pointed down the corridor, the man slipping from the other's grip, bowed low and hurried down the corridor apace.

The two men also bowed their heads to the Duke who was already turning away back toward his chamber, his hand beckoning them to follow. He paused at the door to bellow down the corridor.

"Wine for my Lords, now!"

The men followed the Duke into a wrecked room, the elder limping and leaning on a staff and all stepping around the broken tables and chairs scattered across the floor. A wine jug and goblets lay at the base of the wall, the last of the wine running down it and pooling on the floor. The room was cold, the fire having almost burned itself out; the older man pulled his cloak about him and touched the Duke's hand.

"Duke William, should we not move to the hall and the fireside, you are cold, this room is cold!"

"In a moment, Lord Beaumont. I have news to share and my temper to control before we leave this room … Forgive me, I forget my manners, you are both well?" As the men replied, a servant appeared with a tray bearing wine and cups. William dismissed him quickly, pouring and serving the drinks himself. "I thank you both for coming; your arrival is timely, though my news is not good."

The older man stroked his badger coloured beard. "I can see the news was bad my Lord." He gestured to the room. "But how bad?"

William made a physical effort to control himself as his anger flared again. "That Saxon whoreson! Harold Godwinson … he's taken the English throne."

The younger man looked aghast. "But he swore … he swore an oath as your man, to support you in your claim, I saw it, we all saw it! While he was entertained here as an honoured guest!"

"He did, Lord FitzOsbern but it seems that is what passes for Saxon honour." The Duke growled into his cup. "He will pay for his temerity though, as God is my witness he will pay! … What say you Lord Beaumont?"

Roger Beaumont stroked his beard, deep in thought while the two, Williams looked at him seeking comment. The Duke was about to probe for an answer when the man seemed to snap from his distant pondering.

"Yes … yes, my Lord Duke, he must pay but this must be planned carefully, it will take time. I saw the measure of Harold Godwinson when he was here in 1064, we all did, and a man such as that will not be easily cowed. He was brave, courteous, educated and an able warrior. I'm sorry, Duke William if I misspeak but I think we should remind ourselves of our enemies strengths, we should not allude ourselves as to what we are dealing with."

FitzOsbern took a sharp intake of breath and glanced at the Duke expecting another explosion of temper.

William however just smiled grimly. "Aye, you have the rights of it Roger, we should remind ourselves. He is exactly as you describe. God knows, I liked him greatly, until now."

"So we must teach the Saxon a lesson?" FitzOsbern added. "My sword and my men are at your disposal."

Beaumont held up a hand for pause, his hand once more stroking his beard, his eyes looking down, thinking.

"Did he seize the throne or was he voted in by their council, their *Witan*? If he seized the throne we have a case against him, if …"

"He was voted in Lord Beaumont, the day after King Edward's death."

Beaumont grimaced and nodded slowly, looking the Duke in the eyes. "Its war then, for their *Witan* is lawful and with that support, from some of the greatest in the land, cannot be overturned except by force."

The Duke nodded. "Aye, its war alright! And you don't need to tell me it won't be easy, we'll need more men, have a sea to cross and the Saxons are as battle hardened as we …"

"No matter." Beaumont said quietly and calmly. "My men and I are with you, always!"

William nodded again, a brief smile playing on his lips. "If we begin now we could be ready to sail by the end of the summer."

"So soon, Duke William? This will be a huge undertaking."

"We have to be ready Lord FitzOsbern; we must strike while the iron is hot. I hear that not all accept Harold Godwinson as King and England is yet unsettled and without unity. It must be soon, for I fear, that if I give him too much time, he will bend the country to his will, for the man is well able as my Lord Beaumont rightly attests."

William's anger seemed to have evaporated and he suddenly noticed the cold. Ushering the men out into the main hall he settled them by the fire while calling for food and more wine. He was all urgency and direction now, his ideas, plans even, being quietly but excitedly relayed to the two men.

"I estimate we will need ten thousand men, a mixture of infantry, cavalry and archers."

"So many, Lord Duke? That is a mighty host."

"Aye, but I would not venture with less, if Harold raises the local *Fyrds* and brings his own warriors and his brothers men, he will have good numbers. England is rich in men as well as land and goods. We would need to seek allies methinks, as Normandy alone could not field those numbers, we could put out the call to the Bretons, the Burgundians and the Flemings, as always men will fight for money or the promise of reward."

"What number of ships would we need for such a host, Lord Duke? We would need transports as well as warships if we are to take horses."

"I haven't tallied ship numbers as yet, Lord FitzOsbern but it will be hundreds for I intend to take a fortress with us as well." The two Lords gaped. "We will make it in transportable pieces here and assemble it on arrival in England, thereby giving us a base."

Roger Beaumont smiled whimsically. "Methinks, Duke William that you have expected this state of affairs, these thoughts and numbers were not snatched from out of the air."

William managed a sad smile and sighed. "You are correct my Lord. I saw Harold Godwinson as an able man, an ambitious man but hoped for the best from him in regard to loyalty. However, I have not lived so long by taking everything and everyone on trust, present company excepted." The two men bowed their heads and smiled. "So, I make plans, contingencies, to allow for changes in events such as we see before us."

FitzOsbern shook his head in wonder at his Duke's plans. Roger Beaumont however was once more deep in thought.

"I have an idea which may help your cause Duke William; it will no doubt cost money, as dealings with holy church always do. However I think it could bring men flocking to your banner while being a mighty weapon itself at the same time."

FitzOsbern and William both looked intently at Beaumont. Before they could ask for an explanation, the older man began sharing his thoughts.

"Harold swore his oath on holy relics, to be your man and to aid not hinder your path to the throne of England, yes?"

"Aye, Roger, he did and willingly, he was my guest, my friend I thought. His way of gratitude for me rescuing him from captivity by Guy of Ponthieu."

"So, not just an oath of fealty but a holy oath, before God."

William frowned. "Aye, an oath breaker to me and God."

"So, how do you think Pope Alexander will view that? He being God's embodiment on earth. I think he will see it as an affront to the church and you know these priests, they like to punish."

"You think we should take this matter to the Pope?"

"Why not, Lord Duke? Send the matter and some silver and I am sure you would gain support of the holy church against this heretic who affronts man and God with his oath breaking."

William began to chuckle. "God's bones, Roger you're a wily one, a thinker, I thank Christ you are my friend."

Beaumont smiled. "I may not be able to fight anymore, my Lord." He patted his crippled leg. "But wits can win wars as readily as swords."

"What think you of that, Will?" The Duke asked FitzOsbern, his face losing the frown and his chuckle turning to a laugh. "See if we can bring the wrath of the church down upon Harold Godwinson's head."

The Duke raised his cup to the other two men. "I thank you for your thoughts and offers of support, I need both. This endeavour will not be easy but it is not impossible, I must be up and doing if we are to sail before summers end, seven months just, but then let Harold Godwinson watch out!"

Chapter Fourteen

The court of King Harald Sigurdsson, March 1066 AD

King Harald looked over his ale horn at his guest, taking measure of the man as he pondered the reason for his visit and the message he'd brought. Unlike the Norse with their long hair, the visitor wore his only to his shoulders, his face free of a beard but sporting a long blonde moustache to the edges of his chin. He had an unhappy face, his thin lips twisted into a grimace, his eyes narrow, watching, searching. Harald took a long drink then belched loudly, the man turned, an enquiring look on his face.

Harald growled into his ale. "Tomorrow, my Lord Earl, tomorrow we will discuss your proposal, I'm for my bed." The man tried to speak but was silenced by a raised hand. "Tomorrow."

As the King stood to leave his seat and the hall, those still sober and able rose, bowing their heads in respect. The guest was left at the high table along with Hardrada's *Jarls*, they also eying their visitor with guarded suspicion.

It was late the following morning when Hardrada stalked into the room, his *Jarls, Hearth-weru*, his guest and

143

his retainers all turning from the warmth of the fire and bowing low.

"My Lord Tostig, I will hear your entreaty now, the rest of you may leave."

All turned to go except Ulf, who looked to his King then his guest.

"You too, Master Ulf, I deem I'm safe enough, alone here with our Saxon Earl."

Ulf bowed and followed the others out, closing the door behind him. Harald pointed to a wine jug and two goblets, the Earl filling both and offering one to the King.

"So my Lord, shall we go over this matter again? My wits are no longer fuddled with ale and I trust you have enjoyed a good night's sleep." He gestured Tostig to pull two chairs up to the fire, settling himself he sipped the wine then looked at his guest.

"Now! Do I have things aright? You are an outlaw in your own country, banished from England. The old King, the Confessor is dead and your brother, Harold has assumed the throne?"

"Yes, Lord King, I was ejected from my Earldom of Northumbria and then banished by King Edward before he died, all at the insistence of my brother, Harold."

"Brothers eh? So it will be bitter, no?"

"Aye Lord King, it is. I just want what is rightfully mine."

Hardrada sipped his wine again, looking thoughtful then turned to his guest, looking him directly in the eyes.

"Which is what?" His tone blunt and direct.

"My Earldom back."

Hardrada shrugged. "That's a matter for your brother then, he banished you."

Tostig's face twisted. "My brother is insufferable, his head swollen, he …"

"God's bones, man! Cut to the chase! You haven't risked a long, perilous sea crossing at a time of year when men are still home about their hearths to tell me that! What do you want of me?"

"Support, Lord King, your support, to take back what is rightfully mine."

"You want the throne?"

"No Lord King, I would expect you to take that."

Hardrada was taken aback, though he hid his surprise well.

"But that is the English throne; I have no right to it."

"Neither did my brother but it did not stop him. You are related to the old Danish King, Canute and his sons, Harthacanute and Harold Harefoot, are you not?"

Harald huffed. "Very distantly, hardly …"

"Distant maybe but you still have ties. My brother has nothing, no royal blood, no consent to the throne; he's an Earl, no more than that! Furthermore, you are a King in your own right, take England by conquest."

Hardrada growled into his wine and drank some more.

"And if I was to take England by conquest, why do I need you? I have *Jarls* aplenty who will be seeking land and reward for their men and service."

"I know the country, I know the people, and I can garner support. Not everyone loves Harold Godwinson."

"From what I hear, your brother is an able warrior."

Tostig sneered. "He will die like other men."

Hardrada looked long and hard at his guest. Tostig held the stare, his eyes smouldering.

"I am still at war with Sweyn of Denmark, when the spring is fully here I will resume my fight with him."

"Why fight for Denmark Lord King, when you could have England? It's richer, the climate better and ripe for the taking and unlike Denmark it's not unified."

"Then you take it!" Hardrada snapped.

"I cannot Lord King, hence my visit to you. I need men, monies, support."

"Hah! The truth at last!" Tostig bridled but said nothing. "And if I do invade England, the English will just give me the throne?"

"As I said, Lord King, not all love Harold. The man that took my Earldom, Morcar. He and his brother, Edwin of Mercia, neither want Harold on the throne."

"Then who? There are always others seeking the throne."

"None in England Lord, though the Norman, William the bastard, has designs I hear."

Hardrada looked thoughtful.

"So why not go to the Norman for aid?" Tostig flinched and looked uncomfortable; Hardrada caught the look. "Hah! You've already tried the Norman; I am your second choice"

Reasoning that honesty was perhaps the best policy, Tostig opened up.

"Yes Lord King, I visited the Norman. He is well named."

"Sent you packing did he?"

Tostig shrugged and grimaced. "He has no fleet, how can he invade without ships. You have ships, men and a reputation as an able warrior, Lord King."

"Flatter me not, Earl Tostig, I prefer your honesty. Wine!" he pointed to the jug.

Tostig hid the snarl brought on by the curt command, for he hadn't heard an outright no yet. His pride could suffer further flaying … if it brought him the result he wanted. He refilled both cups.

The fire crackled, disturbing the pregnant silence between the two men. Hardrada quaffed his wine and slammed the cup down.

"You may go, Earl Tostig." He flicked his hand dismissively. "I have much to consider, I need time."

Tostig turned to go, a painted smile and a perfunctory bow given to a King who was already deep in thought, the seeds for conquest planted.

****

"Hah! Eysteinn, where have you been man? I expected you days past." Hardrada shouted, and then went to greet his friend, embracing and slapping him on the back roughly.

"Lord King …"

"Don't Lord King me, Eysteinn! There is only you and I here; we were friends long before I gained this crown." Seeing Eysteinn's troubled look, Hardrada quietened. "You are well? … Inger? … The boys? …"

Eysteinn looked to the floor, biting his lip and hiding his face. Hardrada stood back, his hands resting on Eysteinn's shoulders.

"What is it, Eysteinn? … What man?"

"Inger." Came out in a hoarse whisper. "Inger … Inger is dead!"

"God's bones! … How? When?" Hardrada's voice boomed. Seeing his friend's lost look and slumped stature, he lowered his voice and hugged Eysteinn close. "I'm sorry … so sorry!" Having fought alongside him, witnessed death at close quarters and mourned good friends with him, Hardrada knew the man was not easily moved to grief. However, he also knew that Inger had been everything to him, his world, and a good woman. Harald Hardrada, ruthless as he could be as both warrior and ruler grieved for his friend with equal passion. Leading Eysteinn to a chair near the fire and pouring him a cup of wine, he pulled up a chair next to him.

"Tell me of Inger." He said quietly.

Eysteinn swallowed hard and cuffed away his tears. Hardrada patted his shoulder comfortingly. Eysteinn gulped most of the wine, wiping his mouth on his sleeve.

"It was so simple ... so quick. We'd been at church, she'd insisted on going despite the bad weather. It was cold but dry when we left home, however when we came from Mass and were halfway home it began to rain then sleet heavily. We were soaked through and chilled by the time we reached the hall, nothing odd, or so you would think?

Two days later, she started to cough and suffered pains in her chest but you know Inger, she wouldn't rest, just a cough she said, I was to stop fussing. A day later, she collapsed. We put her to bed, her skin burned as if she was fevered but she shook as if chilled to the bone ..." His voice faltered slightly as he reminisced. "The apothecary came with his potions, Runa, the village 'old mother' came with her herbs and incantations, and then the priest with his misery and his prayers, none could help her." He paused to clear his throat. "The following day she coughed so hard I thought she would break, she brought up yellow phlegm and then blood ... She died the following day, the same day your summons arrived. I had to delay coming ... I had Inger to bury ... my boys ..."

Hardrada gently shushed him, placing a comforting hand on his shoulder again. "Truly, I am sorry. The boys?"

"They are lost, Harald ... men grown and married they may be but Inger was their mother, they have taken it hard."

Hardrada shook his head slowly and refilled the cups, raising his in salute. "Here's to Inger, a fine woman, a good wife and a good mother, may God cherish her."

The pair drained their cups and Harald refilled them.

"Thank you for listening, Harald."

Hardrada waved away the thanks. "You are my oldest and most trusted friend, when you hurt, I hurt, I also loved Inger because she cared for you and we are all the poorer for her passing."

The two men sat for some time without speaking, they drank and stared into the fire. A crackle in the fire broke the silence and Eysteinn cleared his throat and turned to his friend.

"You summoned me Lord King, how can I be of service."

Hardrada didn't answer straight away, the gravity of Eysteinn's situation and that which he was about to reveal giving him pause. When Eysteinn looked up for an answer, the blunt Norseman in Hardrada won out.

"We are going to invade England."

"What? ... Why?"

"Because I can. I have the ships and the men and God knows England is a rich prize."

"Why now?"

"I have King Harold's exiled brother here. He tells me England is not yet unified under his brother, there is unrest in the north and we could exploit that. *Jorvik* or York as the Saxons term it; was ever a Viking city, if we start there; we may even garner some support as many Norse, Danes and Swedes live here."

"Why should they prefer Norse rule over Saxon rule?"

Hardrada laughed. "My good friend, Eysteinn! Always asking the blunt question. If they are unhappy with Harold, maybe I would be a welcome alternative?" He chuckled.

"English politics and English Lords, I would sooner sup with the Devil."

"Well, it could soon become Norse politics and Norse Lords … how would you like an Earldom in England."

"I never count my chickens before they hatch but if you want to invade England, Harald, I am with you. My boys and my men are with you but first tell me of this exiled Earl, this would be turncoat brother. Men like him are not to your or my taste, what does he want?"

"His Earldom back. He claims to be useful in raising support and revolt in the north; once we take England he just wants his Earldom."

"Hmm, a traitor and a false brother to boot …"

"Maybe? Perhaps Harold is the false brother?"

"I doubt it! I haven't heard a lot of Harold but what I have is to his credit, it appears he is brave, honest, good to his friends and followers and even magnanimous in victory to his enemies. I haven't met your guest yet but I like the style of his brother."

"Earl Tostig can wait. I wanted to talk to you about my decision first, for if you are with me, the other *Jarls* will follow."

Eysteinn cupped his chin, deep in thought. "Like the Danes and us, the Saxon's have many ships. I would rather we fight them on the land where our tactics and experience will help, on the sea we are slaves to the wind and the waves and thus chance."

"Aye, agreed, we need to be ashore this time when we fight. If the men see what we are fighting for they will fight all the harder and we will need that edge for the Saxons can be formidable. Tostig tells me Harold and his other brothers also have their professional warriors, their *Huscarls* to stiffen the ranks of the *Fyrd*, we have seen their style when we were in the Guard, do you remember."

Eysteinn nodded. "Aye, they were good warriors … When can we be ready, Harald?"

"This summer, it has to be."

"There is much to do then and I would be up and doing." His voice dropped and he looked sad.

"Aye … I can understand." Harald put his arm around Eysteinn and hugged him. Then with mischief in his voice, he urged him to his feet. "Come; come, let us see what else we can draw out of our Saxon Lordling."

Chapter Fifteen

King Harold Godwinson's court, London. June 1066 AD

"It's an uneasy crown brother, I think it weighs heavy on your shoulders?"

"Aye Gyrth, trouble from all sides it seems. Unrest in the north, the Normans haunting our southern shores and now Hardrada of Norway is rumoured to be seeking to invade and conquer. I must fight for my crown and us Saxons for our country."

"You're not alone brother, you have Leofwine and me, we will never leave you or betray you, unlike that weasel of a brother of ours, Tostig. God grant me that if he comes with Hardrada I get to slit his gullet, bastard!"

"Enough Gyrth." Harold said, albeit gently. "He's our brother, no matter how misguided he is. He blames me for his exile; it was better that than his death I thought, for King Edward was being pushed to that, so to appease the Northumbrians."

The afternoon sun slipped from behind a cloud, casting its glare at the two men causing each to squint and raise a hand as a screen, both electing to move their chairs into the shade of the tree, Gyrth replying while they settled themselves again.

"You're too kind Harold, too forgiving. He would bring the Norse down on us, so brother or not, I would slay him."

"It's easy to kill a man Gyrth, it's the repercussions from it you should consider, it can bring feud and war and without doubt it brings hate, hate from his family but sometimes hate for yourself, hate for what you have done. As much as I am angry with Tostig for his treachery, I do not wish his death."

Gyrth looked at his brother and recognising the steely look did not venture further, seeking instead to change the subject.

"Do you think the Normans will come this summer? Another month or so and the harvest will have to be brought in. We won't be able to hold the *Fyrd* forever."

Harold chewed his lip. "I don't know; is the answer to whether William invades or not. I have reports of his shipbuilding preparations and his recruiting outside of Normandy; his call to arms has gone out to the Bretons, Franks, Frisians and even the Burgundians in the far south."

"So many!"

"Possibly. However, he has to get them here first and if we can attack him at sea or as he tries to land …"

"That's your plan?"

"Yes, we are watching along the southern coast. That is the narrowest point for him to cross. If he sails direct from Normandy, where his ships are being built, I think the channel winds will push him eastwards, which may suit him as it brings him closer to London. I would engage him at sea if possible, if not I would stop him on the beach, before he can gain a foothold. Coming off ship and having to fight as you land will be no easy task. The local *Fyrds* are already mobilised, and I can stiffen them quickly with my *Huscarls* and those of yourself and Leofwine, just as you said. Moreover, William is running out of time, it is almost the end of June, a month a harvest and the Normans, like us; need to bring the harvest in. So, if he is coming it must be soon."

Gyrth rose from his seat and paced. "And Hardrada?"

Harold shrugged. "I'm not sure; he already has many ships and men, along with the addition of Tostig's. He could sail at any time and as the summers are short in Norway he may well come first. Also, he could land further to the north; it would make sense for him as its closer to Norway and Tostig's former seat of Northumberland."

Harold looked away as he spoke, his mind suddenly full of dilemmas, counter plans and thoughts of who, what, where and when.

Seeing his brother struggling with the quandaries, Gyrth looked worried. His brother was always sure, decisive, and clear in his direction, a natural leader of men. Lately, he seemed to have aged, the lines on his face suddenly more evident, deeper, all in the few months since he had become King, the boisterous, fun loving man replaced by a more sombre, serious one. Harold was still looking away as he spoke, as if speaking his thoughts aloud.

"We could have a war on two fronts and at the same time if they come together."

Gyrth nodded sagely. "Yes, all we can do is prepare well and pray to God." Trying to alleviate some of his brother's angst, he asked. "Who is the most able; who do you fear the most? The bastard or the Norseman?"

Harold looked up quickly his lip curling into a snarl, his body coming forward in his chair, his hands gripping the arms. "I fear neither! No man!"

"I didn't mean it like that brother." Gyrth spoke quickly. "Let me put it another way, which is the most dangerous?"

Harold eased back in his chair, the snarl gone as quickly as it had appeared. "I think both are equally dangerous. Some of my *Huscarls* served with Hardrada in the Varangian Guard and they tell me he is a born warrior and a good leader of men. He has fought almost his whole life, from the age of fifteen they say, and has much experience of warfare in many lands against many different peoples; he will have seen and learned much."

"And William?"

"William is also a good soldier; I saw that for myself when I was in Normandy. Remember I fought a campaign with him against Count Conan of Brittany. He is clever, brave and utterly ruthless, for he too has had to fight since he was young. He also wages war differently to us and the Norse; a new way, he uses cavalry, mounted warriors, knights he termed them, as well as foot soldiers along with archers."

"We have archers … well some."

"Aye, but William groups them, concentrating their firepower. They can soften a target, which his foot soldiers or his mounted knights can then exploit."

"I've not seen mounted knights used before."

"They are useful if an enemy breaks formation, after an arrow storm say. However, as long as men stay together, tight in a shieldwall, horses will shy away. They will not run into a solid block of men so the best the knights can do then, is hurl javelins or missiles. With our *Huscarls* to firm the lines and stand fast, William's cavalry will have no advantage."

"A good Saxon shieldwall then!"

"Aye, brother, it's served us well in the past, that and picking our ground." He cleared his throat but lowered his voice. "My one fear that I do have is distance, each could land well apart from the other and I cannot be in two places at once and I do not wish to divide my forces."

"What about Earl Morcar, would he not turn out the Northumbrian *Fyrd* in support, there is much manpower in the north."

"At present I don't think he would support me, well not readily. However, in the face of a threat, from Hardrada say, he might?" He shrugged and gave a whimsical smile. "However, that may change soon, for I plan to marry his sister, Ealdgyth and you know what they say brother, blood is thicker than water."

"What? … But what of Edith?"

"Edith is my woman but not my wife … well, so the church would say. However, according to Danish law we are married under *mos danicus*, the 'hand fast' custom."

"You know the English church don't accept that."

"Yes." Harold laughed; something Gyrth had not seen him do for a long time. "Yes, I know and therefore I will have Edith and Ealdgyth."

"How in God's name will you do that?" Gyrth smirked and chuckled.

"The church says I can't have two wives, so in their eyes Edith is my mistress, which leaves me free to marry Ealdgyth."

"The church won't like that either, a mistress and a wife! What will Archbishop Stigand say?"

"The church will mind its own business and Archbishop Stigand will do as I tell him; else keep his holy mouth shut. He owes me anyway, for I included him at my coronation along with Ealdred, Archbishop of York."

Gyrth looked concerned again. "I wished you hadn't done that Harold, his position is tenuous in the church, the Pope does not love him and he does not hold a pallium."

Harold shrugged. "He is a clever man, a useful man and I saw no harm in it. Anyway, Ealdred has a pallium and he placed the crown on my head."

Gyrth nodded, seemed relieved and chuckled again. "So, you are marrying Ealdgyth, purely for the alliance of her brothers, Morcar of Northumberland and Edwin, Edwin of Mercia?"

"Yes, that and the fact that she is a beauty."

"So is Edith!"

"No argument there brother." It was Harold's turn to chuckle.

"God above, Harold, you have it all."

"And why not? I am the King!"

The pair laughed and Harold called for wine to be brought. As the servant served the wine then departed, Harold raised his cup.

"Here's to the demise of Harald and William."

The pair raised their cups but before either had drunk, Harold slapped sharply at his arm, swearing beneath his breath as his cup spilled the red wine over his hand.

"What is it brother?"

Harold moved his hand away revealing a squashed wasp. "It stung me. They don't usually do that until they become dozy as the summer fades"

Gyrth looked at the yellow and black smear mixing with the red wine. A shiver passed through him, as he thought of the significance of it. Yellow was the colour of the Norman leopard, black the colour of Hardrada's raven emblem and the dark red wine looked like blood but whose blood? Theirs or the house of Godwin's?

Harold was busy trying to squeeze the sting out and did not seem perturbed by it; so hiding his forebodings in his cup, Gyrth said nothing.

Part Three

The Bear, The Raven and The Dragon

Chapter Sixteen

Borg, July 1066 AD

"I'm alright Bjarke, I promise." Eerika smiled as she spoke. "It's normal you know, to be tired and swollen when the child is near."

Bjarke shrugged. "I just worry because your belly is so big while you are only small, your back hurts and your ankles are swollen. I have eyes and can see that."

Eerika reached up, and pulled her husband by his beard down to her height and kissed him gently.

"For a big man, a hunter and a warrior you have a tender heart, Bjarke Orrifostersson and compared to you, everyone is small … and stop worrying."

"You're my wife, my woman; of course I am going to worry. I wished this was all over and done, the baby here and you back to normal. Maybe we should not be having the baby; it's going to be huge!"

"Well you put the baby in there!" Eerika giggled. "Would you rather you hadn't?"

"No …" Bjarke smiled then chuckled.

"Well then! … I expect you put another one in there once this one is born."

"Bjarke smiled. "I'm for bed soon, I need to be away at dawn tomorrow and hunt. Father thinks we will sail within a month and I want to ensure there is plenty meat for you and the baby."

"For the baby! It won't be born with teeth you know!" She giggled again. "And you won't be away that long!"

"I'm not so sure. Father says the King is assembling a huge force, three hundred ships or more, it's not just a raid Eerika, its war and conquest."

"So, our child may grow up in England, for the King is known to be generous to his followers."

Bjarke shrugged. "I'm happy here Eerika, with you, I can hunt and we can raise a family, what else do we need? We want for nothing."

"I'm content also, Bjarke. I was just speaking my thoughts aloud. If the King takes England your father may have to move there with him, you know how he values his council and after your mother's passing, I don't think he sees Borg in the same way."

Bjarke's head dropped forward, his face suddenly sad.

"Oh, I'm sorry, Bjarke! So sorry, your mother's passing is still raw. I was thoughtless" Eerika wrapped her arms around him as best she could for her belly. "If the baby is a girl, we will name her Inger, for your mother."

Bjarke smiled and hugged her, kissed her, then picked her up as if she weighed nothing. Eerika giggling all the while, as he carried her from the fire and the pot she had been stirring, sitting her on the settle, lifting her feet up. Settling himself on the floor his back against the settle his head was still above hers.

"I would be happy to stay here and take care of father's affairs, a Reeve I think they call it. I think Hakon is keen to go to England, should the invasion be successful. So he and Asta would settle there I think; I would miss them both though."

"Poor Bjarke." Eerika said and pulled his head in close and kissing his forehead. "You can't win; you can't have it all, my love."

Bjarke breathed deeply and sighed. "Life changes I suppose, nothing stays the same. Look at us, soon we will be three."

"God willing … and then four, then five, then …"

Bjarke laughed loudly. "I think you just enjoy the practice Eerika."

A playful swipe from Eerika's hand on the back of his head making him laugh more.

The following morning Bjarke was gone at sunrise, slipping from the bed without waking Eerika. Fenrir got up from his blankets on the floor with just a little groan then stretched his legs and yawned widely. Giving his coat a little shake and with his tail wagging, he went towards the bed and Eerika. Bjarke pulled his collar gently, steering him away and out of the room, ruffling his ears as he went. Collecting his bow, javelin and rope, Bjarke and Fenrir made their way through the still silent village, then across the hay meadow into the forest.

It was already becoming hot and Fenrir was panting as he jogged alongside his master, keeping pace with his long strides. Pushing up the steep part of the meadow, Bjarke noticed Fenrir was no longer close and turned back to see him a few paces behind. He watched as the dog caught up, checking how he walked, making sure there was no limping. Fenrir came alongside, his tongue lolling from the side of his mouth and panting heavily. Bjarke cupped a hand and poured some water from his bottle into it, offering it to the dog, as Fenrir lapped it up, Bjarke noticed, as if for the first time, the greying muzzle and streaks of grey on the brindle head above the eyes. Fenrir was very fit but he was getting old, almost eleven in human years, a good age for a large dog, Bjarke let him rest a while after drinking before heading into the forest. The morning passed quietly without sight of a deer or even a scent for Fenrir to latch onto, Bjarke reasoning that with the warmer weather the animals would be higher up the hill, so man and dog pushed on upwards, the climb punishing the lungs and both thankful of the shade from the trees.

The pair crisscrossed the huge hill, searching as they climbed throughout the morning and afternoon and without sight of anything, it was early evening before Fenrir raised his head, sniffing the slight breeze. Bjarke stopped immediately and stared through the trees, finally seeing a small group of deer made up of hinds and yearlings. Selecting a good-sized yearling, he hit it with a single arrow just above the heart; the deer ran on for a few paces before Fenrir brought it down with a nip to the hind legs. The dog held it as it scrabbled on the ground in its death throes, it dying before Bjarke reached it. He removed the head and gralloched the deer quickly, cutting out the heart and liver and feeding Fenrir with it, he keen to be on his way home now, his stomach telling him they had been gone for a long time. Hefting the deer carcase over his shoulders, he set off back down the hill apace, Fenrir following closely behind, the downward trek easier on legs and lungs. Exiting into the meadow, he saw a horseman working his way along the edge of the forest and another down beside the old farmhouse, both riders seemed to be searching for something. Reasoning they may be hunters like himself and perhaps tracking a wounded animal he walked on, cutting across the meadow towards the village. Hearing a shout, he saw one of the riders had turned towards him, raising a hand and still shouting but owing to the distance, he couldn't understand what the man said. The rider held up his hand intimating Bjarke should stop then kicked the horse hard towards him. Bemused, Bjarke carried on walking but altered his course towards the rider. Man and horse were now galloping across the meadow, the man's shouts drifting over the sward but drowned by the sounds of the horse's hooves. Bjarke noticed an anxiousness about the man and the way he pushed the horse, as the gap closed the shouts became clearer.

"Bjarke! … Bjarke! Thank God I've found you!" The man reined up hard, his mount sliding on the grass, the stink of horse sweat strong.

Bjarke felt his heart quicken as he reached for the horse's bridle. "Sven! … What is it?"

Sven threw himself from the horses back. "Eerika! … Eerika, the baby! Quickly, take the horse."

"The baby is here? … But I …"

"Go now, Bjarke!"

Bjarke saw the anxiety on Sven's face.

"They're alright? Eerika is alright?"

Sven paled and took a quick breath before answering. "It's not good, Bjarke, go!"

Bjarke dropped his bow, quiver and javelins and dumped the yearling in the grass, throwing himself over the horse's back. Thankfully, it was a large animal, though it still stepped quickly and whinnied in protest as his weight came on. Dragging the reins hard, he forced the horse about turn towards the village, kicking its flanks hard demanding speed. Fenrir barked once then took off after him, his body stretching as he went to a loping run alongside the horse. Bjarke lashed the reins from flank to flank, then flattened himself against the horse's neck as he sought yet more speed, his heart pounding and his stomach churning. The village was some distance from the farmhouse and the horse had been ridden all day in the heat without pause. Just short of the village, with its heavy load and forced gallop taking its toll, it finally gave up, its legs folding beneath it as it collapsed, throwing Bjarke clear. With no saddle and stirrups, Bjarke managed to leap clear. Stumbling from the impetus as he hit the ground, he went into a forward roll before jumping to his feet and taking off at the run, leaving the animal thrashing on the floor trying to get up. A bark came from behind him; Fenrir, who had been left behind, unable to maintain the horses speed raced after him, catching him up and running alongside. The pair ran on without pause, Bjarke breathing heavy and the dog panting hard, the evening's heat forcing sweat from the man's body, sticking his clothes to his skin and adding to his discomfort.

Reaching his house, he saw a few people gathered outside, the door open and women moving inside. With panic setting in, he bellowed loudly.

"Eerika! … Eerika!"

A man saw him coming and held up his hands to slow and stop him. "Bjarke! … Bjarke, steady, wait …"

Without slowing, Bjarke pushed him aside, heading straight for the door. The others, recognising he was not to be stopped moving to one side letting him through. Stooping under the door head, he pushed into the room. "Eerika!" He panted.

His eyes scanned the room quickly, searching for Eerika. Looking across the room to another door and the bedchamber, he caught sight of at least two women near the bed. Pushing people to one side, he made for the bedchamber.

"Eerika! … Eerika!" His voice dried in his throat, as his mind reasoned what was happening. Runa appeared from the bedchamber and stood in front of him barring his way. Her eyes were wide and wet with tears, her face drawn in sadness. He stopped and stared, her expression saying all that she did not. He went to step past her and she held her arm across his chest. He went to move her arm but she tightened her grip on his shirt, speaking quietly.

"Let the women see to her, Bjarke, please."

Bjarke had a fleeting moment of hope. "She'll recover?"

Runa wrapped her arms around him. "No Bjarke, no. I'm sorry both are gone."

"Christ God, no … no … Eerika … no!"

His strangled cry died in his throat and he fell heavily to his knees as if taking a mortal wound. Runa stepped in close pulling his head to her breast as his heart broke. Still holding him, she quietly ordered then shooed the others out, flicking her hand in brisk dismissal. Bjarke sobbed into her dress, his huge frame shaking, Runa tried to console him with quiet words but lost in his grief he just wept. The dog had followed him into the house but sensing grief and tension had just laid on his bed watching as the house cleared of people. With quiet returning and everyone gone except Bjarke and Runa, Fenrir whined softly then went to the bed and sniffed at Eerika. He pushed his nose against her face and whined again, mournfully. Padding back into the other room he came alongside Bjarke, licking his hand and pushing against him, a low, sad rumble in his throat. Bjarke didn't push him away. Instead, he struggled to his feet, gently easing Runa to one side. His body was aching and sore from the hunt, the fall, the run and being on his knees. He cuffed the tears from his face and looked at Runa. She began talking quietly.

"We didn't know anything until Dagfinn heard Eerika's cries. He tried to help and then ran for me. The baby came quickly; very quickly, Eerika was already in trouble by the time I arrived. The blood loss was too much, she just faded." She saw the questions forming on his lips and pre-empted them. "She was no longer in pain, the baby was out but the damage was great." She saw he was going to speak and again she anticipated his question. "The baby, a boy, died within moments of Eerika."

She looked up at the huge man in front of her, his face haggard with grief, his eyes like slits, the tears still running into his beard. His chest heaved as she finished her telling.

"I need to see her." He managed, his words a despondent whisper.

"Come then, we have done the right thing for mother and child."

Runa led him to the bedchamber. The women had washed both Eerika and the baby and laid them together, covering them with a sheet as if sleeping. Bjarke knelt by the bed, pushing his face against Eerika's, her skin already cold, he cried softly into her hair. Fenrir lay on his bed again, head between his front paws, watching Bjarke.

Darkness was closing before he kissed her gently and then stood and picked up the baby. The little boy looked perfect in every way, limbs and toes all there and a shock of fine blonde hair covering his head. Bjarke groaned softly as he took in the size of his son. Gently laying the child back alongside Eerika, Bjarke's head fell on his chest.

"I've killed her!" He growled quietly. "She was so small and the baby is so large, I've killed her!"

"No, no!" Runa said quickly. "These things happen; child birth is a dangerous time for all."

"I wasn't even here to help; I shouldn't have left her when she was so near her time."

"It wouldn't have mattered, Bjarke, you couldn't …"

"It matters to me!" He roared; Runa jumped back at his sudden fury. He fell to his knees again. "It matters to me … it matters to …" His chest heaved choking off his words. Runa stepped in close again and hugged him, he holding onto her as his heart broke again.

They buried Eerika and the child the following afternoon. Anders and Bjarke digging the grave themselves, refusing any offers of help. The two men laboured without a word or pause, other than a short discussion on the size and depth of the hole as they dug. After a short service in the church, Bjarke picked up Eerika's body, Anders lifting the baby, both bodies wrapped tightly in white linen.

Laying both in the grave, Bjarke added Eerika's leather bag containing her combs, brooches and belt then added her shears, distaff, spindle and whorl. Anders placed two small woodcarvings, one of a bear and the other of a horse, lying them near the baby. Father Gudmund tutted his displeasure at the pagan custom a little too loudly and Bjarke growled and stepped towards him, his fists bunching. The priest held up his hands and backed away in fright. Anders quickly placed a hand on Bjarke's shoulder giving it a gentle squeeze and the big man stopped, glowering his displeasure instead. With the threat gone, the now nervous priest gave his benediction. People and family laid flowers by the graveside then quietly left, leaving the two men to close the grave. When the last of the earth was placed, they laid the flowers on the top, Bjarke at pains to arrange them just so. As he placed the last bunch, he broke down, dropping to his knees by the graveside, his heart broken.

"Eerika ... Eerika was the flower that would die before it could ..." He mumbled before huge, heaving sobs racked his chest while low growls mixed with his gasps for breath as he wept. Anders came alongside, putting his arm over Bjarke's shoulder and pulling him close, his other arm holding Bjarke's head, his own eyes flooded with tears.

The two men sat by the graveside, again without a word until the evening chill had them rise to seek a meal and warmth. The older man pulling the younger close, his arm over his back and steering him towards home.

Hakon arrived at the house in the early evening a week later, bursting through the door like an approaching storm. Fenrir barked fiercely before changing to an excited growl as he recognised Hakon and pushed in close to welcome him.

"Bjarke! ... Bjarke?" He called trying to catch his breath.

"I'm here brother." A voice said quietly from a darkened corner of the room.

Identifying Bjarke in the gloom, Hakon strode across the room and hugged him fiercely.

"I'm so sorry brother, I ... I'm just home from court; they told me what happened as we berthed. I'm sorry brother, so sorry ... I ... Christ! I don't know what to say." The words came out in a rush; Bjarke didn't reply; he just clapped his brother affectionately on the back. "Father doesn't know yet, he is still at court with the King ... I have news for us all in that regard but we can talk later about that. Asta and I want you to come home to us, will you come?" Bjarke still didn't answer. "Come on brother … don't stay here alone." Hakon urged, while trying to raise Bjarke to his feet.

"Thank you brother but no. I'm not great company right now; I don't wish to bring my heartache to your home."

"But we're brothers Bjarke! When you hurt, I hurt. You would do the same for me."

Bjarke cleared his throat. "Thank you, Hakon that means much but I will be alright, I just need time."

"Yes, yes of course. I just don't want you on your own. Come Bjarke, please."

"Thank you Hakon but no, this is my home, I should stay. Anyway, what news from father and the court?"

"It'll keep. You are more …"

"No, Hakon. Tell me please, though I think I know what you are going to say … come on brother, tell me if you will."

Hakon sighed deeply. "We, you and I and Anders, are to summon father's men and marshal the fleet; we are to be at Oslo by the end of next month. We will join father and the King there. It's war and invasion, invasion of England."

Bjarke nodded his head slowly and spoke quietly as if to himself. "Methinks Runa is wiser than she knows."

"What! … what about Runa?"

"Nothing really brother, nothing at all … I'm glad you are home, it's good to see you."

"It's good to see you too Bjarke, Christ God, it is. Now tell me what the old wife had to say, we're brothers, no secrets."

Bjarke sighed deeply. "Most of it doesn't make sense."

"Enough of it did for to trouble you!"

Bjarke shrugged. "I've lost Eerika, that's what's troubling me." He snapped, suddenly irritable and his eyes moistened.

Hakon hugged him fiercely again. There was a long silence then Bjarke cleared his throat.

"I can't remember word for word but the gist of it was."

"Beauty is short lived and passing and the flower will die before it blooms. ... Reputations will be made but lost. ... A harvest is coming not of wheat but of souls. ... Kings and Jarls will lie down with men. ... Angels and Valkyrie will gather the brave. ... Brother will fight brother but the raven, the dragon and the fighting man will give way to the leopard of gold. ... Bifröst, the rainbow bridge will choke with those seeking the Gods. ... The bear that heeds the hunter will not fall but the bear that doesn't, will into the river fall. ...The bridge, linger not on the bridge."

Hakon frowned as he listened. "What?"

Bjarke shrugged again. "I told you ... however, I think Eerika was the flower that died before it bloomed."

Hakon saw his brother's anguish and chose his words carefully. "Maybe brother ... Christ God knows, Eerika was beautiful but the rest ... was the old wife reciting something from the sagas? She loses her mind when she drinks her potions and babbles. Mother always said ..."

"I don't know Hakon." He interrupted. "Think on though, war is coming and men will die, probably many men, perhaps Kings and *Jarls* too? Brother fighting brother, who knows? The raven, the dragon, the fighting man, the leopard? A bear and a bridge" He shrugged again. Hakon also looked lost. "The only thing Runa could explain was Bifröst; it was the bridge to the old Gods."

"Hah! There you go; the old wife's wits are stuck in age's past! Christ knows we have been Christians long enough!" Hakon forced a chuckle. "Come on Bjarke, I'm not taking no for an answer, you're coming home with me." He put his finger over Bjarke's lips stalling the objection, and then pulled his brother to his feet. "Come on big man, Asta, ale, lamb stew and fruit pie await!"

Bjarke smiled at last and followed his brother.

Chapter Seventeen

Oslo, August 1066 AD

Bjarke gazed from the bows as the ship nosed towards the harbour, he felt Fenrir's weight on his legs as the dog leaned against him, it looking down at the water spraying up from the bows as they cut through the small waves. Bjarke had never seen so many ships in one place; scores of masts reared skyward resembling wintered trees, the ships tied to one another ten deep in places, the wharfs completely hidden from view amidst this floating forest.

Hakon came up behind him, reaching up to throw his arm over his shoulder. "God's bones, brother! The King is serious then, there must be hundreds of ships here, so that means thousands of men, he's for making England his."

"Aye ... it looks that way." Bjarke replied quietly.

Ingvar pushed alongside. "Taking a rough count, I make it two hundred and fifty ships which equates to around seven and a half thousand men at least."

Hakon whistled softly. "And that's not counting Earl Tostig's host. He isn't here; we are to meet him in northern England. He's rumoured to have a dozen ships and around five hundred men, a mixture of Saxons with some Scots and Flemish mercenaries."

"What are they worth though?" Kettil grumbled as he joined the trio. "Scots and Flemings fighting for money, they are likely to turn and run at the first sign of trouble."

"I hope not." Ingvar replied. The Saxons should be staunch though, dispossessed men will fight hard to regain what they have lost."

"I'm not so sure Ingvar. Their leader doesn't sound like a great man to follow. I mean, what kind of a man rebels against his brother and his own folk? I wouldn't dream of fighting against you and Hakon wouldn't turn against Bjarke."

"It's power I suppose, or perhaps greed or jealousy? All are capable of driving men mad."

"Well I hope the King isn't greedy when it comes to carving up England, what say you Bjarke?"

Bjarke just shrugged and picked up a mooring rope then turned away readying to throw it. All three looked at Bjarke then each other, the big man hardly spoke at all, he went through the motions of what was required of him, answered when he had to but more often than not, he said nothing. Hakon broke the awkward silence.

"I think we should win it first, and remember, the Saxons are fighting for their homes and families as well as their lives and they won't give in easy."

"Aye but the King knows what he's doing, he's a seasoned warrior."

"True, no argument there, Kettil but so is Harold Godwinson and don't forget the Norman, he's rumoured to be a dangerous bastard and also gathering an army and building a fleet to invade."

"Normans? If they are as soft and weak as the Franks we have nothing to fear from them."

"They're a different breed Kettil, they are descended from Danes. Danes who conquered the western fringes of Frankia, they won't quake and bolt at the first sign of trouble either."

"God's bones, Hakon, you're a prophet of doom!"

"A wise man knows his enemy, Kettil."

The shout to back-oars broke the conversation and the ship turned broadside on, the oars were quickly shipped as ropes were cast, lashing it alongside another already berthed.

Eysteinn was waiting on the wharf for his sons and his ships to arrive. As the brothers stepped ashore, he opened his arms and went to embrace both.

"I'm sorry son, sorry about Eerika." Bjarke nodded. "Hakon sent a message back as soon as he berthed at Borg, I would have been there for you but for the King and this." He gestured to the ships.

"I understand father, you are well?"

"Aye, though better for seeing you both and old Fenrir here." He ruffled the dog's ears as it pushed against him wagging his tail. "Hakon! You and Asta are both well?"

"Yes father."

"Any sign of me being a grandfather yet?"

"No …" Hakon's face fell and Eysteinn grimaced and glanced at Bjarke who looked despondent.

"Christ, curse my tongue! I'm sorry lad, I was thoughtless, I should …"

"It's alright father, honestly." Bjarke said quietly.

The three men looked at each other, the silence heavy. Eysteinn was about to speak when Bjarke cleared his throat and placed his hands on his father's and brother's shoulders.

"We should clear the air. Eerika is gone, the child, my son is gone and nothing anyone or I can do or say will bring them back. Speak freely of Eerika and the child, I would rather we spoke of them and remembered them, than there be a silence and avoidance. However, I cannot speak for Anders; he has lost his only daughter and has taken it hard. I tried to speak to him of Eerika while on our journey here but he could not."

Eysteinn nodded and Hakon looked surprised, it was the most he had heard his brother say since Eerika's death, his previous conversations being short answers, if at all.

"Very well lad, it will be as you wish. Your mother and I both loved Eerika, as we do Asta, despite the pair of them stealing our sons." Eysteinn chuckled attempting to lighten the conversation; when Hakon saw Bjarke smile, he chuckled too.

"One more thing I should tell you father." Bjarke said, though his voice was gravelly with emotion. "If the child had been a girl she would have been named Inger, after mother but as it was a boy, he was named for you."

Eysteinn looked up at his son a sad smile playing on his lips. "God in heaven bless and keep the three of them." He managed.

The discussion was interrupted by the arrival of the King and some of his *Hearth-weru*.

"Hah, Eysteinn! Your cubs have arrived."

The three men bowed low offering their greetings.

Hardrada towered above Hakon and Eysteinn but found himself looking slightly upwards at Bjarke.

"Christ God, lad! What do they feed you?" He gripped Bjarke's bicep and then tapped his chest appreciatively. "If you fight as hard as you are big, England is already won, what say you, Master Ulf?"

Ulf grimaced and growled his reply. "It's not big boys and their dog we need, Lord King, its men, seasoned warriors."

Eysteinn's head lifted quickly, his eyes seeking Ulf. Finding him, he fixed him with a malevolent stare. He was about to speak when Bjarke pre-empted him.

"I may lack your experience, Master Ulf but I'm no longer a boy and I will fight for my King just as you will." His tone civil but sure.

Ulf huffed. "You might be strong, boy but that doesn't make you a warrior."

Eysteinn, Hakon, and even the King swung on Ulf; again, Bjarke was quicker. He held up his hand respectably, requesting to speak while assuming the right.

"Master Ulf, have I wronged you in a former life? What have I done to earn your derision and scorn?"

Ulf growled in his throat and puffed up his chest, his arms folding defensively. "You insulted me!" Hardrada went to intervene while putting a restraining arm on Eysteinn's, holding him back as he made to step towards Ulf, his face twisting in anger but Bjarke was quicker than all of them.

"How so? How did I insult you?" His tone incredulous.

"Offering me back my silver! … I lost the wager but I pay my debts, I don't need some ox-sized plough boy to …"

"That's enough, Master Ulf!" Hardrada snarled. "You forget yourself."

Eysteinn however, despite the Kings restraining arm and vocal support was not to be silenced.

"Aye! Watch your words, Master Ulf. An attack on my lads is the same as an attack on me and as Christ is my witness I will not suffer it … and I fear you not!"

Ulf suddenly looked unsure, with both the King and his first Lord siding against him, it was an argument he couldn't win.

"I meant no insult to you Master Ulf. I was trying to behave as I was taught. You tried bravely and lost, no shame there, I won the strongman's money, not yours thus I ..."

"Enough Bjarke, don't feel you have to explain your actions to this." Eysteinn's voice rose along with his anger as he stabbed a finger close to Ulf's face.

Ulf bridled at the venom and the pointed finger. Stepping back quickly, his hand dropped to his sword hilt. Eysteinn snatched his seax from its sheath and stepped forward.

"That's enough! ... Christ God, I say enough!" Hardrada roared.

All around, men stepped back, for Hardrada in anger was a terrible sight. Towering above all except Bjarke, his body seemed suddenly broader, larger, his previous happy visage twisted into a snarl.

"You dare to reach for weapons in my presence?"

The words thundering out as he glared at Ulf then Eysteinn. Ulf moved his hand away from his sword hilt and Eysteinn sheathed his seax. Hardrada, making a physical effort to control his anger, lowered his voice.

"Lord Orri, I will deal with this. Master Ulf, you have heard Bjarke Orrifostersson's words, he has declared he intended no insult to you; I too am at a loss as to how you came by that notion anyway. So, you will apologise, apologise to Lord Orri and Bjarke, this ends now!" Ulf hesitated. "I said now! Obey your King, damn you! Or I ..." Hardrada's hand dropped to his sword hilt.

Ulf dipped his head to Hardrada and then to Eysteinn. "My Lord, I apologise."

Eysteinn nodded slightly in acknowledgement then flicked his head in the direction of Bjarke. Ulf grimaced slightly and turned to Bjarke. Bjarke offered his hand. Again, Ulf hesitated but hearing an intake on breath from Hardrada, offered his own hand. The pair shook hands, though Ulf pulled his away quickly.

"By your leave, Lord King. I have matters to attend to."

Hardrada sighed and waved him away. He urged Eysteinn and the brothers onwards along the wharf.

"He's a strange man and a prickly one; I have had trouble with him and his pride before. He sees an insult where there is none."

"Why tolerate him then, Lord King?"

Hardrada shrugged slightly. "He's an able man, a good organiser, reliable …"

"There are others, surely?"

"Like as not, aye … but you grow used to folk, you come to rely on them despite their other failings."

Eysteinn ushered Bjarke and Hakon ahead and out of earshot then turned to Hardrada speaking quietly.

"Useful or not, Lord King and with respect to you and your authority. If he causes trouble for me and my family again, I will kill him. I raised my boys to be respectful to others, else prepare for the consequences that can follow; it seems Master Ulf has no such respect."

Hardrada chuckled lightly. "Fair enough Eysteinn, fair enough. I have known you and trusted you for most of my life, with my life, so you matter, your boys matter. If however you do kill him, be prepared to replace him … with yourself!" Hardrada laughed when Eysteinn looked shocked. "When we take England, I will need you more than ever anyway, so commanding my *Hearth-weru* as well as being my first Lord will be no great addition of duty."

"Lord King, when we take England and all is settled I would seek a quieter life, time to enjoy my boys, I have already been away so much, the hearth is calling."

"The hearth! …You! … Christ God, man! You are but a year or two older than me! The hearth!" Hardrada shook his head and smirked. "And stop, Lord Kinging, me!"

Eysteinn raised his eyebrows and managed a tight smile. "Once all is settled, Harald, I would have a little peace."

"I'm for a little peace myself, Eysteinn but to ensure that, I need good men, strong men, like you beside me."

Eysteinn smiled slightly, appreciating the sentiment. "We need, we must, bring younger men on Harald, train and entrust them as we cannot last forever!"

Harald looked thoughtful as the pair walked on. "I have a proposal for you, a proposal that may put some vigour back into you." Harald threw his arm over Eysteinn's shoulder. "Not at the moment though, out of respect for Inger."

"Not another woman, Harald?"

"No, not any woman Eysteinn, my daughter, Maria. A marriage, when the time is right of course." Eysteinn looked up quickly, surprise evident on his face. "Don't say anything at the moment Eysteinn, I know Inger's death is still raw and you are hurting greatly but I must plan for the future. You are my closest friend, I would make you family."

"Harald, I …"

Harald put his finger to his lips. "Not now, Eysteinn, not now. Between you and me, eh? Just us."

The pair walked on, closer to the ships now and amongst the men loading supplies onto the vessels. Some called a greeting others bowed. Some, knowing the King and Eysteinn from earlier days came to talk of the invasion and when it was likely to be underway.

Later that evening when Harald and Eysteinn were settled over a meal and ale and with a room to themselves, Harald brought the invasion date back into the conversation.

"We leave on Friday week, the last Friday of August but we are not going direct to England."

"What! ... Where then?"

"The Orkneys first. We collect the Orkney *Jarls* and their men, then we sail south down the east coast and meet with Earl Tostig and his ships at the river *Tine* in Northumbria. After that, we sail south for the Humber, from there inland and upriver towards *Jorvik,* we will make our base there for it is the most powerful city in Northumbria and the most likely to offer us support. Not all men love Harold Godwinson it would seem, if Tostig is to be believed."

"Do you trust him then? This turncoat Saxon Earl."

"Enough to see us into England. His local knowledge and such will be useful and he only stands to gain by allying himself with us ..."

"And after that?"

Harald chuckled. "Well, if he behaves himself and does as he's told, I may let him keep his Earldom. However, any sign of treachery or trouble from him and I'll gut the bastard! Think on though, it makes sense landing in the north as he suggests, it's well away from Harold Godwinson, the Saxon fleet and London. I'm told he is engaged off the south coast at present, along with the southern counties *Fyrd,* seeking the Norman, the northern *Fyrd* is not yet been summoned for the men are busy bringing in the harvest."

"So…, the place could be right, no opposing ships to try and hold us off and the timing could be right as the northern *Fyrd* is not yet raised. *Jorvik* you think, may side with us and Harold is in the south of the country and could well be busy fighting the Norman?"

"Hopefully yes, and if Harold and William tear themselves to pieces it will be easier for us to defeat the winner of the two."

"No wonder you are confident Harald, this is all falling into place."

"It would appear so." Harald smiled over his wine cup. "But let's keep everyone guessing as to when we leave and where we are headed first."

"Agreed."

"And here's to a short war for once." Eysteinn raised his cup.

"God willing. A short war to suit old men."

The pair laughed as their ale horns nudged together.

Chapter Eighteen

The Raven at Fulford, North Yorkshire, 20ᵗʰ September 1066 AD

The wind roared off the sea, fanning the flames and black smoke from the burning houses and driving it against the rising cliffs behind. Most folk had fled at the sight of the Norse fleet, the bodies of those that hadn't, littered the pathways and wharf. The tiny fishing hamlet of Scarborough was being raised to the ground, a lesson to anyone else daring to question the will or the right of Harald Sigurdsson to be King. Looting had produced little in the way of reward for the effort, the exercise really doing nothing other than to relieve the boredom and sharpen the senses of men who'd suffered a long sea voyage.

The long ships pushed off from the beach and turned south, the stiff onshore breeze forcing the men to row to hold the ships clear of the rocks. Bjarke, sombre faced, was at the rudder, holding it firmly against the steady throb of the wind and tide.

"What's your thoughts brother?" Hakon asked as he offered Bjarke a flask of ale. Bjarke shook his head to the drink. "Are you alright, little brother?"

The big man gurned his face. "Was that necessary?" He flicked his head back towards the smoke. "They were just simple folk …"

"They refused to acknowledge the King, saying they already had a King."

"Which is true."

Hakon stepped closer. "Shush brother, The King didn't like their tone and he wouldn't thank you for yours."

Bjarke shrugged. "I just don't like ordinary folk being trampled by the aspirations of powerful men."

Hakon chuckled. "Christ God, Bjarke, for a man that could force his will on almost anyone you have a gentle heart."

"I don't mind fighting warriors if I have to and I will follow and serve my King because you and our father do but burning houses around folk's ears does not leave a good taste in my mouth."

"There will be warriors to fight soon enough methinks, we are sailing for *Richale* and from there we march on *Jorvik*, the King would secure it first, giving us a base in the north here. There is a rumour that the northern Earls will try and stop us."

"Well, once the fighting is done, I'm for home."

"What? Why would you go home after …" Hakon cut his words short as he saw his brother frown.

"After Eerika's death?"

"I'm sorry Bjarke, I meant no …"

Bjarke held up his hand silencing his brother. "I just want to go home is all, it's my home, your home, and I like it there, I like us being there."

Hakon stared at his brother for a moment; he saw the raw hurt of Eerika's death in his eyes and the lost, despairing look of a man who needed something to hold onto. His heart ached to see Bjarke so unhappy, yes he had a tender heart, always putting others first and Hakon counted his blessings that he had a brother who loved him and would defend him no matter what the cost. Putting his thoughts aside of settling in England, he threw his arm around Bjarke.

"Alright brother, when this is done we will go home, I promise."

For the first time in a long while, Hakon saw Bjarke smile.

Having reached *Richale*, the first long ships were tying up all along the river's edge with their masts stowed and sails folded. Some were drawn up high on the banks trying to make space for others which continued to arrive throughout the day, filling the river. Men spilled onto the grassy bank in their hundreds, strapping on their mail and weapons then began their march north towards *Jorvik,* those still arriving ordered to follow on once they had docked. Thus, the Norse army broke into three columns, spaced apart by their ships arrival time at *Richale*. As the first Norse column neared *Jorvik*, scouts reported a Saxon army under Earls, Morcar and Edwin gathering outside a small hamlet, Gate Fulford and blocking the road into the city.

Hardrada and his leading column advanced up a gentle rise where they scanned the terrain before them. The land lay wide and flat to the north and east and was predominately marsh, it was devoid of large trees, being covered in sedge, tall grass, reeds and stunted bushes instead. To the left, and flowing from the north was the river Ouse, on its way to *Richale* and the sea. At a right angle to the Ouse and directly in front of the Norsemen was a small beck, which drained from the broad marshland into the river. North of the marsh *Jorvik* was visible, smoke from the house fires rising lazily above its old Roman walls into the morning sky. All along the opposing beck bank, standing out brightly amongst the greenery was the banners and shields of the Saxon army, the warriors numbering in their thousands.

"Quite a number, Lord King!"

"Aye, Earl Tostig, a good number!" Hardrada growled. "Not keen to support Harold you said, hah! That looks like good support to me." He spat on the ground.

Tostig's lips twisted into a snarl. "Those banners are the Earls Morcar and Edwin, Lord King. Morcar is the bastard holding my Earldom of Northumberland and Edwin is of Mercia. I'm told that my brother's made a timely marriage to their sister, Ealdgyth. Thus their sudden loyalty and support, blood is thicker than water it seems."

"Aye, so it seems! Let's hope your blood doesn't turn suddenly loyal."

"Lord King! My loyalty is to you and …"

"Save it, my Lord! I've heard it many times." He snapped. Gaining silence, he lowered his voice. "Tell me what you know of the land hereabouts."

Tostig hid his distaste at the question of his loyalty and told of what he knew.

"The ocean tide is full at present, Lord King, thus the beck and the river are flooding and forming a strong barrier against us. The land is marshy to our right as you can see; that and the river giving the Saxons protection on either flank. However, we need to watch our left flank as the tide recedes and the river level falls, as access to an army's rear for us or the Saxons becomes possible over the mudflats once the tide recedes."

"So, if we engage and keep the Saxons busy along the beck until the tide falls, we could march around their flank and engage their rear?"

"Yes, Lord King."

Hardrada stroked his beard, deep in thought. "Very well, you and your men and my less experienced troops engage the Saxons in the marsh and along the beck bank. I will await my best troops coming up and then lead them around the Saxon right flank once the tidewater falls, then we'll crush them between us."

"Yes Lord King. We will have some time yet anyway, as the beck will be too deep to cross until the tide begins to turn, I will commence my attack then."

Bjarke and Hakon were in the last column to leave the ships, it was led by their father and consisted of veterans and the professional warriors of Hardrada's and Orri's *Hearth-weru*. As they approached Fulford, the sounds of battle came drifting towards them. Marching over the rise they saw the battle raging across a wide front in the marshes and noticed that the Norse ranks were being steadily pushed back. Messengers arrived at the run with orders from the King. Expecting to reinforce the men fighting in the marsh, they were surprised when the scout led them off to the left flank where the beck joined the river. The tide had fallen, exposing the mud flats of the river and beck and the Norsemen poured across it, floundering through the calf deep mud and up onto the Saxon side of the beck, Hardrada and Eysteinn at their front. With Harald's raven banner flying at their head, huge brightly painted round shields and gleaming mail, the cream of the Norse army came on with war horns blaring and a huge roar. The Norsemen charged, rolling up the Saxon right flank and hitting their rear like a sledgehammer. Bjarke had his shield slung on his back and his long-axe ready, Hakon and Ingvar protecting either side of him, Kettil following to his rear. The Saxon ranks splintered under the terrific incoming rush of steel, wood and muscle. Men, weary from wading through the mud and water of the marsh, and a battle that had raged for hours, were surprised and overpowered by the fresh Norse troops and turned to flee. The Saxons nearest the river and led by Earl Edwin ran first seeking the safety of *Jorvik's* walls, Morcar, unaware of his brother's retreat fought on and suffered the heaviest casualties as the Norsemen cut his army to pieces in the mire.

As evening closed in, the Norse ceased their pursuit and the slaughter stopped and both sides began to count the cost. Though the Saxons had suffered defeat, the casualties on the Norse side were considerable. As the tide rose again to flood the beck, the water collected up the bodies choking the waterway and turning it red.

Bjarke, Hakon and Ingvar had remained unscathed but Kettil had suffered a wound to the shoulder, Bjarke was busy cleaning and dressing it, just as he'd seen his mother do so many times before. Despite the heavy losses, the Norse were in good spirits after their victory and the men were jovial as they settled down to eat and rest, they camped in the open field as the unseasonably warm autumn had kept temperatures high. Excitement ran through the camp when word spread that envoys had arrived from *Jorvik* bearing the keys to the city gate and a note of acceptance of Harald Sigurdsson as their Lord and King, it seemed that northern England at least was going to be cheaply won. Bjarke and the others gathered to watch and listen to the King deal with the envoys, the business to be done in the open air, in view of all.

Torches mounted on poles the height of a man illuminated the camp, the flames flickering in the light breeze and driving the darkness back with their orange-yellow glow. The area around the King's tent, lit up brightly so all could see the supplicant Saxons bend the knee to their conqueror. The envoys had come soon after the fighting finished and before many of the Norse had washed themselves or cleaned their weapons, thus it was a fierce and much bloodied looking reception the envoys stepped through to reach the King. Nervous of the warriors and unsure if their embassy would be accepted and their lives and city spared, the men fell to their knees, their heads bowed before the grim and giant King. Proffering the keys and papers of the city, they mumbled their surrender. Harald boomed his reply so his warriors could hear.

"I accept your submission and recognition of me as your King, thus I will spare your lives and *Jorvik* a sacking. Send the hostages and supplies to me at Stamford; we move there tomorrow for space to camp, you may go."

The envoys; surprised and relieved at their treatment got to their feet; bowing repeatedly to the King's already departing back. They were jostled by the warriors as they passed through the crowd, suffering head slaps, kicks and jeers as they went. Reaching where they had left their horses, they found them gone. More kicks and hurled stones urged them to go homeward, which they did at the run.

The Norsemen broke camp and moved out to Stamford the following morning, setting up a more substantial camp in the lush meadows by the Derwent River. The army was divided now, half here in the meadows near the village of Stamford and the rest guarding their ships berthed at *Richale* all awaiting the arrival of the promised hostages and supplies from *Jorvik*.

Eysteinn had wanted to keep most of the army together with only a small guard left on the ships. Hardrada however, insisted that with the Northumbrian Saxons slaughtered at Fulford and the Earls Edwin and Morcar fled, and *Jorvik* suing for peace there was nothing more to fear. Moreover, Harold and the southern *Fyrd* were reported to be still occupied in the south and hundreds of leagues away, thus there was no need to keep the army all together. It was easier to supply and feed men in smaller numbers and less taxing on the land and people roundabout, people who would soon become his subjects. Eysteinn had taken charge of guarding the ships, while Hardrada and the rest of the army camped here awaiting the hostages.

Chapter Nineteen

Stamford, North Yorkshire, 25th September 1066 AD

The day had dawned bright and cloudless, the early autumn sun remaining surprisingly hot. The Norse warriors were scattered in groups across the meadow resting, drinking and eating, else repairing their gear or playing *Tafl*. With the might of the Northumbrian *Fyrd* slaughtered at Fulford the atmosphere was relaxed, the men fearing and wary of nothing. The meadow was large and lush and dotted with late summer poppies and foxgloves; it rose gently upwards from the river that flowed along the bottom. The river was not wide, being only four to five fighting spears in width but it ran deep, a wooden bridge, low railed and wide enough to take an ox cart was built across it.

Bjarke heaved his mail shirt over his head, dropping it beside his long-axe and helmet in the grass. He sat down heavily before easing onto his back and stretching out; Fenrir sat beside him, his tongue lolling and he panting with the heat. Bjarke beckoned him to lie down beside him, the dog settling himself while giving a low rumble in his throat as if appreciating the rest, his head resting on Bjarke's leg. Bjarke closed his eyes against the sun's glare while enjoying the late morning warmth on his body. The sweet smell of the meadow filled his nose along with the occasional waft of roasting mutton. A bee came close, it's wing drone loud then becoming distant as it flew on seeking the last of the late summer flowers. With the serenity of his surroundings his mind began to drift towards sleep, he was only dimly aware of the tapping of a woodpecker way off in the distance and the low murmur of men close by as they talked quietly and relaxed.

He awakened to the sudden movement of Fenrir's head and a low growl, followed by the thud of footsteps close by. Opening one eye he saw Hakon, Ingvar and Kettil making their way towards him, Fenrir stood, his tail beginning to wag as the men closed. Bjarke sighed at the disturbance then sat up to greet his brother and friends.

"Sorry to wake you, big man but we think you will appreciate this." Ingvar said as he hefted a leg of mutton.

Bjarke smiled and nodded while Fenrir pushed himself against Hakon, licking his hand and pushing his head up seeking a pat or an ear scratch. As the three men laid down in the grass alongside Bjarke, Ingvar passed him the meat; he was hungry and took it gratefully. Drawing his seax, he went to cut the meat into portions but Hakon stopped him.

"We've already eaten brother; we couldn't find you so saved you and Fenrir a piece, here, there's ale too. It's Saxon piss but it's better than nothing."

Bjarke tore at the meat, taking huge mouthfuls and swilling it with the ale. Chewing noisily, he cut a large piece of fat and meat offering it to Fenrir, the dog taking the meat gently then wolfing it down.

"Your wound Kettil, is it healing?" He asked between biting and chewing.

"Aye, it's sore though, I think the bone is broken." Kettil instinctively touched the bloodied rent in his leather shirt on his shoulder. "I'm in your debt though Bjarke; that Saxon would have had my head off if you hadn't deflected his axe."

"No debt, Kettil. We all look out for each other"

"What do you think of England, Bjarke?" Hakon asked as he dropped his sword belt and rolled onto his back, closing his eyes against the sun's glare.

"Beautiful."

"A kinder climate than home, eh?" Ingvar added. "It's late in the year, yet feel the heat of the sun." He lifted his head and stretched his neck, enjoying the warmth on his skin. "And one more fight and I think it will be ours. Christ! Within a month or two we could all be wealthy men."

"And what would you do with all that wealth, brother?"

Ingvar laughed hard, causing the others to look at him seeking the reason for his merriment.

"Well brother?" Kettil pushed.

Ingvar smirked. "Well, when I get my Saxon Manor I'm going to take me a Saxon wife ..."

"You already have a wife, Ingvar." Kettil interrupted, sounding confused.

"Aye, in Borg. That doesn't mean I can't have another here." He laughed again.

"The church won't like that, nor will Dagmar!" Hakon said as he sat up from the grass.

"The church can mind its own business and Dagmar will never know."

"You're not bringing Dagmar here then?" Kettil asked.

"No, I'm planning on spending my time between here

and Borg, two homes, so two wives!" The three men looked at him amidst headshakes and chuckles. "Don't you think about doing it Hakon, you stick with our sister."

"No argument there Ingvar, no one comes near my Asta, she is all I need. Kettil however, needs a wife." He laughed and dug Kettil in the ribs.

"Aye, true!" Ingvar agreed. What do you want Kettil?" He asked. "A sylph like Saxon girl or a big titted heifer? There will be plenty of both to go around if we keep killing their men, even someone as ugly as you will have your choice."

Kettil thumped Ingvar in the thigh. "Be careful brother, lest my tongue slips and Dagmar hears of your scheme, then you know what will happen, she'll have your balls for ear rings!"

Ingvar chuckled and rubbed his thigh. "Brother, I had no wish to offend, pardon my ill-chosen words." He bowed his head, laughed and laid back in the grass. "So … a Saxon princess for me, a fine Saxon girl for Kettil, Hakon to remain a good and honourable husband, so what for you, Bjar …" Ingvar stopped short. All at once, the three seemed to remember Bjarke's anguish and notice his silence. Looking around they saw he was still sharing his meal with Fenrir, a sad gaze on his face. "Christ! I'm sorry, big man, I didn't mean …"

Bjarke just raised his hand, nodded slightly and carried on eating while doling more meat to Fenrir. The uncomfortable silence and looks exchanged between the other three were interrupted by a wailing war horn.

Heads turned and bodies sat up from the grass seeking the source and reason for the noise. Another horn sounded, and then another. The four men rose quickly to their feet, hands shielding their eyes from the sun and looking about.

"To the south." Bjarke said as he pointed.

The men turned to look and saw a huge dust cloud trailing away to the south.

"A deputation from York?" Kettil suggested.

"No, York is southwest of us, that dust is coming direct from the south and that's a lot of people or animals on the move, it's no deputation." Bjarke said, his tone quiet but serious.

"Who then? The rest of the army from *Richale*?" Kettil offered.

"Could be? But the King was happy to leave us in two parts and we have heard nothing to say different."

"True, Hakon. And it would make more sense to move us south toward *Richale*, not for them to come here, after all, any further opposition is going to come from the south."

Bjarke was gazing to the southern end of the meadow and saw a horseman gallop up to a group of men, shouting and then pointing southwards. The men began strapping on weapons and rousing their comrades, a sense of urgency becoming apparent. The horseman rode on to other groups, still shouting and pointing back southwards.

"Saxons!" Bjarke said, giving the last of the mutton shank to Fenrir and reached down for his mail.

"What! ... It cannot be! We've just slaughtered the bastards, and the rest are in the south of England, leagues away."

"Are they, brother?" Bjarke said as his head disappeared into his hauberk. "I'm not so sure."

"Normans then?" Kettil ventured. "Have they landed in the north like us?"

The four began arming themselves as they spoke, apathy and banter suddenly forgotten.

"Normans or Saxons, we have a fight coming." Bjarke muttered as he fitted his helmet. "Where's your mail and helmets?"

The three men stared at him, sudden looks of hopelessness on their faces.

"Back at *Richale,* on the ships!" Hakon muttered as he hung his head.

"Shields then?"

Kettil picked his up from the grass while Hakon and Ingvar raised open hands. Bjarke looked about and saw that many men were in a similar predicament. The seeming completeness of their victory and the hot weather had seen most of the warriors leaving their heavy hauberks, shields and helmets back at the ships. The horseman was now coming in earshot, his mount throwing up dust and dry grass as he forced it across the meadow at speed.

"Saxons! … Saxons, to the south and coming on apace!" He bellowed and rode on shouting warnings to those further back in the meadow who still looked unsure.

"Christ God!" Hakon swore. "How … how?"

No one deigned to answer him. While in the distance, the first screams of men and clangs of steel could be heard.

"Mother of God!" Ingvar drew his sword. "Battle is joined!"

"Do we fight here? What do we do? Where is the King?" Kettil couldn't hide the panic from his voice.

Another horn sounded, deep and long. The four looked to see where the sound came from and saw Hardrada's raven banner being raised in the middle of the meadow. Men began hurrying towards it, the four setting off in that direction immediately. Hardrada stood by the banner, easily distinguishable by his height, a long-axe in one hand, his other waving his men to him and forming them into a shieldwall up and down the gentle slope of the meadow, anchoring it at the riverbank at the meadow bottom. Hardrada's *Jarls* and Captains were doing their best to sort men with shields and mail to the front, placing those without behind. As the four men and the dog ran up to the wall a Captain saw them and directed them up the slope to the end of it.

"Big man! You with the long-axe, hold the open end of the wall for us." He pointed up to the top of the slope. Seeing Kettil's damaged shoulder he pushed him towards the rear ranks. "Give him your shield, lad, he could better use it." He gestured towards Hakon. "You! Watch the big man's flank."

Hakon nodded as he helped Kettil slip the shield from his back then followed Bjarke and Fenrir up the slope to the end of the wall. Ingvar stepped in next to Hakon and drew his long-seax. When the Captain went to move him, Ingvar smiled grimly. "I'll grab a Saxon shield, sir. These men are kin!"

The Captain nodded and moved off continuing to order and sort the wall as best he could.

The rattle of weapons and sounds of breathless men eased as the wall came into form, men settling as they recognised order coming out of what had been surprise and chaos. At the front of the wall, Hardrada pushed through the ranks and turned to face his men. Clad in a full hauberk to below his knees and a magnificent helmet adorned with golden eye-rings and nasal bar, he seemed even larger than before. The sunlight flashed off the helmet and his mail seemed to shimmer like tiny ripples on a breeze blown lake, his long-axe resting casually over his shoulder. His blonde-grey beard hung to his chest and pulled into a tight plait. Another man stepped out beside him, not nearly as tall but broad of chest and similarly garbed in mail shirt and helmet. The helmet this time was conical, the nasal bar, rim and rivets were of gold and worn over a mail coif. The man carried a magnificent sword and a long, kite shield, the face showing a rearing black lion on a yellow field.

"The Saxon Earl, Tostig, I guess? He has balls then?" Hakon muttered to Bjarke.

Bjarke just nodded slightly, his hands resting atop his axe head in front of him.

"Time yet for treachery." Ingvar hawked and spat.

"It looks like he is going to fight." Hakon replied.

"Aye, but who for? This all looks very convenient to me; where in Hell did the bloody Saxons appear from?"

The talk was interrupted when they saw men appearing at the far end of the meadow. Some in groups, others in one and twos, some injured and being helped by their comrades, others walking or trotting but all glancing warily behind them as they made for the relative safety of the Norse wall. The dust cloud was very close now as was the noise of horses, men and metal. Suddenly the skyline darkened with horsemen, the sunlight reflecting from their mail, helmets and spearheads. In the midst of them mounted on a pole was an effigy of a huge golden dragon, its mouth wide open, its long tail lifting and flapping gently behind it in the breeze. Next to it, a crimson banner with a white fighting man emblazoned on it.

"Christ God!" Hakon muttered. "That's Harold Godwinson's banner! There, look! The warrior on the flag."

"Treachery! I told you, Saxon bastards!" Ingvar snarled and spat into the grass.

The Norse watched as the meadow quickly filled with Saxons, first hundreds and then thousands. The horsemen pushed forward, coming closer as more men came up behind them, their ranks growing deeper and wider and extending past the Norse wall, the Saxon *Thegns* and Captains quickly dressing and forming their lines into a dense wall. The Saxon horsemen were quite close now and dismounting, the horses being taken by handlers and led back through the ranks, the men taking up spears and shields, swords or long-axes.

Seeing the Saxon lines were overlapping his and while the Saxons readied themselves, Hardrada pulled the open end of his shieldwall at the top of the slope, back into a large curve. This helping stop the overlap and screening the small wooden bridge at the bottom of the meadow, which lead across the river into another meadow that also sloped gently upwards from the river. Maintaining the anchor at the riverbank, he slowly backed the whole shieldwall closer to the bridge.

"We would have been better on the other side." Hakon grunted. "Atop that slope, with them having to come up at us."

"Aye, true! But there was no time. Those bastards appeared from nowhere and if we try and cross now, they'll slaughter us." Ingvar replied, his tone bitter.

"Enough!" A grizzled Captain growled as he pushed into the line next to the four men. "We do the slaughtering! The King has made the best move he could considering the space and time allowed. The wall is solidly anchored at the riverbank so we can't be outflanked there; we hold this end of the wall and have negated their overlap by bending our ranks. Furthermore

… if push comes to shove, we can cover our withdrawal over that bridge and reform on the other side. I tell you lads, I've been with the King in tighter spots than this and we both still live!" He laughed then spat.

"Gods bones, lads! They're just Saxon goat turds!" An older warrior growled as he leaned on his axe. Those that heard him began to laugh. "They'll be shitting themselves facing Hardrada, I tell you! … And we have a dog" He reached down and patted Fenrir. "He'll eat the bastards instead of that bone!"

The atmosphere close by changed as men chuckled or smiled grimly and took heart from the older man's words, while Fenrir continued to gnaw determinedly at the lamb shank.

Hakon nudged Bjarke. "All good brother?" Receiving no response, he turned to find Bjarke staring trance like down the meadow at the bridge, the fingers of one hand rubbing the bear claw at his neck. "Bjarke! All good? … Bjarke!" Hakon clasped his brother's shoulder; Bjarke turned slowly, his eyes full, his face pale and a slight quiver on his lips, which he tried to hide by chewing them. He let go of the bear claw and threw his arm over Hakon's shoulder then hugged him hard.

"I love you, brother." He managed, and then turned himself and Hakon to the front, silencing Hakon with a sad smile and a shake of his head. A horn droned again, stopping Hakon from further questions as a lone horseman pushed out from the Saxon ranks, he rode towards Hardrada and Tostig.

The horseman kept his mount to a walk and stopped it just a spear length from Hardrada and Tostig, he took a moment to study the mailed giant before him. He bowed his head to both.

"Lord King, Earl Tostig. A final offer before we drive you from our land."

Hardrada laughed lightly then gestured politely that the horseman should continue.

"Earl Tostig, if you return to the King's peace now, your banishment shall be lifted and your Earldom will be restored to you."

"Is that so?"

"Yes, that is so. By order of King Harold." The rider's voice was firm.

"And my Lord King here?" Tostig gestured to Hardrada. "What will, King Harold give him?"

The horse stamped and tossed its head as if sensing the tension between the men, the rider taking a moment to settle his mount.

"Well!" Tostig snapped. "What will King Harold give my Lord King?"

"Seven feet of good English earth, or more as he is taller than other men."

Hardrada laughed loudly and spat, the laughter replaced by a snarl. Tostig grimaced and waved the horseman away. "You have your answer!"

The horseman stared for a moment, his look impassive. Then inclining his head to both men, he turned his mount about. As he neared the Saxon ranks, he raised a fist and with a rattle of metal and wood, the ranks came to attention. Brightly painted shield faces turned to the front, the warriors with mail coifs quickly tied the ventails closed across their mouth and chin. At the same time, the Norse ranks stiffened and closed tighter, death was coming.

"Insolent jumped up, Saxon bastard!" Hardrada snarled at the departing rider then turned to Tostig, hooting loudly. "Hah! ... He had big balls, I'll give him that!"

"Aye, he has ... for that insolent Saxon bastard was my brother."

"What? ... Harold? Harold Godwinson?"

"Aye, the same, my brother." He sighed.

"If you'd said, I could have gutted him."

"That's why I didn't say, Lord King. I have sinned enough without being complicit in my brother's death."

Hardrada threw his head back and roared with laughter. "Christ on the cross! I will never understand you Saxons ... Let's to it!"

Chapter Twenty

The Meadow

The shouts of the *Jarls, Thegns* and Captains had died away, the meadow now eerily silent. Norseman and Saxon stared over their shield rims at each other, the distance separating the two sides less than a javelin throw. Some men fidgeted, just wanting the battle to begin and the tense, nervous, bowel churning tension to be over, others mumbled prayers or just stared. Some wept softly; some puked or quietly pissed themselves, some that had it, swilled ale. The older, more experienced warriors' gripped their shield handles tighter or took the chance to wipe sweat-slicked, weapon hands on their trousers, before renewing the hold on their sword, spear or axe.

Hardrada and Tostig looked to the far end of the meadow and the still arriving Saxons joining the rear of the thousands already formed up.

"Master Ulf!" Hardrada bellowed and the man stepped out from the front rank. "Send runners to Lord Orri at *Richale*. Tell him to come now, with all his men and bring any mail or weapons the men left on the ships and that he can carry."

"My Lord King! That's almost fifteen mile!"

"Just do it, man! This isn't going to be over quickly."

Ulf dipped his head then stomped off down the line bellowing names and raising his hand in summons. Hardrada and Tostig pushed back into the leading rank of their shieldwall. A lone shout came from the ranks

"Harald! … Land-waster! Land-waster!" A sword banged twice on a shield and the call repeated again, followed by two more bangs on the shield. The call was taken up by those closest and growing louder and louder, becoming a roar as more men joined in, bolstering their courage, the thump on their shields becoming a co-ordinated deafening beat. Fenrir left the bone and stood, joining in the din with loud barks.

The Saxons began singing, the song broken every so oft by the chant of "Out, out, out!" and the clashing of weapons on shields. The hellish din grew louder as if the enemies sought to outshout or out-sing the other. Then, after a huge cheer from the Saxons, came the rush. The Saxons came on at a trot, which quickly became a run and then a charge, a low rumble from thousands of feet filling the air. Men howled like wolves as they came, the ranks flowing across the meadow like a silver wave flooding up a beach. The ranks bunched tighter, fear of death and injury pushing men closer to their comrades, their painted shields a blur of colours.

The Norse front rank crouched on one knee, emitting a loud 'Hah!' as they locked shields tight and the clatter of wood loud. Their comrades behind slipped shields over the top of their crouching brothers, emitting another 'Hah!' Top and bottom shields interlocking.

The Saxons hit the wall at speed and with an almighty clash of wood and metal. A huge groan emitting from men on both sides as flesh and blood absorbed the impact, the wall bending and flexing, then straightening as the Norse pushed back. Push and shove began, men straining and heaving behind shields while hand axes came over the rims to chop at heads. Some men died as the heavy blades split or crushed helmets and smashed skulls, spraying blood and splattering grey-pink brain tissue into the air. The axes that missed heads then sought to hook or pull shields down else batter them aside. Swords and short spears probed over the rims seeking faces and throats. Long-seaxs and short swords, the most useful weapons in a shieldwall, sought gaps between the shields else probed beneath, seeking stomachs, thighs, knees and groins.

Blood misted in the air as throats were slashed open, spraying shields and men in hot, sticky, red rain. Strings of blued entrails spilled onto the ground from stomach wounds. Heads and limbs littered the ground becoming trip hazards while bladders and bowels were hacked open, adding more liquid and a new stench. The grass was now slick with blood, piss and shit and slippery from the trampling by thousands of feet as the two walls forced one another forward and back. The noise was deafening. Metal on metal, scraping and clanging. The slap and crack of wood as shields clashed and the unholy sound of men screaming in pain as metal sliced flesh, chopped limbs and smashed heads and shoulders to bloodied pulp.

At the end of the Norse wall, Bjarke and the others were the last to engage, the opposing Saxons having the furthest to travel. Owing to the distance, the strongest Saxons or those keenest to shed blood outpaced their comrades and came at the Norse wall at the run but in a ragged vee. Bjarke stepped out of the wall, Fenrir following, his bone forgotten, he barking hard and baring his fangs at the advancing Saxons. Bjarke hefted his long-axe into a figure of eight swing. The first Saxon running into it before he could stop or duck. The axe hit his shield with its full force, smashing it back into the running man knocking him clear off his feet, the second swing chopped into the sprawled man's chest bursting mail links and burying itself almost head deep. Hakon and Ingvar stepped quickly to either side of Bjarke, guarding him as he wrenched the axe free and swung again at the next men. The next Saxon angled his shield trying to deflect the axe away; instead, it glanced off the shield face and took half of his head with it. As he fell, his comrade ducked low readying and watching for the return swing. Concentrating on the axe, he was easy prey to a slash across the back of the legs from Hakon's sword, the man fell into the grass, one leg almost off at the knee and the other opened to the bone. Bjarke stepped forward again, the long-axe humming through the air like winter wind in the trees, killing two men with one huge swing. Blood fountained as bodies broke, Bjarke roaring his defiance as he kept up the scythe like swings. More Saxons were arriving as others caught up to their faster comrades; coming in greater numbers, they forced the three Norsemen back into the shieldwall. Some ran past the end of the wall, seeking to get behind the Norseman, Bjarke turned to face them.

"Hakon! Ingvar! Watch my back!"

Clear of the wall again, Bjarke had room to move and swing his long-axe. His huge strength forcing it around in circles above his head or changing to figure of eight as the Saxons tried to close in on him. Hakon and Ingvar attacked the first Saxons that tried to get behind him or beneath his swing, while Fenrir, skulking on the flank helped turn men back, the size of the dog and its snarling maw discouraging them. Suddenly a dozen arrows flew past, no higher than head height and thumping into the oncoming Saxons, some stuck in shields, others found their mark in flesh and men fell and rolled in grass, some coming behind tripping over the fallen. The Norse Captain had located a handful of archers and sent them up to the end of the wall to help Bjarke and the others hold it. A small but withering hail of arrows ensued, forcing the Saxons to slow their headlong run, seeking instead to close their shields again against the incoming missiles. The pressure eased on Bjarke and the others as the Saxons slowed from a run to a trot and finally to a walk, their leader shouting himself hoarse for the men to close up. A trail of bodies behind them testament to the accuracy of the small arrow storm. When most of the arrows hit only wood, the archers ceased firing, saving their arrows for surer targets. Bjarke, not giving the Saxons a chance, attacked. Stepping in front of the shields, he swung hard, the long-axe smashing into the shields and knocking two men over with the force. Swinging the axe back over his left shoulder he brought it down hard over his right, into the gap in the shields, cleaving one of the men on his unshielded side, almost cutting him in two. Four men to his right broke from, the shieldwall to rush him. Swinging the axe behind him again, he dropped onto his left knee his body crouching. As the axe came over his right shoulder, he aimed for the legs of the oncoming men, hitting them just below the knees. The axe hacked the first man's legs off, broke the bones of the second then raked along the shins of the others. All four went down in a tangle of bodies, destroyed limbs and shields; Bjarke stood and brought the axe down hard finishing each man as writhed on the floor.

As he killed the last man, a sharp command brought the Saxons following behind to a halt, speed and recklessness replaced by a fast thickening wall and long probing spears. Someone was using his head. Bjarke hefted the long-axe again as the wall came on slowly, each step accompanied by a loud 'Hah!'

"Back here, Bjarke! Quickly." Hakon shouted.

Bjarke glanced behind, then front again and stepped backwards towards the Norse wall and his brother. The Norse wall also stepped back, it having to give way to the sheer pressure of more and more Saxons pushing forward as the meadow continued to fill with them.

As the Norse sought to disengage, the Saxons took the chance to draw breath. Having arrived at the trot, skirmishing with the first Norsemen and then committing to battle almost without pause, a brief rest was welcomed. As the Norse stepped back, they shrank their shieldwall, closing it to a tight semi-circle in front of the small bridge. Men on both sides taking the chance for a drink. The dead from both sides already lay thickly, like a long tideline of debris. Some men still moved amongst the carnage, others crawled or staggered from it back towards their own lines. The stink of blood, shit and eviscerated bodies rose in the heat and carried on the light breeze, already drawing flies.

The Saxons began pushing forward again, they stepped through the carpet of dead and dying, killing any wounded Norsemen on the way. Their own wounded being helped by servants and slaves once the warriors had passed. Hardrada glanced back at the bridge and the meadow across the river and then summoned Ulf.

"Master Ulf. Begin shrinking the shieldwall from behind, send the men over the bridge and have them reform across that rise in the opposite meadow. Do it quickly, before the Saxons close again."

"Aye Lord King!"

"Scatter what archers we have along the riverbank on the opposite side; once we are over they can help hold the Saxons back from crossing too quickly, we need time to reform."

"Aye Lord King." Ulf shouted for the Captains and began relaying his orders.

Soon the first Norsemen were peeling away from the rear of the wall and funnelling over the bridge. The narrow wooden structure had the warriors packed tight as they trotted over, a queue began to form waiting to cross. The Saxons, seeing the Norsemen filtering across the bridge hefted their shields again and came at the Norse wall at the run. They knew that once on the other side the advantage would rest with the Norsemen and by the time they forced the bridge, Hardrada could have his men drawn up on the rise. Thoughts of attacking uphill into the face of a Norse shieldwall held little appeal.

The two sides clashed again with renewed vigour, the Saxons eager to finish it quickly, the Norse holding their ground while they fed men across the river to the other meadow and a better position. Bjarke, Hakon, Ingvar and Kettil were still at the end of the wall and now near the riverbank, furthest from the fighting but also furthest from the bridge.

"Christ! This is going to be touch and go!" Ingvar yelled above the roar as the Saxons hit the front of the wall. "We'll be almost the last to cross!"

Just then, the Captain who had positioned them earlier came running up.

"Go lads, go! There's no one here to fight yet, so go. Once you're across, make for the rise on the other side, we'll stand there."

The four men and the dog set off for the bridge at the run, joining the bunched column of men trying to cross. As the semi-circle of Norsemen shrunk and the Saxons pressed closer, arrows, javelins, throwing axes and slingshot rained down on them, the mass of men, many without shields or mail making for easy targets. Ingvar stumbled and fell forward, Hakon falling over him. Bjarke pulled Hakon back up to his feet with one hand then reached down for Ingvar. A bright-fletched arrow was lodged high in his spine. Bjarke used both hands to lift him but stopped when Ingvar let out a bone-chilling scream. Lowering him gently he pulled him to one side, as the press of warriors trying to cross the bridge would see him trampled. Ingvar howled as Bjarke pulled him clear.

"Can you get up? Can you stand? … The arrow's not so deep!" Bjarke lied, shouting above the noise.

Ingvar's face contorted in agony as he tried to move, his voice panicked. "My legs! … Christ! I can't feel …" His words cut short as he gasped for breath.

Hakon and Kettil squatted alongside, Fenrir also stopping to wait. Hakon shielding Ingvar as best as possible with Kettil's shield.

"I'll carry you!" Bjarke said, passing his long-axe to Kettil.

The Norse ranks were thinning fast now as more men crossed the bridge, the rain of missiles becoming heavier and the Saxons pushing closer.

"We have to go … now!" Hakon shouted.

Kettil grunted and spun to one side dropping his sword and Bjarke's long-axe, the hurled wooden club that hit his head lying on the ground next to him.

"Hakon! Help Kettil, I'll get Ingvar." Bjarke shouted as he reached for Ingvar. "I'm sorry but we have to go." Ingvar yelped as Bjarke lifted then heaved him across his shoulder, then bent down for his long-axe. "Come on!" He urged Hakon.

The Norse wall was almost gone by the time the four reached the bridge, the Saxons less than a javelin throw away. Hakon was struggling with an unconscious Kettil, while trying to shield them from the arrows and missiles. Bjarke was striding out for the bridge, then realising Hakon was behind, turned around looking for him.

Seeing Hakon struggling under the weight of Kettil, his shield and weapons, he ran back to him, Fenrir following. "Come on! For Christ's sake, come on! Here …" He urged, while thrusting his long-axe into Hakon's hand and lifting Kettil from him, crouching and putting him over his other shoulder.

"Bjarke! You can't carry them …." Hakon flinched as an arrow flew past.

"Come on!" Bjarke urged, turning back to the bridge.

They were almost on the bridge when Ulf stepped in front of them. Raising his shield from the missiles, he shouted from under it. "Leave those two and get across the bridge! You're needed in the …"

"I can manage them sir …"

"Do as you're dammed well told, boy! Leave them!" Two arrows thumped into the bridge handrail, quivering in the wood while a sling stone bounced off Ulf's shield.

"Sir, I can be over …"

"They're useless if they can't fight, leave them!" Ulf snarled.

"No!" Bjarke made to step around him. "I won't tell you again, you oversized oaf!" Ulf stepped in quickly, backhanding his shield towards Bjarke's chest but hitting Kettil's suspended legs instead. He raised his hand axe to swing.

Bjarke, surprised by the blow stumbled backwards, off balance. Fenrir jumped at Ulf, biting the arm holding the axe and growling as he savaged it, his weight dragging the man down to his knees. Fenrir pulled and shook Ulf's arm, pulling him along the ground, his teeth biting the mail shirt, then leather bracer and finally flesh as his jaws closed over his hand. Ulf shrieked as Fenrir bit to the bone. With his other hand wrapped in the shield straps, he couldn't get up and Bjarke stepped forward, stamping down hard on the shield repeatedly, the force breaking Ulf's arm and driving the man down.

"To Hell with you! ... Bastard!" Bjarke bellowed.

Still holding Ingvar and Kettil on his shoulders, Bjarke stepped closer to Ulf stamping hard on his back now, forcing him right to the ground. Ulf gasped loudly as the air was driven from his lungs

"Off Fenrir! Away!" Fenrir backed away as Bjarke stamped on Ulf's weapon arm, breaking bones and forcing a howl from him. Ulf finally let go of the axe and Bjarke stepped in close and stamped twice on his neck, snapping it like a dried twig. Hakon, looking back from the middle of the bridge just gawped.

Without pause, Bjarke stepped onto the bridge urging Hakon on. The last few Norsemen were crossing now, handfuls at a time. The Norse archers assembling on the other bank were loosing arrows across the river at the Saxons and managing to hold them back, the Saxons having to reform their shieldwall in defence against the arrows. Bjarke hurried Hakon and Fenrir across in front of him.

"Run, run! I'm right behind you!"

On the opposite bank the Norse were trotting uphill from the bridge to the rise and reforming their shieldwall. On the riverbank, the archers were still holding the Saxons back while urging the last groups of men over.

Bjarke was almost off the bridge when he suddenly stumbled forward, as if he'd been pushed, almost dropping his load, his face twisted in agony. Trying to walk on, he fell onto one knee, Ingvar groaning horribly at the sudden jolt. With a roar, he powered to his feet again, readjusting the injured men over his shoulders but forced to walk now, a Saxon arrow, slipping through the slit in the rear of his hauberk, lodged deep in the back of his thigh. Hakon, seeing his brother's plight dashed back toward the bridge, Fenrir following.

"Get back! ... Hakon! Get back!"

Hakon ignored him. Stepping alongside, he held Kettil's shield over Bjarke's back covering him. Reaching the end of the bridge, Bjarke had to go down on one knee again, his double load and the arrow lodged deep in his back thigh sapping his strength. Hakon and another warrior lifted Ingvar from him. Kettil was coming to, blood still trickling steadily from his head wound which ran down Bjarke's mail shirt. Kettil tapped Bjarke on the back.

"I'm alright ... I think I can walk." Bjarke set him down; Kettil stumbled as he sought his balance but managed to stand.

"Come on!" Hakon yelled at Kettil and Bjarke while trying to help carry Ingvar. "Fenrir, here!"

Ingvar groaned. "Put me down! For the love of Christ, put ...!" His words strangled by the pain. "Leave me!" He gasped, blood and froth dripping from his lips. Hakon and the warrior made to carry on.

"Please, please … go! … Go!"

"I'll carry you!" Bjarke growled as he ducked as more arrows whipped past.

"No … no! I … the pain!" Ingvar was almost weeping now. "Go!"

Hakon pulled Bjarke away while pushing a distraught, unsteady, Kettil onwards. Ingvar dragged himself towards a post that carried the bridge's handrail, his legs trailing uselessly. Pulling himself to a sitting position but wary of the arrow, he leaned his back carefully against the wood. He coughed then gasped hard for breath, his face twisted in agony, his eyes full. He coughed more blood and froth then drew his long-seax and looked past the dead and dying men littering the bridgeboards towards the other end of the bridge.

The last of the Norse warriors died at the entrance to the bridge and with a loud roar, the Saxons began to cross.

Chapter Twenty one

The Bear and the Bridge

Hearing the Saxon roar, the Norse archers loosed again then turned to run across the meadow towards the safety of their shieldwall. Bjarke and the others also heard the roar and turned to look. The Saxons were running across the bridge now. With the Norse arrow threat gone, they would be over and into the meadow in moments.

"Run! ... Run!" Hakon bellowed, still pushing Kettil in front of him, then looking back, urging a badly limping Bjarke to hurry.

Bjarke glanced up at the Norse wall and the distance to it. He looked back at the bridge and the Saxons streaming onto it, the warriors jammed shoulder-to-shoulder, tight against the handrails and trampling the dead and wounded as they came. The Norse archers turned to loose the odd arrow at them as they ran. While Ingvar, propped against the handrail, raised his long-seax in defiance, waiting for death to come.

Bjarke was hobbling now, his trousers wet against his leg. He stopped and let out a loud, bear-like roar, a roar of frustration and pain. Hakon heard it and turned around.

"Come on Bjarke … we can make it!" Bjarke dropped his long-axe in the grass and went onto one knee. Reaching behind, he snapped the arrow shaft off, grunting at the pain. "Christ God, brother, come on! Else they'll catch us!"

"No! … No they won't!" Bjarke growled as he picked up his long- axe, stood and turned back towards the bridge. Fenrir following.

"Bjarke! … Bjarke! What the …"

"I love you, brother." He called without looking back as he limped back towards the bridge using his long-axe as a support. "Fenrir! Stay!"

Hakon's despairing cries were drowned out by the shouts of the Saxon war cries and their feet thumping over the wooden bridgeboards. Pushing Kettil onwards again, he ran after Bjarke, grabbing him by the arm.

"Bjarke! Come on, for the love of Christ …"

"Go brother! Now! … Fenrir, go!"

"It's not far, I'll help you …" Hakon beseeched as Bjarke pushed him away, striding out as best as the wounded leg would allow. "Please!" Hakon begged, as he and Fenrir followed after him, he reaching again for his brother's arm only to be pushed forcibly away.

"Go, Hakon! … Help Kettil, take Fenrir and go!" Bjarke bellowed and glared at his brother, his face haggard and his eyes full.

"No!" Hakon wailed. "No, no, no!" He fell to his knees in the grass, tears streaming down his face. Bjarke seized Fenrir by the collar, pulling the dog back and pushing him into Hakon's hand then walked back to the bridge.

The Saxons were three-quarters of the way across now and Bjarke increased his pace, stumbling and hobbling towards the narrow bridge entrance. He reached Ingvar and the edge of the bridge just as the first Saxons were paces away. With a roar, he swung the long-axe into the first men. The axe took the first man's head clean off, chopped into the next man's neck bursting through the mail coif smashing his clavicle and driving on into his spine. The dying man pushed into the two men next to him and knocked them into the handrail, one falling over Ingvar's legs. Ingvar stabbed the man twice before he could get up, while Bjarke killed the other with another axe swing.

The second row of Saxons roared their hate while stepping over their dying comrades, the delay giving Bjarke a chance to swing the axe again. The first two warriors stepping clear of the dead, died quickly. Bjarke's axe hit the man's shield with full force, his arm bones snapping under the blow, the axe blade deflecting up from the shield boss and sliding over his mail shirt, hitting him in the chin. His head was forced backwards as his jaw smashed and his face was cut away. Bjarke barrelled into the other man, knocking him backwards. Then spinning his body around and bringing the axe around with him, angled it down into the sprawling man. Ingvar stabbed upwards from his sitting position and took another man in the groin, Bjarke bringing the axe shaft heel, up sharply into the other man's face destroying his teeth, upper jaw and nose, he falling backwards adding to the pile of bodies now partially blocking the bridge.

The next row of Saxons came on undaunted, pulling their shields tightly together, heads dropping low, only their helmets and eyes showing above the rims. Short swords angled over the top as they stepped towards Bjarke. They were obstructed and thus delayed by having to climb over the bodies of their dead and dying brothers. As they stepped across, Bjarke swung again, using the full length of the shaft to reach over the bodies. The axe only reached the shields but the force of the blow broke the small wall, wood splintered and cracked, men's arms were broken with one shield being hooked from the man's hand. With the defence gone, the men stepped back while Bjarke stepped onto the dead bodies to close the distance, swinging again. Instead of pushing forward to attack and get under the axe's swing, they panicked and tried to evade the axe blow. The Saxons couldn't back away further as their comrades were packed tightly behind and being pushed on by yet more men coming onto the bridge. Bjarke chopped the row of men into bloody ruin.

The bridge end where Bjarke stood was now choking with bodies and helping block it. Cries had gone back through the Saxon ranks to stop the push forward but not before another row of men had gone down to Bjarke's long-axe. With a moments respite in the attack, Bjarke reached down and lifted the dead Saxons off Ingvar's legs. Ingvar looked up, his eyes wide in awe at the destruction he'd witnessed, his face twisting with pain as the movement sent spasms up his back.

"Christ Almighty, big man!" He gasped, spraying more blood. "That's slowed the bastards up!" He laughed manically and pointed at the Saxons readying themselves for another push; then made chicken noises before a cough and a gasp cut him short.

The Norse archers had seen the destruction and the stalled Saxon advance and now came back to the river's edge, readying their bows to add support to Bjarke's defiant stand. When the Saxons began to step forward once more, the archers loosed, hitting three men and stalling the advance again, men quickly crouching behind their shields once more. Hakon watched, while holding back a straining Fenrir by the collar

With the Saxons stopped and seemingly undecided, Bjarke took a chance. Stepping over the dead towards the Saxons, with powerful swings he chopped some of handrail away on both sides of the bridge, making gaps just in front of the dead men. Then dropping the axe he began hefting more of the dead Saxons into the heap, the bodies making an obstacle to just above knee height. His wound shot bolts of pain through his thigh as he worked, he doing his best to disguise the injury. The Saxons finally pushed forward again, their shields held as a screen against the arrow fire. Bjarke picked up and hurled a dead Saxon at the oncoming men. He roared as the body flew. It hit the bridgeboards with a thump and rolled, stopping at the oncoming men's feet and stalling them again. Eyes peered over shield rims to see a huge warrior, his face partially covered by the eye ringed helmet, his mail shirt red with blood and the long-axe again held horizontal across his thighs, waiting for the men to come and fight.

Everything seemed to stop. An eerie silence fell, quiet enough to hear the river flowing around the bridge supports. Bjarke stood unmoving. Ingvar waited with his seax and a hand axe. The Norse archers waiting with arrows laid on the string. The Saxons stalled and undecided. A Saxon warrior pushed through the ranks, his commands carrying easily in the silence.

"Front row, shields up! … Left flank, shields up! … Right flank, change your shield hand and cover yourselves till we're across."

The Norse archers quickly took advantage as the men moved their shields into position, sending arrows into the mass and dropping another six men to the bridgeboards. With a final clash of wood, the shields closed.

"Advance!"

The Saxons stepped forward again, punctuating each step with a loud, 'Huh!' The men standing on the dead rather than risking breaking the wall

The Norse archers looked for gaps in the shields but with the men under firm command and the slow, steady advance, gaps were small and chances of a shot fleeting.

"Huh! … Huh! … Huh!" the Saxons edged closer

Bjarke stepped up to the barrier of bodies. He winked at Ingvar and gave a sad smile. Ingvar smiled back through blood-frothed lips and nodded while grasping the axe and seax firmly. Bjarke noticed the colour was fading from Ingvar's face and he looked weary, blood was pooling from the wound in his back onto the bridgeboards where he sat, his chin and chest covered in red froth. Ingvar tried to speak but only bubbles and air came out. His eyes flickered and his head fell forward, the axe falling from his hand. Bjarke sighed, snarled, then ducked and grimaced as a hand axe flew past, narrowly missing his head and drawing his attention back to the oncoming Saxons.

The Saxons stopped in front of the barrier of bodies, the men wary of stepping across and exposing themselves to Bjarke's long-axe. Two war spears thrust out from between the shields fast as striking serpents, one glancing off Bjarke's mail, the other missing but spoiling his axe swing and forcing him to one side. One warrior in the front line breaking the wall to step over the dead while Bjarke was distracted.

Bjarke dropped his axe and seized both spear shafts, pulling hard. The surprised holders were hauled forward, knocking two men in the front rank over the dead bodies, the falling men hitting the one advancing warrior off balance. The sprawling warriors let go of their spears. Bjarke using the butts to jab at the shields to hold the men back, while kicking and stamping at the fallen warriors, breaking legs and crushing necks. Men screamed as bones snapped, while one warrior in the shieldwall collapsed as the spear butt slid over the rim and destroyed his face. Leaving the injured warriors as another obstacle, Bjarke dropped the spears and grabbed for his axe. With the madness of battle on him, he smashed into the shields again, men groaning at the impact. The front ranks backed quickly away, terrified of the giant warrior, his strength and the destruction he wrought. Men stumbled, knocking into the warriors behind, some losing their balance and falling through the gap in the handrails into the river. Bjarke followed the retreating wall, swinging the long-axe with herculean strokes, destroying shields, mail, helmets and men.

The Norse archers cheered as the Saxons hit the water. Up on the meadow rise, where the Norse shieldwall was forming, a huge cheer went up as they realised the Saxon advance was stalled.

Hardrada pushed to the front of his men to see what the cheering was about.

He squinted, watching as the long-axe rose and swung and a body or two would fall, while others fell from the gap in the handrails into the river. Those in mail, sunk like stones, others without armour swam for the Saxon bank. Some surfaced then sank again, others calling for help as they drowned. Having driven the Saxons back, past the gap in the rails, Bjarke stopped, breathless.

The Saxons stopped, awaiting orders or leadership, unsure what to do. The sun-bleached bridgeboards showed bloodied boot prints and pools of scarlet that leaked and dripped through the gaps in the boards into the river below. The only way forward was over their dead and dying comrades, across a bridge littered with weapons, limbs and offal from the fallen, then to face the huge warrior with the long-axe that killed them before they could close on him. Bjarke also waited, thankful of the chance to rest, he at pains not to show it. His thigh with the arrowhead in it, felt as if it was on fire. He watched, as the Saxon side of the riverbank filled with warriors, hundreds of them, no, thousands, a sea of silver mail, spear points, coloured banners and brightly painted shield faces … he was going to die here. Leaning on his axe, he eased some of the weight from his wounded thigh; to the watching Saxons he appeared casual and calm, completely unafraid.

In reality he was very afraid. His heart pounded in his chest, his hands betraying a slight tremor, which he sought to hide with his lean; a shake coming in his leg of which he wasn't sure came from fear or in response to his wound. He glanced at the sky and found it blue and cloudless, the sun bright and hot on his face. It was quieter now, just the odd bellowed order and the cries of the wounded, both fading as he thought of Eerika and his son and what might have been. Of his mother and her fierce love for both him and Hakon, and for his father, a good man, and he managed a sad smile.

Cheers starting up from the Saxon ranks drew him back to reality. The warriors ranks rippled, men being jostled and pushed to one side as a huge Saxon, head and shoulders in height above his comrades, stepped out from the front row of shields. The cheers grew louder as the man stood clear, a long-axe in his hand. Bjarke stood up from his lean, eying his opponent, the 'would be'

Saxon Champion. The warrior's face was hidden beneath a bushy, grey-black beard and a magnificent iron helmet; it edged around the rim and face and crossing the crown in engraved brass bands, ending in a highly decorated nasal bar, a mail aventail covering his neck, two long cheek pieces hung at the sides, clanking as he walked. His broad body shrouded in a mail hauberk to his knees. Bjarke hefted his axe, holding it horizontal across his thighs taking a moment to assess the man. He was big, though not as large as himself but with thick arms and a huge chest that spoke of strength and power. He looked older, perhaps in his mid-forties, which meant experience but could also mean he would tire quicker. Sadly, Bjarke knew he was in no position to take advantage of that, he was already tired and hurting badly, this man looked fresh and unbloodied.

The Saxon was eying Bjarke, noting his size while peering at the face under the eye-ringed helmet, assessing it for age. He held up his hands, silencing the cheers.

"I'm Oshere Carlson, *Thane* of *Dunholm*, who might you be?" The man spoke in Norse, though with a heavy accent, his voice boomed above the tense, pregnant silence and low gurgle of the river.

Bjarke raised his head high. "I'm Bjarke Orrifostersson, of Borg."

"You're blocking my King's bridge, Bjarke Orrifostersson!"

"Then move me!" Bjarke grinned.

"Very well!" Oshere hefted his axe then paused; he laughed and pointed. "Christ on the cross, you're just a boy!"

"And you're an old man!" Bjarke retorted.

"I expected a warrior of some renown; you don't look old enough to be away from your mother!"

"Old enough to send you to meet yours again, old man!"

The Saxon laughed again, seemingly enjoying the banter. "You're insolent boy; it seems you need a lesson in respect."

"I was taught respect and told it to give it to those deserving of it, all I see in you is an old goat fart that blows hard."

The Saxon laughed again. "Are you as quick with that axe as you are with your tongue, boy? Or are you just a bumbling lump of Norse, pig shit?"

"Come and find out, you Saxon, sheep humper."

"I will! … I will!" Oshere smiled grimly. "Say your prayers boy. It's a good day for spreading Norse pig shit on bridgeboards."

Bjarke hefted his axe above his shoulder and crouched slightly, ready. He was unable to hide the grimace and slight reflex shake from his leg as his wound objected. The Saxon saw it and stopped to look again at Bjarke.

"Did you shit yourself there, boy?"

"If I did, I'll use that grey beard of yours to wipe my arse."

The Saxon just chuckled; it seemed he had fought too many fights to be drawn on by insults. "Shall we clear the way a bit? Move some of these poor lads out of the way so we can dance?"

"Do what you will, old man. I won't soil my hands on Saxon shit!"

The Saxon raised his eyebrows and grinned. Holding up a hand, seeking pause, he planted the long-axe in the wood and began moving some of the dead to the side of the bridge. He threw the dropped weapons and shields into the water.

"There! I don't want a clumsy farm boy like you falling over. I would kill you fairly." He smiled, spat on his hands and pulled the axe from the wood.

Back on the Norse side of the river, Hardrada had his men were formed in a circle, crowning the low ridge, the men's attention on the drama playing out on the bridge below. The archers remained at the bankside, also watching, Hakon and Fenrir watched from half way up the meadow. On the middle of the bridge, the two men stalked one another.

Bjarke attacked first, the Saxon letting him come. Bjarke swung fast at the man's chest. The Saxon stepped back quickly. Bjarke carried the missed stroke on, spinning around and dropping into a crouch, bringing the blade low, aiming at the man's shins. The man jumped as the axe whooshed under his feet. The Saxon powered in, his axe raised to split Bjarke like cordwood. Bjarke brought the axe around again, opening his hands to hold it defensively like a quarterstaff as he stood up. His axe shaft caught the Saxon's descending shaft, a loud crack coming from the wood. The Saxon however, managing to kick him on the shins of his wounded leg. The sewn in, steel plates of the man's boots had Bjarke groan and step away.

"That's for your bad manners, boy!"

Bjarke swung again, fast. Driving the man back towards the handrail, trying to pin him against it. The Saxon however, was wily and gave ground, letting Bjarke work, then held his axe up to block Bjarke's swing. Bjarke expected to cut the shaft clean through, instead it chopped into the boiled leather reinforcing, which the man had fitted on half of the shaft just beneath the axe head. The force however did, knock the axe sideways and down. The Saxon let his axe ride with the incoming blow and as both axes passed, he spun about, kicking Bjarke hard in the back thigh. Bjarke cried out as the arrow head was forced deeper, his leg buckled and he went down on one knee.

He expected the man to step in and finish him but managed to raise the axe shaft defensively again. Instead, the Saxon stepped back.

"Get up boy! I don't need to steal a victory. Try again."

Bjarke felt the cold fingers of fear in his heart. He was badly hurt, weary and this Saxon knew his trade. He got to his feet, trying to hide his pain and tiredness. He managed a curt nod of the head to his opponent, the man smiled and nodded back. The two men circled again. On the Norse bank, the archers began to shout, it wasn't cheering this time, more like a warning. Bjarke however didn't dare take his eyes from his opponent. He was vaguely aware of the whoosh of some arrows flying under the bridge and then the Saxon bowmen retaliating and loosing back but he kept his attention on the big Saxon.

The bridgeboards creaked slightly beneath his boots as he stepped, then suddenly there was pain. Excruciating pain, hot and twisting, deep in his groin, wringing a pitiful cry from his lips. He didn't understand what had happened, his body suddenly rigid as the pain froze his movements. He cried out again as the spear that had been rammed into him from beneath the bridgeboards was dragged out, taking the breath right out of him. He felt his blood spatter heavily on his boots as if tipped from a cup. He staggered a pace, dropping his axe and fell heavily to his knees; his hands instinctively holding his groin, the hot blood running between his fingers. The Saxons cheered but his opponent dropped his axe, stepping across quickly to him. The man held him as he sagged forward, his lifeblood pooling quickly around his knees.

"That wasn't my doing lad! Christ knows it wasn't! … A coward's blow." The man sounded angry.

Bjarke gripped the man's mail shirt for support, his blood soaked fingers slipping on the metal links. The man still trying to hold him up. The Saxons began running past with a loud roar, the bridge was open. Bjarke felt his grip slackening, his fingers losing their strength; he felt cold, so very cold and his eyes heavy. The man laid him gently to the bridgeboards. Supporting his head, he slipped Bjarke's helmet off and saw how young he was. He shook his head.

"Reputation was not worth this, lad."

Bjarke's eyes flickered at the word, reputation. Runa's words flooding back, another piece of it making sense. His body began to shake, as if with a winters chill.

"So cold … I'm so …"

A shadow across him had him glance up. A tall man, resplendent in mail shirt, coif and conical helmet looking down at him, the helmet bearing a circlet of gold around its rim. He untied the ventail, showing a long, blonde moustache. He unclipped his cloak and laid it over Bjarke.

"Though you cost me dear, I respect your bravery. Peace lad … I'm sorry."

Bjarke didn't hear. His eyes stared, glass like, his pallor fading to white.

Harold Godwinson ran his hand over Bjarke's eyes and shook his head. "Come Oshere, let's finish this."

Chapter Twenty two

Orri's Storm

Hakon let out a long piercing cry when he saw Bjarke fall. "No … no … no, Christ God no!" He was unsure what had happened but looking up saw the archers loosing arrows under the bridge and then what looked like a large, wooden washtub with a dead man in it came floating out.

Tears were running down his face as he cried softly and mumbled. *"The bear that heeds the hunter will not fall but the bear that doesn't, will into the river fall. …The bridge, the bridge, linger not on the bridge …* Oh brother! Why wouldn't you listen, now what am I to do?"

Fenrir barked loudly and Hakon looked up to see the Saxons were clear of the bridge and coming up the meadow apace.

"Oh Christ! … Fenrir, heel!" Hakon was up out of the grass like a startled hare and raced towards the Norse wall.

Hakon and Fenrir slipped into the shieldwall, the first javelins already flying overhead towards the oncoming Saxons. Shouted commands went up from both sides, the Saxons to hold and form a wall and the Norse to close up and stand fast. The Norse began to sing. For a moment the fight was static, the clatter of wood loud as shields locked together while missiles flew and whipped overhead and some men fell to the grass. Then with a roar, the Saxons attacked.

Long-seaxs stabbed over and under shields, axes chopped at heads and arms and hooked at shields and men died. The trampled grass quickly became slippery with blood and entrails as the Saxons wore the Norse wall away, pushing it slowly back up the incline, a pace at a time. A sudden groan from the Norse ranks was followed by urgent cries for the King. Hardrada was down, an arrow transfixing his throat. Men stooped to help and shield his body while Hardrada's *Hearth-weru* roared their defiance and fought more fiercely, forcing the Saxons back a few paces. The Saxons however, sensing victory were not to be denied and hurled themselves back at the Norse push, the fighting rising to a fierce intensity. Amidst the madness and slaughter, Hakon and Kettil stood shoulder to shoulder, Fenrir alongside, stepping back and forwards as the shieldwall pushed forward or fell back. Kettil was tiring, his shoulder wound sapping his strength and his head wound dulling his senses. He never saw the long-seax that slipped between the shields and stabbed his heart. He sagged quietly against Hakon, still held upright by the tightness of the warriors. As the wall flexed again he slumped to the grass, Hakon groaned as he felt then saw Kettil fall. Screaming hate, he launched a vicious attack at the opposing Saxons beating at the shields and heads with his hand-axe, Fenrir followed him, fangs bared and savaging any warrior Hakon put down. The Saxons backed off, wary of the berserk rage of the Norseman and his dog with long fangs and bloodied face and maw.

The battle raged all afternoon, the shieldwalls separating only for men to draw breath and ease their wounded back through the ranks. Those that had water or ale drank, Hakon removing his helmet liner and tipping some water into it for Fenrir. After one such respite, King Harold pushed his way to the front of his men prompting a huge roar and a clashing of weapons on shields, his *Huscarls* alongside him in a dazzling show of kite shaped shields, swords and long-axes. With their King in sight and renewed vigour, the Saxons threw themselves at the Norsemen again, breaking a hole in their shieldwall and striking deep into their ranks. Suddenly, a great cheer went up from the Saxons while the Norse backed away again, the news filtering through the ranks that the Earl Tostig was down.

The Norse shieldwall was shrinking now. Leaderless, their position and situation untenable, men sensed their demise, with no chance to run and nowhere to run to, men pushed closer, fear producing a fierce defiance and savagery. Hakon was battered and bruised but still without serious wounds, he too was weary, his nerves frayed, the battle having raged since before midday. Early evening was coming on and he wondered if he could survive until dark where the possibility of escape and survival may eventuate. Just as the Saxons closed again, a war horn wailed above the clash of arms and cries of men. Appearing out of the trees to the Norse left flank, Eysteinn Orri and his men from the ships at *Richale,* came on at the run. The embattled Norse ranks erupted into a ragged cheer, Hakon's heart lifting as he saw his father's banner. The Saxons, suddenly unsure, stalled as the Norse ranks swelled rapidly with the new warriors, then had to brace themselves quickly as the newcomers went to the attack almost without pause. The incoming Norse warriors were all well-armed and protected by mail shirts, their impetus and almost berserk fury forcing the Saxons rearward, back down the meadow. The reinforced Norsemen took fresh heart at the arrival of their brothers and their *Jarl* and followed on in their lee.

The Saxon war horn blew in short blasts and King Harold and his *Huscarls* pushed forward of their ranks, forming an arrowhead of mail and steel and breaking the oncoming Norse impetus, scattering men off to the flanks and holding their rush in check. Hakon was unable to reach his father; he still tightly packed within the wall, he could only follow the red and black banner as it moved above the swirl of men. The fighting seemed to standstill with neither side gaining ground, then just as the sun was casting long shadows Orri's banner went down, followed quickly by a cheer from the Saxons. Hakon's heart sunk, more of Runa's prophecy seemingly falling into place. *'Kings and Jarls will lie down with men. … Both Angels and the Valkyrie will fly, gathering the brave.'*

Orri's men had already done the impossible, having ran almost fifteen miles from *Richale,* in their mail and carrying their weapons and those of their brothers, they'd committed immediately to battle. Had the Saxons not held them, they may well have carried the day. However, flesh and blood can only withstand so much and in the face of the Saxon defence, 'Orri's storm' was stalled and contained. Thereafter, the Norse vigour seemed to falter, ground was given slowly as the Saxons pushed forward again, Harold and his *Huscarls* at the fore. As tiredness took its toll, the sides paused to rest again. Men disengaged amidst curses and threats, some sinking to their knees in the grass holding wounds closed else supporting broken limbs. Others leant on their shields or weapons and rested or snatched a drink. Harold held up his hand and stepped forward into the dead ground between the two armies while sheathing his sword. He gestured the two warriors back into the line that stepped after him. A hush fell over the meadow as men watched and listened.

"Norsemen! … Brave, Norsemen! I say enough!" He shouted. There was some grumbling from the Saxon ranks. He turned briefly to snarl back at his men. "Silence there!" Turning again towards the Norse, he continued. "I say enough! … Enough killing for one day. Your King, Your *Jarls* and my brother, all lie dead on this field. I would kill no more of you …"

A low growl ran through the Norse ranks then a shout. "Come! Kill us then! … Come, if you think you can."

"You know I can kill you all … will do, if …" The growl came again. "Listen to me!" He shouted. "If death is what you seek, I can offer it here, now … If however, you wish to leave; you are free to go, back to your ships and on to Norway, never to return, under pain of death. Alternatively, if you wish to remain here, you will serve me. You have until the sun touches the hills to decide."

Harold turned back to his men.

Gyrth pushed forward to his brother.

"Brother! Lord King, we can slay them all here, they're beaten! They know it!" He pointed to the Norsemen.

"Aye, I'm not blind Gyrth!" He snarled, forcing his brother back apace and quietening him. "At what cost though? What cost? How many more men? Christ knows we have paid a heavy price already, men I can ill afford to lose."

"But …"

"But nothing! Think man, use your wits! If they're content to go, I will let them, if any stay and wish to serve me, I will welcome them. This battle has been costly enough."

"What of vengeance for our dead, recompense for the burning and thievery done?"

Harold took a moment, inhaling deeply and chewing his lip trying to contain his temper. He began again, his tone lowered, his words precise.

"Both sides have lost Gyrth. They, their King and their *Jarls*, their brothers and friends. We ... us, our brother ... Christ have mercy on me ..." He gasped, Gyrth saw his brother's anguish and horror on his face, was about to ask but Harold held up his hand silencing him and carried on. "Our men ... our men have lost their brothers, kin and friends; I think that makes us all equal. As for recompense, I think I can suffer Scarborough being burned if it stops this carnage now."

His steely look silenced Gyrth. The younger brother bowing his head and remaining silent.

"Lord King! ... King Harold!" A voice called from the Norse ranks.

Harold stepped to the front again, watching as a much-bloodied Norseman stepped forward. The man unsheathed his sword slowly and Harold stopped, the Saxon shields clattering dully as they closed together, swords quickly raised over the rims again. The Norseman stuck the sword in ground and stepped forward to Harold, his arm outstretched, his hand open. The Saxons lowered their shields.

Harold shook the man's hand then stepped past him, pulling the sword from the ground he handed it back. The Norsemen looked on quite amazed.

"Those of you, who wish to leave, go now!" He pointed southwards. "My men will escort you to your ships. Those of you who wish to stay and serve me, we make camp here tonight. See to your wounded and dead."

As he turned away, the Norseman asked. "If we serve you Lord King, how will we live?"

"The same as my own *Huscarls*, by my grace and from my purse. I have Danes and Swedes amongst my men as well as Saxons, why not Norsemen?"

As the Norsemen relayed Harold's words back to his colleagues, a great number that were originally looking to leave stopped and turned about. There was some brief handshakes and discussions amongst the Norsemen as the groups separated. Hakon, taking Fenrir by the collar and joining the men electing to stay.

Harold detailed mounted men to escort the departing Norsemen back to their ships at *Richale,* while allotting those remaining to a place in the meadow to camp. With the sun almost set, the men used the precious twilight to search amongst the carnage for the wounded, the dead having to wait until the morning light for burial. As they moved amongst the slaughter, all the men took the chance to garner extra weapons or mail, the dead having no further use for it and both commodities being too expensive to leave. The two nations eyed each other warily, the Norsemen still expecting to be slaughtered on a whim, the Saxons distrustful of their new, would be, allies.

Hakon asked Fritjof and Brynjar to find his father's body then took Fenrir and set off back towards the bridge seeking his brother. Stepping through the sea of bodies, he followed their trail down the incline towards the river. With the fighting being over in this area some time ago, he was spared the calls and cries of the wounded, nearly all he passed being dead. He scattered crows and ravens as he walked, the birds waiting until the last minute before taking to the air with sharp, objectionable cries and much wing flapping before landing again the moment he'd passed by. The birds seemingly prepared to risk the approaching darkness so to feast on the dead. Twilight was well advanced by the time he reached the bridge, the light fading and changing to darkening shades of blue. Fenrir was walking ahead, his nose to the grass, sniffing.

Fenrir walked onto the bridge scattering more birds as he stepped around and over the bodies, his pace quickening, Hakon hurrying after him. Fenrir stopped and began pushing with his nose and then licking at a body, small whimpers coming from him. Before Hakon could reach him, he was already throwing back his head and howling, the pitiful, distraught wail carrying over the meadow. Hakon came alongside and found Bjarke. Dropping to his knees beside Fenrir, he stared at his brother's face. Apart from the brown blood splashes, it was as white as driven snow, his eyes closed, and a look of peace on him. Hakon wondered about the rich looking cloak that covered him as he eased it away looking for the wound that had killed him. Seeing nothing on his chest or throat, he looked lower and saw Bjarke's trousers and boots coloured darkest red and the dark-stained bridgeboards where the blood had splashed and pooled. A lump came in his throat and his chest heaved, unashamed tears flooded his eyes and coursed over his cheeks, Fenrir's despondent howl dropped to a whine and he pushed against Hakon, licking at his face. Hakon reached down and with a great effort pulled

Bjarke to a sitting position where he wrapped his arms about him holding him tight, his heart breaking.

"Oh brother, brother." He wept.

He was unsure how long he knelt holding his brother's corpse, though the darkness was now complete and he beginning to shiver from the cold, Bjarke's body stiffening within his embrace. His weeping had stopped now, only the occasional sob and snatching of his breath disturbing the peace. Suddenly, a gruff voice called out of the gloom.

"Leave him be boy or I'll kill you!"

Fenrir growled at the sudden intrusion and Hakon lowered Bjarke to the boards and drew his seax. He turned to the voice, and saw a big man appear from the shadows, broad chested and heavily bearded, an axe in one hand and a flaring torch in the other, the orange flames dancing on the brass edging of his helmet.

"Put the knife down boy, else you and your dog will be dead before you stand … I won't tell you again. That warrior was a brave man and I won't have him robbed!"

Hakon threw the seax down, his other hand grasping Fenrir's collar holding the growling dog back.

"Stand away boy!"

Hakon ignored the threat, his renewed anguish loud in the silence as he whispered a blessing for his brother, it almost unintelligible amidst fresh sobs.

"What in Christ's name, boy?" Came from the big man.

"He … he is … he was, my brother!" The words a shouted, hoarse, rant.

Fenrir was now snarling and growling, and forcing himself between the big Saxon and Hakon.

The Saxon spoke again but this time it was quiet and without malice. "If you settle your dog, I'll help you bury your brother."

Hakon looked up quickly, his head shaking as if he didn't believe what he heard. "Help me?"

"Aye lad, help. I'd not leave such as him here for carrion and looters to pick over." The big man planted the axe in the boards. "Settle the dog."

Hakon pulled Fenrir back, tapping his snout gently and quietened him. He cuffed away his tears and tried to settle his breathing. Fenrir however, still putting himself between the Saxon and Hakon. The big man approached slowly. His hands held up, open, showing no weapons and offering no threat, Fenrir still growled low in his throat and Hakon quietened him again.

"Did you ... did you kill him?"

"No lad, I fought him but I didn't slay him, his death was not by my hand or my doing. The man who killed him is in the river somewhere, dead. Your archers feathered him like a cockerel after he speared your brother from beneath the bridge."

Hakon went to get up and struggled, his legs weak, his muscles cold and stiff, he had to use the pull of Fenrir stepping toward the Saxon to help pull him to his feet. The big man steadied him as he stumbled.

"I'm sorry for your brother lad ... believe me I am. He was a brave man."

Hakon nodded and held Fenrir as he sniffed at the Saxon and finally settled.

Working beneath torchlight, they buried Bjarke back from the riverbank and beneath the spread of a large willow tree. Using discarded hand axes to chop the roots and a broken sword and their hands to scoop out the dirt, they managed a shallow grave. Hakon drew Bjarke's antler-handled seax and pushed it into his hands.

"If Christ God's angels don't find you brother, the Valkyrie will and Odin and Ullr will not be disappointed." He undid his helmet strap and removed it, the cold air tingling his scalp and cooling the sweat on his brow. He laid it next to Bjarke. "Fair trade bother." He said as he managed a sad smile. "I will take yours to remind me of you." He picked Bjarke's eye-ringed helmet up and fastened it on his belt.

They backfilled the grave then covered it with large stones from the river to stop wild pigs and wolves digging it up, the big Saxon adding a roughly made cross at the grave's head, the two branches bound together with a hide strip. As he knocked it into the ground, he saw Hakon watching and spoke quietly

"I saw a crucifix around his neck lad; he has two chances of salvation now." He also managed a sad smile.

"Aye …" Hakon sighed. "My mother would be glad to see that, there."

The two men stood back and bowed their heads, each quietly whispering a prayer into their chests. The Saxon crossed himself and stood back, as Hakon finished his prayers he turned to find the big man with his hand open, his arm extended.

"I'm Oshere Carlson, *Thane* of *Dunholm*. I would know your name and more of your brother."

Part Four

The Dragon and The Leopard

Chapter Twenty three

York and the road to Hastings, October 1066 AD

The moment dawn had broken, the day after burying Bjarke, Hakon had sought out Fritjof and Brynjar and news of his father's body. He had been somewhat surprised and impressed to learn that Harold had taken over the burial of the Norse notables, seeing they received an honourable and decent Christian internment. Sadly, however, the scale of both Stamford and Fulford and the numbers killed; saw many of the ordinary folk left where they lay, stripped of anything of value their bodies left as food for birds and wolves.

It was a strange relationship, a Norseman and a Saxon, Hakon Orrifostersson of Borg and Oshere Carlson, *Thane* of *Dunholm,* the pair inseparable since the battle at Stamford Bridge. The two men sat in the great hall in York, at a victory feast to celebrate the Saxon victory and to remember the dead. King Harold however, insisting that it was also to remember all who had perished, thus attempting to dilute any ill feeling from the Norsemen assimilated into his army's ranks. There had been some hostility, scuffles and even bloodletting amongst the survivors of both sides as men had lost brothers, fathers and friends, Harold and his

Thanes doing their best to defuse it, explaining that the Normans were the threat both nations now needed to worry about.

Oshere and Hakon sat quietly, eating. The Saxon's size and reputation ensuring no one questioned or bothered Hakon, he being easily identifiable as Norse by his long hair. Fenrir also drew stares and whispered comment, though again no one looked to venture too close as the dog looked as formidable as the big Saxon.

Over the days since the battle, Oshere had asked Hakon of his decision to stay in England. Hakon explaining that with his father, brother, and friends all dead and nothing to show for their sacrifice, he would wait until he could return home with something other than grief. How could he explain to his wife and people the losses of their men folk, Bjarke's bravery then death but his survival. Thus, home and his beautiful, Asta must wait until he could return there with some honour.

The two men were talking quietly when a messenger entered the hall, he grimy from the road and weary looking, his clothes dishevelled. Stopped by the guards, he drew attention from all by his frantic struggle and his shouts for the King. Harold saw the commotion and summoned the man before him. The hall fell silent, watching as the man relayed his message in hushed tones into the Kings ear, his state and agitated demeanour didn't bode well. Harold's face betrayed little, though a slight snarl was noticeable before the messenger finished. Harold clapped the man on the shoulder and ushered him to a seat, calling for food and ale for him, returning to his place at the table he remained standing and didn't need to ask for silence.

"My Lords, *Thanes*, fellow Saxons and Norsemen. It seems we must be up and doing once more, William and his Normans have landed at Pevensey, in the south." The hall erupted with shouts and anger, men shook their fists and brandished seaxs, food and ale suddenly forgotten, Harold called for quiet. When the hall was silent, he began again. "We march tomorrow; so eat and drink your fill but rest, for it may be sometime before we can sit and sup at peace again. We move quickly, for I would box this Norman up in the southeast before he causes further damage, he is already laying waste to our villages and slaughtering our people." The furore in the hall rose again, the warriors from the south especially wanting to know where exactly William and his army were.

Oshere turned to Hakon. "We'd best look for sleep lad, it's a long march south, two hundred mile or more to London at least, from there I know not how far."

Hakon nodded and stood to follow Oshere out of the hall, Fenrir at his heel. The best accommodation had been taken by the nobles, the rest of the army having to sleep where they could, with Harold forbidding any harassment of the locals; many were reduced to sleeping in the streets or outside the city walls in the meadows. Oshere, being a *Thane* and able to pay, had secured accommodation and for the last few nights a stable in an inn courtyard had served. With the amount of men in York, the stable was a luxury and with the cold autumn nights the two men very content with a roof over their heads, clean straw and the warmth it gave.

Dawn found the city like a disturbed anthill, horses, carts and thousands of men funnelling through the southern gate onto Ermine street, the old Roman road and marching southwards. Harold's main concern now was raising more men as they marched and catching William sooner rather than later and before he could push northwards towards London. Seeking speed, he, his

Huscarls, Gyrth and his nobles, all mounted, went ahead of the army in a bid to raise the southern shires, leaving his army under Leofwine to follow on as fast as they were able.

Oshere had a servant, a horse and a small pony that carried his supplies, weapons, mail and helmet; it now additionally loaded with Hakon's war gear, most of which had been supplemented from the dead on the field. Hakon walked alongside Oshere's mount, his hand hooked into the stirrup strap when the horse went to a trot, the army moving at a brisk pace, the servant, Wulfric, following and leading the pony by the bridle. Fresh word had come that William remained ensconced well south of London and working out of a secure base in the Hastings area and from where his men continued sacking and burning villages and slaughtering the local populace. It was also reported that he had burned all his ships, with any thought or chance of retreat gone, the 'bastard' clearly intended to win England or die in the attempt. Despite the ill news, both Harold and the army were confident of victory. To his men, Harold was a great warrior and a war leader of renown, Harold himself was enjoying a confidence boost having just beaten Harald, reputed to be one of the greatest warriors of the age.

The unusual relationship between Oshere and Hakon was fast becoming friendship, the big Saxon sharing all he had including his horse, the pair taking turns to ride and walk. Oshere asked nothing in return other than knowledge of Hakon's home and his brother. Wulfric however, was the opposite. While following his Master's orders and caring for him and his Norse friend, the man's manner to Hakon was perfunctory but cold. Hakon thought little of it, reasoning the man had perhaps lost someone in the recent battles and thus his feeling towards the Norse was understandable. The army was well south of Lincoln and settling for the night when trouble came. Oshere had gone to find a Smith, the horse having thrown a shoe, he sending Wulfric and Hakon on bidding them set up camp by the roadside and wait for him there.

Just before dusk they'd found a site, Hakon had gathered wood for a small fire while Wulfric skinned a pair of rabbits and a hare. The man never spoke to Hakon, so silence in the small camp was complete; Fenrir lay with his head between his paws watching. Hakon noticed a nervousness in Wulfric; he seemed tense, glancing up from his work repeatedly as if expecting something, any sudden noises from other camps close by making him flinch. Hakon was on his knees, bent low over some dried grass and twigs and striking flint to steel then nurturing the tiny flame into life. He discreetly drew his seax and laid it beside him. Heaping dried leaves onto the growing flame, he watched Fenrir, the dog remained settled, his eyes beginning to flicker then closing. Hakon looked at Wulfric again; the man seemed even more agitated than before. With the fire taking hold, Hakon went to a crouch, resting his hands on his knees. Fenrir's ears suddenly flicked up.

Hakon's eyes swept the small area. Fenrir's nose twitched and he growled low in his throat. A twig snapped and Wulfric threw the rabbits down and dashed from the camp. Fenrir stood; the growl now loud barks. Hakon snatched the seax up just as four men burst into the camp area. The men came quickly but silently, obviously his murder was to be done quietly and without drawing the attention of others. The first man launched at Hakon raising a hand axe, the second brandishing a club, the third with a long-seax having to square up against Fenrir as the dog stepped into fight. At the rear, the fourth man was momentarily crowded out by his comrades, as the camp space was so small. Hakon powered to his feet, ducked beneath the swinging axe and stabbed the man's belly with his seax, the man's forward impetus driving the blade deep. The man yelped as Hakon twisted it quickly so it didn't stick in the flesh. He pushed the man to one side but was hit on the upper left arm by the second man's club, the aim at Hakon's head spoiled as he was forced to step around his wounded comrade. Fenrir was driving the other two men back. His reactions and movements quicker than theirs, his head switching from one to another, teeth bared, his head lunging if they dared step close. Hakon was knocked sideward from the force of the club's blow, stumbling, losing his balance and hitting the floor. The man stepped after him raising the club for another strike. Hakon rolled quickly and lashed out with his feet, kicking the man in the ankles and bringing him to the ground. Hakon was on him instantly, forcing the seax towards his chest, the man seizing Hakon's wrist to hold the blade away. He dropped the club, it hanging by its wrist strap as his fingers grabbed for Hakon's throat and windpipe and locked on. Hakon gagged as the man's fingers clamped then tore at his throat. Fighting the impulse to pull the man's hand away, he drove two fingers from his other hand, hard into the Saxon's throat and the man instantly released him, his hand instinctively going to his own throat. Taking advantage of the man's pain, Hakon forced down with the seax while clubbing his hand and smashing it into the man's face. The Saxon's nose crumpled under the blows, his lips bursting, as teeth were knocked loose. Hakon forced the seax down further, driving it between the clavicle and top rib, where it lodged. The man screamed as the blade went slowly deeper. Hakon left him and jumped to his feet stepping alongside Fenrir.

The dog was stepping back and forth as the men moved trying to get close to strike. Hakon had no weapon now so had to stay close to the dog for protection. The man with the long-seax slashed at Hakon's belly and he jumped backwards, the blade cutting his shirt and slashing his skin but not going deep. With only the one man facing him now, Fenrir went to the attack and leapt, his full weight knocking the man off his feet, the man's swinging club hitting Fenrir in the back hip, most of the power however had gone from the blow. Fenrir's weight drove the man to the ground and as he sprawled, Fenrir's teeth sank into his throat. The man's cries were cut short as the dog shook and ravaged his throat, its fangs tearing and ripping.

The Saxon driving Hakon back realised he was on his own and took fright; taking his chance as Fenrir finished killing the other man, he turned to run. Hakon, being breathless and shocked was content to let him go. He looked around the camp area, the warrior with the seax in his rib was dead, and the man Hakon had stabbed was holding his belly and trying to crawl away. Hakon stepped after him and stamped hard on his lower leg breaking it, the man howling as the bones snapped. With his enemy stalled, Hakon stepped alongside his head and stamped on his neck, there was a sound like a dry twig snapping and the man fell silent.

Hakon pulled Fenrir away from the other Saxon, the man was clearly dead. His throat and face a bloodied, torn pulp. The small campsite resembled a battlefield, bodies covering the ground and blood staining the grass.

Hakon sat down heavily, catching his breath and hugging Fenrir close. He was still stroking the dog when Oshere found him. The big man appeared out of the gloom, drawing his long-seax; he stepped quickly amongst the carnage.

"Hakon! … Hakon, are you alright? What in Christ's name …"

Hakon just raised a hand, his other holding Fenrir as the sudden intrusion had set him snarling and barking again. Oshere stopped while Hakon settled the dog.

"I'm alright, Oshere but as Christ is my witness, I'll skewer that bastard, Wulfric!"

"Wulfric? Where is he anyway?"

"Long gone, if he has any sense, bastard!" Hakon spat.

"What happened?"

Hakon explained Wulfric's furtive movements and then the attack. Oshere listened and nodded sagely.

"I knew he didn't like you, but murder?"

Hakon shrugged. "It's to be expected I suppose, up until a week ago I was your enemy."

Seeing Hakon shaking with the shock of it all Oshere sat down beside him and threw a heavy arm over his shoulder, hugging him close.

"Four of the bastards eh, they were going to make sure of you then?"

"Aye, without Fenrir I'd be a dead man. He held two off and then savaged one."

"God bless Fenrir." The big man smiled and gently patted the big dog's head. "I'm sorry lad; they wouldn't have dared if I was here. Are you hurt?"

"No, no, a sore shoulder and a flesh wound is all." Hakon pointed to his belly and bloodied shirt.

"You should wear your leather shirt at least, lad. I thought you would have learned that lesson at

Stamford." Oshere chuckled and dug Hakon gently in the ribs. Hakon just sighed and nodded.

"I should go, Oshere …"

"Go where?"

"Just go! Away from here, I should have gone home."

"Well you didn't and I'm glad you stayed. I respected your brother for his bravery and I like you. Things will settle soon enough lad. The next battle against the Normans will see to that, anger will be directed there, you'll see. Come on, we may as well eat those rabbits, the dog can have the hare now Wulfric's gone."

"If he comes back, I'll kill the bastard." Hakon hissed.

"No you won't lad." Hakon looked up quickly, a snarl twisting his lip. "I will! … Now, let's move these bodies and eat."

Oshere hobbled the horse and pony while Hakon roasted the rabbits. The rabbits were plump, the men washing them down with bread and ale and made for full bellies for the two men, Hakon feeding the hare to Fenrir. With supper over, Hakon built the fire up, happy at the flames driving back the darkness, the light and warmth bringing him some comfort. The men spread their blankets close to the flames, Hakon settling Fenrir next to him and laying seax, sword and hand-axe in easy reach. Oshere did likewise.

"Oshere?"

"Aye lad?"

"Wulfric hated me and my kind and he wasn't even a warrior, why are you so accepting of me, shouldn't you hate me?"

"Hate is a powerful word lad and not to be said lightly. Men fight, it's the nature of it methinks but we have to live in peace at some time and you and me, we are not so different."

"But we invaded, attacked …"

Oshere smiled. "You're people aren't the first lad and no doubt, won't be the last. The Saxons invaded after the Romans left, and then my people came."

"Your people?"

"Aye, I may be third generation Saxon and have a Saxon Christian name but my surname, Carlson, its Danish. My folk hailed from *Haithabu* over a hundred years past then settled in *Dunholm*." Oshere chuckled. "We all piss in the same pot, Hakon. Saxon, Dane, Norseman, we're all here, you're just the most recent arrival is all, well, bar the Normans." He chuckled again.

"Huh! Now we fight them."

"For the moment, aye, but there have been Normans here for many years anyway, look at our last King, he was more Norman than Saxon."

"It's all madness and waste, a waste of men's lives!"

"Aye, you're not wrong but it is what it is, as we say … Anyway, tell me of your dog, Fenrir here, he dealt to that other bastard with the club, is he a war dog?"

"No, a hunting dog, my brother's dog." Hakon's voice thickened. "My father bought Fenrir and Garmr for Bjarke and me when we were boys."

"Garmr?"

"Aye, Garmr was from the same litter and was mine, he was killed by a wild boar years ago. Fenrir was Bjarke's dog but we practically shared him, my brother would … my brother …" Hakon swallowed hard, his eyes filling.

Oshere smiled trying to lighten the conversation; he pulled a mead bottle from his pack and filled two horn cups passing one to Hakon. "Fenrir is just like your brother then, a protector. Bless them both."

Hakon managed a smile. The pair gulped the mead, it was sweet and strong, Oshere poured another after which Hakon felt much better.

"Sleep lad, you know the dog will wake us if needs be." Hakon nodded and settled into his blanket, sleep didn't come easy but as Fenrir relaxed and closed his eyes Hakon fell asleep. The men were not disturbed further and slept until dawn, the pair up and moving at first light.

Chapter Twenty four

Southern England October 1066 AD

"Lord Duke, was burning the ships necessary? Should we lose, we …"

"There's the essence of it, Lord FitzOsbern, lose! I will not entertain the thought of it and now, neither will the men."

"We either win or die here then?"

"We win."

William FitzOsbern was troubled. "My Lord, you read the message and council from Robert Fitz Wimar, the Confessor's old Steward, for us to stay behind our fortifications and let Harold come to us."

"And give him time to gather more men and the local *Fyrds*? I don't think so! Reason it out man, Harold has won at Stamford but at what cost? Hardrada and his Norsemen would be no milksops, no walkover, he must have lost heavily and what of the men lost at the previous fight, Fulford? Moreover, he disbanded the local men in the south as we sailed, it will take time for them to re-muster especially with the harvest still coming in, late as it is. Also, the remainder of his army from Stamford will need time to get here. So, we strike now; take the fight to him, before more men come to his banner!"

"You'll march on London?"

"We'll march for it but he'll come out, he won't let us close on him methinks? He's aggressive, a fighter is Harold."

"He's in London!"

"Yes, two days past."

"Christ God! Has he grown wings and flown south?"

"He's no laggard, I'll give him that! I understand he's come ahead of his men and is again calling out the local *Fyrd* while he waits for more of his men to come from the north. Thus, I would draw him on now."

FitzOsbern knew that once William's mind was made up, argument was futile and he moved on. "What from here then, my Lord?"

"Increase the burning and slaughter hereabouts, this is Harold's land, his tenants, it all adds further insult to injury. However, we march soon, we can't stay here indefinitely, we will need more supplies, and the men need a fight."

A servant appeared at the tent entrance. "Lord Duke, Bishop Odo is here."

"Send him in." A tall man in his early forties stepped into the tent dressed in full mail hauberk but wearing a huge golden cross at his neck. "Hah! Odo, all is done?"

"As you commanded brother, the message to the usurper has been dispatched."

FitzOsbern looked bemused. "A message to Harold, my Lord, why?"

Odo smirked and William laughed. "A request by the Pope. An olive branch, that Harold will never accept but we must be seen to offer. In short, if he submits to my claim as King, I will let him keep his Earldom."

"It's a good offer, considering he's a usurper."

"Exactly! If he takes it, it would save much bloodshed. He won't of course, but we have been seen to offer it and if that keeps the Pope on my side, I'm happy."

"So, we fight with good conscience and the Pope's blessing." Odo added and the three men smiled.

****

"Please Harold, for the love of God … wait! Men from the north are still coming in and we have the time. William is the one who needs a battle, not us! If we employ a scorched earth policy we could starve him, wear him down …"

"No! My people have suffered enough. I'll destroy him now, before he slaughters more folk and burns more of my land!"

"But that's what he wants, he needs a …"

"Christ God, Gyrth, I'm neither blind nor stupid! I know what he's doing and why but we will fight, I stopped Hardrada and I will stop him. We'll have men enough if I can work this to suit us."

"What do you mean?"

"Catch him unawares, look what it did to Hardrada. We'll march towards Hastings, late coming folk can catch us up. Remember, I Know William, Gyrth, he won't wait, he's not unlike myself in character. Now that he's ashore and established he will seek to strike, he has to; I would hit him first. We march the day after tomorrow; the meeting point is the old hoar-apple tree near Caldbec hill, I have passed the word for all to assemble there."

"As you wish, Harold. However, can I ask that you let me command in this fight?"

"What? … Why?"

"Hear me out brother, if you will. If I lead this, you could remain in London and marshal our late come men as they arrive; a rallying point. It also removes the stigma of you being oath sworn to William, which the Normans took to the Pope to raise him against you."

Harold's face twisted into a snarl. His fist smashed into the table-top sending cups and jug bouncing, his words forced from between his teeth.

"Christ on the cross! How many more times must I say it! I swore to serve William as his man while in Normandy! … I did not, ever! Swear to support him in a bid for the English throne."

Gyrth stepped back at the outburst. "I know brother, we all know, it's a Norman ruse but the church, the Pope …"

"Damn the church and its poking into affairs over which it has no business and damn this Pope! Damn him to Hell! I wonder how much silver William gave him for his support!"

Harold in anger was a fearsome sight and Gyrth chose his next words carefully.

"That aside Harold, let me fight, for if by chance the Norman wins, you are still here and as I said can rally the men still arriving, my life or death matters not, yours does, you're our King."

Harold's temper disappeared as fast as it surfaced and he smiled at his brother.

"Your life does matter Gyrth, greatly, especially to me, our mother and also to your people. I thank you for your offer but how can a man lose when he has a brother like you to support him." Harold smiled and clasped Gyrth's arm warmly. "However, I am the King and must therefore be seen to lead. I doubt not your ability to command and lead the army well but this is my country, my crown, I have a duty to defend it."

Gyrth smiled. "Thank you Harold, your words mean …"

Raised voices in the corridor coming closer cut Gyrth's words short.

"My Lord, you cannot enter, the King …" Was heard outside the room.

"Out of the way man, I want to see my brother." The door burst open and a young man in his early thirties stepped in.

"Leofwine! By all the saints." Harold exclaimed and stepped forward to embrace his younger brother. "You have made good time from the north."

"The weather is still fair, the roads dry and God is good, so here I am, along with my *Huscarls* and many of your men." He chuckled as Gyrth stepped up to also embrace him.

"Welcome brother, it's good to see you … I vouch William would not say the same!"

All three brothers burst into laughter.

"Aye! But he'll find out just as Hardrada did, not to fight with the Godwinson brothers."

The three brothers were dining when a servant announced a messenger. "Lord King, my Lords, an emissary from Duke William."

A black robed priest stepped into the room, he cast a nervous glance at the three men but Harold waved him forward. The man bowed low to Harold and then to the two brothers.

"Lord King, My lords, I have a message from my Lord Duke, William of Normandy."

"Speak father, what does Duke William request?"

The man swallowed nervously and despite the cool evening, his brow and face was wet with sweat.

"Lord King, Duke William has an offer to make."

Gyrth sat up quickly in his chair, his lip beginning to snarl, his hands gripping the chair arms. Harold placed a restraining hand over Gyrth's and squeezed. "Go on father." The man struggled to find the words but Harold was patient, he smiled. "Speak freely father; there is nothing to fear here, my fight is not with you but your Duke."

The priest nodded and blurted the message. "Lord King, the Duke offers you your Earldom in return for your handing the crown to him, as it is his by …" Gyrth jumped up from his seat. "God's bones how dare he …"

The priest stepped back in fright at the outburst.

"Gyrth, sit down." Harold said quietly. "Go on father."

The priest swallowed again. "My Lord Duke reiterates his claim to the crown, Lord King. However, he would have you as his Earl; he remembers you and he were fiends, brothers in arms. No fight need to take place if you give him what is his by right."

The priest's voice tailed off as he finished the message, his hand quickly mopping at his wet brow.

Gyrth and Leofwine were like guard dogs ready to slip the leash, the insult to their brother demanding defence. Harold however, had a hand on each ones shoulder, quietly restraining them.

"Father, sit please. There is wine in the jug; can I have food brought for you?"

"Thank you … thank you, Lord King, some wine would be most acceptable."

The man gratefully took a chair, poured himself a cup of wine, quaffed it and refilled it quickly, his nerves clearly on the raw. Harold was quietly settling his brothers, his hand held up to stop their agitated whispered tones. He watched as the priest gulped more wine while casting furtive glances at the three brothers and around the room. Harold broke the silence.

"I won't detain you overlong father, you have a way to travel back to your Duke. My answer is this; tell the Duke … my friend, that he should not promise that which is not his to give and I will offer him this. He can return to Normandy unmolested, along with his men and my blessing and without bloodshed … if he recompenses my folk and myself for his men's transgressions." The priest paled. Harold held up his hand for silence. "Should the Duke fail in either of these duties I say watch out William, let the Lord God judge between thee and me! I am the lawfully anointed King of the English, both before God and my people and I will not suffer him and his kind here … do you have the gist of it father?"

"Yes … yes, Lord King."

"Good. I will bid you good day and safe journey. You may go."

With the priest gone, Harold turned to his brothers. "A change of plan, we march tomorrow."

"I thought you said the day after tomorrow, we still have much to do." Gyrth queried.

"I did, but that priest has seen the preparation, the men and our disposition, all of which he will relay to his masters. A man of God he may be but such as he misses nothing, he will have been briefed as to what to look for. Thus we march tomorrow."

****

Oshere, Hakon and Fenrir reached London that same evening. Both men, being from more rural areas were quite in awe of its size, the amount of people and the squalor. The city was full to bursting with residents, warriors and displaced folk and their livestock from the southeast, that had managed to evade the Norman despoliations. Leading the horse and pony by their bridles, they pushed their way through the crowds of people, noses wrinkling at the stench from the gutters in the streets. Old, dilapidated stone buildings from the Roman period stood in various states or repair, some crumbling to rubble others that retained their roofs had been added to or repaired with wood, the usual material of choice for the Saxons. The Roman buildings were interspersed with wooden sheds and huts, giving a chaotic look to the city. With evening drawing in and weary from the road, the two men sought a bed for the night. Again, with the amount of people within the city, the best accommodation had been taken by the wealthy and the cost of anything close to a bed had risen dramatically. Securing a loft above an inn and stabling for the horse and pony, the two men dropped their gear beside the thin straw mattress's that passed for their beds. A luxury after days on the road and sleeping in fields and woods. Hakon settled Fenrir at the foot of the short ladder leading to the loft.

"We best look to our weapons lad, we may not have another chance."

Hakon nodded and laid his weapons and war gear out on the floor. The sword, hand axe and seax were his, the eye ringed helmet, Bjarke's. The mail shirt was Saxon and taken from the field at Stamford, as was the kite shaped shield, Oshere suggesting it would draw less attention especially seeing Hakon insisted on wearing the Norse style helmet. With oil and whetstones' the pair set about the blades, carefully smoothing out nicks and honing the edges back to sharpness. The amount of weapons between them took some time to complete; Hakon stretched his back as he sat upright from finishing the axe.

"All done, methinks."

"Weapons, aye lad. Now to check the mail."

"The mail?"

"Aye, any repairs we need and can do, can only help, obviously anything major will need a Smith at it but small breaks are not bad to fix and worth the effort. Let's have a look at that hauberk you picked up, I'm guessing there will be some damage."

Spreading the hauberk, Hakon fingered the rent in the centre of the chest and rubbed at some of the dry, caked blood ingrained in the mail links.

"I hope I fare better than the last owner." He said gloomily.

"Here lad." Oshere fished in his pack and pulled out a small coil of steel wire passing it to Hakon. "Tie it off at the top of the rent and weave it through the links, which will pull it together."

Hakon did as he was bidden, Oshere finishing tying off the wire and neatly securing it using a small pair of pincers. "That needs to be smooth lad, so a blade doesn't catch on it."

"You brought pincers!"

"Aye lad, I haven't lived this long by not being careful." Oshere looked fondly at the pincers. "I've carried these since I was your age, all the way to Constantinople and back."

"You were in Constantinople?"

"Aye, and all over the east, fighting wars for money. I was in the Varangian Guard. I returned home about twenty-five years ago."

Hakon gawped. "You would have known my King then, Harald Sigurdsson; he was there about that time."

"Aye, I did." Oshere said wistfully. "He was a fine warrior, a good leader of men. Despite being my enemy of late, I was sorry to see him killed."

Hakon went quiet, his gaze locking absently on the wall. "My father … you would likely know my father then?" He asked quietly.

"Your father?"

"Aye, he served with the King." Hakon's voice dropped low, his eyes filled as he thought of his father. "My father, Eysteinn Orri." He managed, though his voice was now just a rasp.

"God's Bones! Eysteinn … Eysteinn Orri, you're his son?"

"I am. My brother and I are his foster sons."

Oshere gripped Hakon's arm a rueful look on his face. "Another good man gone to God." He shook his head slowly. "Your father saved my life in Sicily, when we fought for George Maniakes against the Arabs. I was knocked down by this." He slipped his shirt from his shoulder, revealing an old javelin wound. "Your father killed three men that came to finish me, then hauled me out of the shieldwall … he called me a dozy Saxon oaf, bless him!" Oshere chuckled at the thought.

Both men seemed lost for words, after a long silence, Oshere spoke first.

"I asked your brother his name before we fought, when he said Bjarke Orrifostersson, I didn't make the connection." He shook his head very slowly. "Christ, lad! It seems I have a duty well beyond friendship to look after you and I am glad I didn't slay your brother. Come, before we bed down for the night, tell me of your father."

Chapter Twenty five

The Hoar-apple Tree

Oshere and Hakon had both slept well, secure in the loft and guarded by Fenrir. They'd enjoyed a good breakfast of porridge followed by fried ham and bread washed down with ale.

They set out just as dawn broke joining a long, straggling column of men headed southeast towards Hastings and the muster point at the Hoar-apple tree, the Normans and battle.

Oshere yawned and belched. "When this is over lad, what do you think of coming north with me, to *Dunholm*? If you like it, you could send for your girl and the pair of you are welcome to make home on my manor."

"If the King will release me, I will take your offer wholeheartedly as I have lost my appetite for war and home without my brother, mother and father will no longer be the same. You're confident we will win this fight, Oshere?"

The big man smiled down from atop the horse. "It'll be a hard fight, Hakon, I've seen Normans before, back in the east, they are doughty fighters, however our King is a great warrior too and we know the country, which has to count for something."

"You have lost many men at Fulford and Stamford though … on account of us!"

"More men have come and are still coming; I think we can match William's numbers, seven to nine thousand men they reckon he has but the King must be confident if we are moving up to meet them."

Hakon nodded and was quiet for a while. He took a moment to look at the column of men and decided there were at least some thousands on the move. It was a cosmopolitan mix of; ordinary folk, peasants with just a spear and pieces of leather armour, Yeomen with better equipment, a helmet, spear and shield. *Thanes,* with their mail coats and weapons and some retainers armed at their expense and then the great Lords with their *Huscarls,* the professional warriors with their heavy armaments, grim looks and confident swagger.

"How far do we march this time?"

"Not nearly so far as we have come, I'm told." He chuckled. "Forty to fifty miles, depending on where we find the Normans."

"So battle is coming in two or three days?"

"Aye, about that I would say."

The pair marched on in silence for a while. When Oshere dismounted and gave the horse to Hakon, the younger man struck up conversation again.

"I know you to be a *Thane*, and you clearly have status and property and with that will have come folk and men who owe you service. I've only ever seen Wulfric, I hazard the others fell at Fulford or Stamford?" Oshere looked up as Hakon settled in the saddle, his expression curious as to where the conversation was going. "I only ask because I don't wish to bring you anymore trouble. If your men are dead, will your folk accept me as readily as you have? You have fed me, looked after me, shared everything you have; others may be bitter as my people have brought much death and injury to yours."

Oshere didn't answer immediately. "I brought five warriors south to Yorkshire with me as required by the size of my land. Three fell at the Fulford fight and two remain but wounded, they're ensconced at a small farm west of Fulford, recovering, we'll collect them on our way back north."

"Surely that will bring trouble then?"

"I doubt it Hakon, the three dead lads were all single men and professional warriors they were in my employ but not local men. The two wounded are local and thankfully likely to recover, both are Danes, incomers like yourself, they know how it is. I told you, the north is mixed through with many races, Saxon, Norse, Swedes and Danes; God knows we're a mongrel lot." He chuckled. "We muddle by, usually the world just leaves us alone to get on with life, we have some trouble with the Scots now and then and that keeps us all pulling together so don't worry about it. Anyway, it's my manor and I want you there."

"What of your family then, what will they think of a Norseman and his wife at your table?"

Oshere's face showed a frown and sudden sadness but he recovered from it quicker than Hakon could ask the reason.

"My table is a lonely place, Hakon. My wife, Elswyth is gone, she died two winters ago. My son was killed in the wars in the east; he had no interest in the farm but followed in my footsteps and joined the Varangian guard." Oshere shrugged. "What could I say? Don't go; I forbid it! … I had no wish to be a hypocrite and he was a man grown with a mind of his own, all I could do was train him as best I could and then give him my blessing and wish him well. When news came of his demise, Elswyth was never the same, Osbeorn was our only son, our only child and thus she took it badly and died that winter, the grief I think was too great."

"I'm sorry Oshere, you have lost much."

"No more than you." The pair walked on some way before Oshere spoke again. "This will be my last war. I'm growing old Hakon, and am ready for some peace and would have young folk and life about me in my autumn years. Just come with me lad, we'll make a life."

"I never thought of farming, I've helped in the fields and such but don't know much … I can hunt though, Bjarke and I spent all of our young life in the forest. When I look back now that is where and when I was happiest."

"The hunting is good in the north, Hakon. Deer, goats, wild boar, ducks and rabbits, wolves if you want some excitement and a nice pelt, the land is full of life. We have forests and fells, river and moor. The weather is cooler than in the south here but we have good long days in the summer, its good country for a man to settle in and the people are good folk!" He laughed and drew a grin from Hakon.

Fenrir barked and stood out of the column looking back the way they had come. A thunder of hooves saw a separate column of men cantering up the side of the road, raising dust as they came, a large banner fluttered above the riders showing a white wyvern on a red field. The horses were of high quality, as were the men on their backs. Big men for the most, sporting long moustaches and mail coats, their weapons, and gear stowed behind them on their mount, kite shaped shields slung on their backs.

"That's reassuring." Hakon said as the horses thundered past.

"Aye, *Huscarls* by the look of them. That banner means it's one of the Godwinson brothers and his warriors."

The long, irregular stream of Harold's army grew as the day progressed, men joining it from the surrounding countryside else catching up with the column from London or the north. Hakon glanced at the mile marker stones as they passed, doing the maths and calculating how much further they needed to march.

The third day out from London saw the column beginning to bunch up and thicken as men slowed their pace, watching and listening for news from the scouts. Hastings and the area the Normans were said to be in was close and thus battle was not far off. Early evening saw the army at a halt, for on a small hill, standing by itself, a twisted, misshapen and ancient apple tree stood, its limbs having never suffered a husbandman's saw were drooping to the ground, the main trunk all bent from the wind, a few bright green apples remained amongst the sparse leaves. As the light faded, the mounted scouts were returning in ones, two's, and small groups, when one of the riders slowed to thread through the men, Oshere held up a hand to halt him. The rider, recognising a *Thane*, stopped the horse.

"My Lord?"

"What's happening warrior?"

"Normans, Lord!" He pointed southeast. "Large patrols of them, way more than just usual scouting parties, they are obviously wary."

"They've seen you?"

"Yes Lord, it was sheer bad luck. We saw them first and fell back out of sight but one of our lads had his horse flounder in the marsh and couldn't get it out. Its whinnying brought the Normans to see what was afoot."

"Damn it! It would have been good to have stolen a march and surprised them."

"Aye, Lord, I hear the King is not best pleased."

****

"My Lord Duke! … My lord Duke!" The leading horseman pulled his mount up hard outside of William's tent. Leaping from his saddle, he thrust the reins into one of the startled guard's hands. William appeared from within the tent followed by William FitzOsbern and Roger Montgomery.

"What is it?"

"Saxons my Lord! Thousands of them!" He shouted all too loudly.

"William grabbed the man by his jerkin and pulled him inside the tent.

"God's bones, man, keep it down! … Now! Where precisely, and how many? Don't just tell me thousands!"

"To the rear of the low hills to the north my Lord, my best guess is nine or ten thousand men."

"Aha, and are they on the move or going to camp?"
"There was no sign of them settling my Lord; they were just amassing with more coming in from the London road as we watched."

FitzOsbern tried to speak but William cut him off, holding his hand up for silence, his attention not leaving the scout. "Now, think on but carefully mind, from what you have seen, how is the army made up? Archers? Horse? Heavy infantry? Farm boys?"

The scout was about to blurt his answer but William held up his hand. "Think soldier! … Think carefully!" He turned from the scout to FitzOsbern and Montgomery and spoke quietly. "My Lord FitzOsbern. Rouse the camp, but quietly, no horns or shouted commands, have the men arm themselves and be ready. If I know Harold, he may try to attack us immediately."

"As you wish, Lord Duke." FitzOsbern slipped from the tent.

Roger looked doubtful. "Surely, the Saxons wouldn't risk an attack this late in the day; it will be dark within the hour. It would be chaos for them as well as us?"

"Local knowledge could count for much and Harold … Harold is a confident and able commander. I cannot afford to take the risk, Roger."

"But if battle is joined tomorrow, the men will be exhausted from standing to arms all night."

"Better tired, than dead! The Saxons cannot be fresh either; they've raced from the north of the country to here in a few days so they too must be weary. They too will have suffered a guarded night as they can also only guess at our intent. Remember, Harold knows me to be as belligerent and vigorous as he." William turned back to the scout. "Now, man! What can you tell me of the makeup of this Saxon host?"

"From what I saw, Lord Duke, there were very few archers amongst their host and the horseman were not knights, the animals seemed to be used as transport rather than as cavalry. There was a large number of heavily armed warriors, big men in mail shirts; I imagine them to be Harold's or his Lords personal retainers. There was also many ordinary folk, some better armed and armoured than others."

William looked thoughtful. "And you are sure of their numbers?"

"As best I can be, Lord Duke."

"Very well. You may go"

William followed the man out of the tent and noted with satisfaction that the camp was readying, the men helping each other into their mail and buckling on weapons. Harold would not catch him napping! He called for his armourers. William was already dressed in his leather trousers and shirt and raised his arms above his head so the hauberk could be slipped on. As the mail fell into place across his shoulders, the two armourers looked aghast, it was back to front. William, seeing their concern chuckled.

"Fear not, it's no omen, no ill sign, how can we lose when we have the Pope's banner and blessing and God on our side? Think no more of it." The two men smiled and continued their work, while deep inside William's mind he was troubled.

****

Harold swilled his wine, his face bitter. "Damn it! If William knows we are here, he'll be ready for us, mark my words."

"Is it not for the best brother?"

"How so?"

"A night attack is always risky, much could go wrong you know that."

"Aye, Gyrth but with our local knowledge and surprise, I would have risked it … still, the chance is gone, I must think anew. We will march early; I want us in a good position, on some high ground where we can place our shieldwall to negate William's cavalry. As long as we stay together behind our shields on a hill, the Normans can throw what they like at us, they will never move us."

"Men are still coming in Harold; can we not delay, even for a day or so?"

"No, strike while the iron is hot. Our father always told me that and from what the scouts say our numbers are about even with the Normans but we have the advantage anyway, of home ground and knowledge and give me a Saxon *Huscarl* over a Norman knight any time. Tomorrow at dawn, Gyrth, we'll teach William and his Normans a lesson, you'll see."

"Pull your hauberk on, Hakon, it's not comfortable to sleep in but it's better than trying to find it and fit it in the dark while being attacked."

"Do you think they'll risk a night attack?"

"I doubt it, without local knowledge, it would be a huge risk but from what I've heard, William is clever and does things people don't expect, so let's be ready, just in case. We haven't come all this way to die in our sleep."

Hakon shrugged into the leather lined mail shirt, ignoring the stink of stale sweat left behind by its previous owner. Lying his weapons alongside, he settled Fenrir next to him.

"I tell you, Hakon, I do sleep better with Fenrir close by, he'll wake us if trouble eventuates."

"Aye, you're not wrong Oshere. Fenrir has saved me before now … he and Bjarke made a formidable pair." Hakon smiled as his eyes stared vacantly, reminiscing. Oshere saw the look.

"I'm sorry for your brother, Hakon. I can see you were close."

Hakon snapped back from his memory. "Aye, brothers by tooth and claw my father said, Christ knows we had some scrapes." He smiled again. "My poor mother never knew if we would come home whole or in pieces." He chuckled. "She was fierce, kind and loving, bless her heart, she raised us well!"

"Happier days?"

"Aye! Methinks Bjarke had the rights of it too, he just wanted to stay at home, raise a family and hunt."

"Then the ambitions of great men came along and here we are."

"Aye, here we are."

The pair settled down for sleep with Fenrir laid between them. Around them, the Saxon army was also settling, men still wary of the Normans close by but thankful of the chance to rest after the continuous march.

Chapter Twenty Six

The morning, 14th October 1066 AD

The Saxons were on the move at first light and before the sun was clear of the horizon. Harold was anxious to be in a good position and thus most men breakfasted as they marched, chewing on bread, cheese or cold meat, if they had it. Being late in the year the morning was chill and damp and men pushed along at a good pace, keen to put some warmth into their bodies. The grass was wet with dew underfoot and the shadows still holding as the army pushed forward to find the Normans. The Saxons hadn't gone far when a scout came cantering back along the column his arm pointing behind him.

"Normans! … Normans! Directly ahead of us, two miles distant."

At the head of the column, Harold conferred with his outriders.

"Beyond the next hill, Caldbec, you called it? There is room for us to stand and make our wall?"

"Yes, Lord King. There is a long hammer shaped crest called *Santlache ridge,* just below it, which slopes down into a marshy area. We will reach it first if we move quickly and the Normans will have to attack up it, at us."

"A marsh you say? The weather has been unseasonably dry of late, how wet and boggy is it? Will it cause William problems?"

"It's not a marsh like the fen, Lord King, it's no great water margin and with the dry weather we've had, the best we can hope for is soft ground but it's not a great place for cavalry and with the hill to surmount the Normans will be disadvantaged."

"That will do, have the men move up quickly we need to be in position before William, he will not want to be in this marsh if he can make the hill, we need to hurry."

"Yes, Lord King."

Harold ground his teeth and muttered to himself. "Damn you, William of Normandy you move fast! But as Christ God is my witness you'll not make that hill and you will not move me off it."

****

William was riding amongst his men, chatting and making light of the coming battle when his scouts told him of the Saxons up ahead and the likelihood of battle shortly. Urging his men on, he called up his commanders.

As the Normans exited the sparse woodland, they looked across the sward to the gently rising hill beyond and the Saxons manoeuvring across the top of it. Thousands of men were on the move pushing and shoving themselves into position across the hillcrest. The Saxons were a blaze of colour with brightly painted shields and the morning sun dancing off their mail coats, while above them a great number of gaudy banners lifted gently in the morning breeze. The golden dragon of Wessex was amongst them, along with Harold's personal banner of the fighting man and the Wyvern of the house of Godwin. The Normans stared up at the coloured mass, the rising hill and the fast forming shieldwall. William glanced up at the assembling Saxons and then at his own army still spilling onto the field.

"What think you, my Lord Duke? Do we have at them before they form up?"

William was still assessing distance, numbers and the ground and answered FitzOsbern without looking back. "No Will, though they are not yet arrayed and vulnerable, so are we. This soft ground is not best suited for our knights and if the Saxons throw us back down the hill before we are properly drawn up we could be in trouble. Array the men as we planned; three lines, archers and crossbowmen in the front, the infantry behind and the knights to the rear."

"Yes, my Lord." FitzOsbern spurred away calling Captains and Marshalls to him while pointing out the disposition of the troops.

William watched from his saddle as both armies deployed. Overall numbers appeared similar but his advantage of mounted knights was being somewhat negated by the rising incline and shieldwall and the soft ground he found himself on. As his lines settled, he rode along their front.

"Men of Normandy, Britany, Flanders and those who have come from further afield, hear me. This is the day and the battle we sought, this is the day we make ourselves Lords of a new land." Some cheers came back at him. "All we need do is break that Saxon wall and we will have victory … fear them not, they have no unbroken record of victory such as mine and no cavalry to match our own. Be strong, be valiant, we will carry the fight to them seeing they will not to come to us. They are weak in resolve and their King is a false sworn, oath breaker, where we have God, the Pope and righteousness on our side. I have not brought you this far to gamble on a win, we win this day because God favours the just, the Pope says it is so!" He pointed to the Pope's banner held by his standard bearer, Count Eustace of Boulogne who rode alongside another man who bore Williams personal colours of a golden leopard on a crimson field, together they trotted along the front rank as cheers and a loud roar of approval rose up to meet them.

****

The Saxons spread along the crest of *Santlache ridge*, the men tightly packed into the restricted space, warriors still arriving funnelled into the rear ranks making a huge, solid block of men. Harold stood in the centre beneath his planted banners and waited until his lines settled themselves. Gyrth was off to his right with his *Huscarls* and Leofwine to the left with his, ensuring a solid line of mail and shields were being presented to the Normans below. Oshere, Hakon and Fenrir found themselves in the front rank and just to the side of Harold's *Huscarls*. Harold saw William addressing his men and also stepped forward, walking the front of his shieldwall.

"Men of England hear me! We are here today to once more defend our land and homes from a rapacious invader. Yes, we are many different races, Saxon, Dane, Norse and Swede but we live together and thus must fight together against an invader who would take all." Growls rose from the ranks. "I say this ends today! William comes with false tales of a promise of the throne and men at his back who have already done much slaughter and thievery hereabout; that is the style of him and his mercenaries, for that is what most are. I say God is on our side, God will see us delivered of this Norman filth. Stand with me, stand here on this ridge, firm and strong and together we will throw these Normans back down the hill and then from England itself!"

A huge roar came back at him followed by cheers and then a banging of weapons on shields, Fenrir, caught up in the tension and excitement of the din carrying to the Normans below added to it with barks and wolf-like howls.

Oshere leaned on his long-axe and looked at the Normans and then at Hakon.

"Well lad, we're here, just these Normans to see off and then we have a long walk home. Can you manage another couple of hundred miles?"

Hakon was watching William and the Norman banners as they progressed along the ranks; he paled and swallowed nervously when he saw the golden leopard.

"You alright, lad?" Oshere queried when Hakon didn't reply.

Putting Runa's dire prophecy from his mind he nodded and looked away while settling Fenrir as the shouting died down and men readied themselves for battle to commence.

"That's a lot of archers down there, I've not seen that many used together before, and what are those strange looking things, next to the bows?"

"Crossbows, they fire short bolts, I've seen them in the east they have good range but are slow to load. Keep behind your shield Hakon and close to me, a good shieldwall makes for good defence against arrows. Keep Fenrir in tight, under your shield."

The shouting had died away now and men had taken to their devotions. On both sides, priests moved amongst the men calling out prayers and making the sign of the cross. Some soldiers fell to their knees, their hands clasped together, praying aloud, while others bowed their heads and mumbled quietly into their chests, some held up their swords, the hilt and cross guard making a crude crucifix. Hakon raised his crucifix to his lips and kissed it, Oshere bowed his head low as he leaned on his long-axe and mumbled his prayers into his beard.

As the priests withdrew men took a moment to study their enemy, some chatted loudly hiding their nerves in talk, others stood quietly while one or two vomited, many had a sudden need to piss. Ale and wine skins were passed around and shared; men shook hands amidst grim jokes. A sudden loud and brassy call of trumpets from the Norman ranks caught everyone's attention, the Saxons answering with hunting horns and a loud aggressive roar and a banging of weapons on shields.

As the noise fell away, commands of 'loose, loose!' heralded the whoosh of wind over feathers as the archers let fly against the Saxon ranks. The shafts arched upwards in a dense cloud, going black against the bright morning sun then fell onto the raised shields of the Saxon wall. A loud clatter and thudding like that of summer hail followed, along with the odd scream as a shaft slipped through the wooden roof. Another half-dozen salvos followed but to little effect to the Saxon front rank, the only casualties being some of the men without shields at the rear of the wall. When the arrow storm stopped, the Saxons let out a mighty cheer and lowered their shields, jeering at the Normans. William wasted no time and ordered his heavy infantry up the hill, the mail clad and helmeted men coming on in a broad line with their shields raised, swords and spears sticking over their shield rims. The Saxon archers; spread across the front ranks appeared from behind the safety of their comrade's shields and loosed into the advancing Normans. Negotiating the hill and the uneven ground the Norman infantry made for reasonably easy targets as they could not form a cohesive shieldwall and soon wounded and dying men began to litter the slope. As the Normans pushed on, stepping over their dead and injured comrades they came within javelin range then throwing stick and axe range, the maelstrom of missiles slowing their advance as more men fell. Thus, it was a ragged and breathless attack that clashed weakly with the stout Saxon wall.

The whole of the front Saxon rank was engaged now; the Saxons having the advantage of higher ground beat down into the attackers with a ferocity that prevented any piercing of the line. Spears struck out, swords stabbed from under shields while the long-axes of the *Huscarls* chopped ruin into the Normans. Oshere laid about him with his long-axe, destroying shields, heads and limbs and scattering the Normans within its reach, Hakon darted forward with his shield guarding Oshere's flank and dispatching any wounded that fell beneath the axes blows. The hill seethed with men packed almost shoulder to shoulder, hacking and pushing then falling as they went down under the Saxon onslaught. The melee raged for almost an hour, the ferocity only easing as men wearied and leaving the Normans no further than the front of the seemingly unbreakable Saxon wall. As flesh and bone reached its limit, the attack faltered. William, seeing the difficulty and the waning charge had the recall sounded. The Normans began backing away, some Saxons stepping after them before they were barked back into line by their comrades. With the Normans falling back the Saxons began rattling weapons on their shields again and the cries of 'out, out, out!' rent the air.

"Alright lad?" Oshere shouted to Hakon above the din.

Hakon grinned from behind his shield. "That hurt them!"

"Aye and the more bodies on the hill the better, that will make it difficult for their knights to press home a charge."

Trumpets sounding again interrupted the diatribe and all along the line shields raised and locked together once more. The Norman archers fired another half-dozen salvos, again to little affect before being commanded to cease. At the foot of the hill the Norman cavalry began moving, the horses were not large, more like ponies but each held an armoured and lance wielding warrior on its back. They came on at the walk and then the canter, the mounts being spurred hard as they reached the bottom of the hill and their pace slowed. Above the rumble of hooves, the knights roared their war cries of 'Saint Denis' and 'Normandy' as they came on. The Saxon bowmen took advantage of the slowing targets and sent arrows whistling down the hill, emptying a few saddles and killing a number of horses. As the knights came closer, the hill kept them to a canter and they suffered the same missile storm as the infantry, men, and horses went down either to arrows, stones and javelins or tripping over the bodies of the infantry. Upon reaching the Saxons' shields, the horses shied away from the unmoving mass and their riders had to content themselves with hurling lances, maces or hand axes into the solid mass of men.

"Watch my side, Hakon!" Oshere bellowed as he stepped forward a pace and brought the long-axe down on a rider. The heavy blade broke through the chainmail, chopping the Norman's sword arm off and cleaving his ribcage, the man rolled off his mount backwards in a shower of blood. Hakon held his shield high in defence as another knight rode in with his lance lowered at Oshere. Suddenly the man was catapulted from his horse as it was tripped by a Saxon spearman. The knight hit the grass and lay still; the horse stumbling over then falling on top of him whickering horribly as it went down. The Norman charge began to falter again, the knights unable to make any dent in the wall and struggling with their mounts as they shied and stepped along the uneven ridgeline. Again, the trumpets sounded and the knights began to disengage, arrows and javelins followed them down the hill emptying more saddles. On the Saxon side, the wounded were helped or passed back through the ranks while the dead were eased out the front, adding to the Norman dead on the hill. With all three attacks having failed and the Norman knights falling back in some disarray the Saxons began singing, punctuating each verse with the cries of 'out, out, out!'

The lull in the fighting had men snatching a drink and helping the wounded back into the safety of their ranks. A Norman knight pushed out from the lines and walked his horse up the hill towards the Saxons. Slinging his shield on his back he drew his sword and began to swing it dextrously in circles before flicking it high in the air and catching it again. Steering his horse with his knees he continued up the hill whilst increasing the display with his sword. Having caught it a few times by the hilt he changed to catching it by the point then proceeded to balance it in his gloved hand before throwing it high once more and catching it by the hilt again. Men from both sides cheered as he performed.

"Who in God's name is that?" FitzOsbern growled.

"Whoever it is, he's buying us some time." William answered.

"It's Taillefer of Bayeux, brother." Odo said. "He's a strange man but a brave one."

Taillefer was now close to the Saxon line and shields rose as he approached. Suddenly a Saxon darted from the wall and jabbed a spear at him. The Norman dodged the blow, caught the spear in one hand while deftly swinging his sword to decapitate the Saxon. Spinning the spear in his hand, he spiked the head like a turnip and held it aloft. The Norman ranks exploded into cheers while the Saxons growled, two men stepped forward to attack the rider. Taillefer spun the spear, flinging the head off it and quickly jabbed at the first man who literally ran onto the spear point, the second man he killed with a sword slash to the face. As the Norman ranks erupted at the display, Harold growled.

"Somebody kill that bastard before he fires the Normans up again."

Some *Huscarls* went to move forward but Oshere was closer and quicker. Brandishing his long- axe, he stepped towards the knight. Taillefer turned his mount and spurred it, trying to ride the wrong side of Oshere's axe. The big man stood his ground and chopped the axe into the oncoming horse, splitting its head and neck almost down to its withers. The horse collapsed in a welter of blood and Taillefer went down with it, Oshere stepping in and decapitating him with his next blow. Dropping his axe in the grass he picked up the helmeted head in two hands and showed it to the Saxons, they cheered loudly as he turned and hurled it down the hill towards the Normans.

FitzOsbern looked at Odo and shook his head. "Damn it! That's bolstered them even further!" He turned to find William but found him gone and already organising the archers and the infantry for another attack.

Regrouping his men, William launched both infantry and cavalry at the Saxon line. However, pushing up a hill covered in bodies, blood, gore and severed limbs proved difficult and the attack met with the same result as the first and the Bretons on the Norman left flank lost heart and turned to flee. The cavalry overtook their infantry, riding over the small hill previously at their backs; they rode straight into a deep-banked stream and the soft marshy ground. Men and horses went down like ninepins, the infantry following on compounding the chaos. A cry went up from the Norman ranks that the Duke was also down and then the Saxon line broke, the men running downhill chasing after the fleeing Bretons.

Hakon whooped loudly and went to follow but Oshere seized him by his sword belt.

"Whoa lad! Stay by me!"

"But they're fleeing, they …"

"Maybe! If they are, we will have plenty time to catch them. Look! The rest of their army still holds." He pointed to the Norman centre and right flank. "This isn't over, believe me!"

Chapter Twenty seven

The Dragon and the Fighting Man must give way to the Leopard of Gold

William scrambled up from his dying horse. Badly shaken he took his servants mount while bellowing for his standard-bearer. Forcing his helmet back and pulling the ventail down to expose his face, he rode along the front of his men.

"I'm alive! … I'm alive! What madness is this, you flee from men that you could easily slaughter!"

Odo and others reined in alongside, corralling and shouting at the men urging them to hold while pointing at William. The rout slowed and stopped as men's nerves steadied at the sight of their Duke. Almost without pause, William led a detachment of cavalry directly at the fast approaching Saxons, who in loose order on the open ground were now easy pray for knights who rode at them slaughtering most of them. Some ran for the small hillock in front of the stream making a stand but the Norman knights swept over it, killing them all.

"Close up! … Hold there! … Close those ranks!" Harold Bellowed.

Back on the hill, the commands relayed over the Saxon lines and men closed up once more. Hakon looked at Oshere, shocked at the sudden turn of events, his lips forming words but no sound came out.

"As long as we stand firm Hakon, we are unbeatable, once we break and the enemy counter attack … well?"

Hakon, recognising what would have been his demise nodded slowly then had to face front as William now had the Normans coming back in full force against the Saxon wall. With their Duke fighting alongside, the Normans threw themselves at the Saxon wall again; the line flexed and bent under the impact but stubbornly refused to break. A hurled mace smashed into Hakon's helmet knocking him backwards and stunning him. Oshere roared and swung his axe at the mace thrower, the heavy blade chopping clean through the man's thigh and on through the saddle into the horse's ribs. As the animal collapsed whinnying and the man screamed, Oshere turned to find Hakon.

"Hakon! … Hakon!"

He reached down to grab Hakon who was on one knee holding his head, Fenrir was to one side pushed in close trying to shield Hakon from the chaos surging about him. The side of the helmet was dented with part of the eye guard broken away, Hakon's face was cut and bleeding heavily but his eye was intact.

"I'm alright!" He held out a hand seeking a pull up then gave a nervous laugh. "God bless, Bjarke!" He pointed to the helmet. "It would have been my eye if I'd had my old helmet on."

Oshere smiled, nodded, and steadied him on his feet. "Keep your shield up eh!"

Again, with the Normans making no headway, William pulled his men back but in an orderly withdrawal. It was now early afternoon and both sides were exhausted the battle having raged almost nonstop since nine-o-clock that morning.

Oshere pushed some bread at Hakon. "Here lad, eat! It's going to be a long day, they'll come again as they have no choice, they need to either beat us or die in the attempt."

Hakon tore at the bread hoping it would stop the nausea he felt rising in his stomach and swilled it down with some water then lifted his hauberk to piss. All along the line, men ate and drank what they could while others helped the wounded who groaned and cried. The grass was heavily trampled underfoot and slick with blood, the place stinking of sweat, ruptured entrails and emptied bowels. Men helped one another to bind flesh wounds while keeping an eye on the Normans who were doing likewise, the knights taking the chance to water their horses. Before long, a droning trumpet blast saw the knights remounting and the Norman infantry reforming.

"They're coming again! … Shieldwall!"

Men refitted helmets and hefted their shields; shuffling closer together again, they gripped their weapons as the singing started up once more, for at the base of the hill the whole Norman army was now advancing.

"This is it Hakon, the final push methinks, it's now or never for the bastards!"

"Then we go home!"

"Aye lad, then we go home." Oshere hugged Hakon roughly then joined in the singing.

The Normans reached the Saxon wall again and the fighting intensified, the Normans desperate to break the line and the Saxons fighting like demons to hold it. William was unhorsed again as a *Huscarl's* axe beheaded it but quickly remounted as a knight offered his own horse. Another hour of fighting saw neither side advantaged, and with exhaustion claiming all, the Norman trumpets signalled a withdrawal and men began falling back. The withdrawal quickly became what appeared to be a rout with men and horses streaming away down the hill. The Saxons roared and cheered, euphoric as they sensed victory and a huge part of the front line broke away with hundreds of men rushing after the Normans, whooping and howling like wolves as they gave chase. At the base of the hill however, the Norman cavalry about turned and rode back through their infantry straight into the oncoming Saxons, who in open order were easy targets for the oncoming knights.

"Christ God! A ruse. The bastard is aptly named!" Oshere shouted. A huge groan came from the men on the ridge as they watched their colleagues being slaughtered to a man.

The shieldwall closed again but this time the huge gaps left by the others saw it shrink dramatically. Gyrth and Leofwine pushed their men closer to Harold, Oshere and Hakon finding themselves absorbed into the *Huscarls* ranks. Meanwhile, below the ridge, not a Saxon remained alive and the Normans were massing to attack the shieldwall again. Hakon sensed desperation amongst those left on the ridge, they were quiet now and the looks on men's faces had gone from fearful hope of survival and victory to a grim realisation that death was coming instead. He squatted and hugged Fenrir who turned to lick his face, he offered his hand to Oshere who shook it while nodding respectfully and giving a sad smile.

"I'm sorry lad, maybe you should have gone home. If you have a chance, you …"

Hakon smiled ruefully as he interrupted. "No fault of yours Oshere, this was foretold long since, we cannot cheat fate. The dragon and the fighting man must give way to the leopard of gold."

Oshere looked quizzically at Hakon, not understanding. He shrugged. "It would have been good, lad, you would have liked *Dunholm*."

"Arrows!"

The shout and clatter of raised shields halted the conversation as men took cover beneath the wooden roof, while below them the Norman cavalry were once more forcing their mounts uphill their infantry following on. The sun was sinking now, the light fading to a pale wash of pink and blue as evening approached. The arrows fell thickly as the Norman archers intensified their fire and more men went down, moments later the Norman horse swamped the Saxon line forcing their way into the gaps. The *Huscarls* fought back savagely, momentarily stalling the horsemen but were forced steadily backwards as the Norman infantry came up behind their knights. The combined push forcing the Saxons into splintered groups. Gyrth went down to a Norman knight's lance, Leofwine following shortly after as the Normans flooded the ridge with horses and men. To the Saxon rear, men were already peeling away and running for the cover of the forest while Harold's *Huscarls* closed tighter about their King, Oshere, Hakon and Fenrir going with them as the Saxon ranks shrunk.

A sudden rush at Harold by five Norman knights split Oshere and Hakon apart as the horses forced through them, Oshere killed one man and his horse as they passed but Hakon went down to a sword stroke to the shoulder and neck. The four pushed on to attack Harold as Oshere rushed to Hakon's side. He had to push Fenrir away as the dog stood over Hakon's body with teeth bared. Cradling Hakon in his arms, he saw the sword

---

slash had ruptured the mail coif forcing broken links into the deep gash and blood was sloshing over Hakon's shoulder.

Oshere had to stand again, swinging his long-axe to fight off two infantrymen as they followed on in the knight's wake. Swinging high and letting the long-axe shaft slide through his hands he lengthened his stroke, the blow took one man's head off, the axe carrying on to smash into the other's shield, breaking his arm and shoulder and knocking him off his feet. As the man hit the ground, Fenrir leapt in to savage him, the man screaming as the dog ripped and tore at his unarmoured neck and face.

"Hakon … Hakon!"

Hakon's lips moved but no sound came out; his body shook slightly as his eyes flickered.

"Stay with me lad, stay with me! We're going." Oshere hissed as he lifted Hakon bodily.

Seeing two more Normans approaching, he lowered Hakon's body to the ground again and snatched up his long-axe, the men seeing he was uninjured and ready to fight and the snarling, blood-maw'd dog alongside, decided there was easier men to kill and veered away. Oshere looked about quickly and saw that Harold was down, the four knights hacking and stabbing at his body and that now, only small groups of *Huscarls* remained on their feet. The Normans were already killing anyone on the ground that moved and looting the dead of mail and weapons. Seeing all was lost; Oshere hefted Hakon over his shoulder, the lad groaning at the rough handling, then snatched up his long-axe and attempted to get off the ridge, Fenrir running alongside. All around him, small fights were still ongoing, horses whinnied and reared as they were forced over the dead and dying as the knights swept in on the few remaining *Huscarls*. Oath-sworn to die by their King, the *Huscarls* took a terrible toll of the Normans and their horses but inevitably, their numbers dwindled as the Normans kept coming. Oshere and Fenrir dodged through the chaos, man and dog slipping off the ridge and into the nearby forest.

It was already becoming dark beneath the trees preventing any large-scale chase by the Norman cavalry. Oshere laid Hakon down in the bracken and leaves, the lad's blood all over his hauberk and Oshere's hands. Fenrir pushed in close lapping at Hakon's face. Oshere eased the dog to one side and saw the wound was deep and Hakon's pallor white, fishing in his pouch; he stuffed a clean rag into the gash. Hakon whimpered and Oshere realised that the clavicle and top ribs were also smashed; he wet another cloth and mopped Hakon's face. Hakon blinked then opened his eyes.

"We need to keep moving lad, I'll carry you."

Hakon nodded weakly. He stifled a cry as Oshere picked him up again and placed him over his shoulder. The pair set off into the gloom, Oshere stumbling over roots and uneven ground and wringing strangled cries from Hakon as the movement jogged his broken bones. Oshere could hear the sounds of other men as they forced through the forest but so far no sounds of fighting or horses in hot pursuit. Running on deeper into the forest and total darkness, crashing into low branches he fell more than once. Breathless, he hurried on, desperate to be as far from the battle as possible and didn't see the ground falling away steeply in front of him. Men and dog rolled and tumbled headlong down the steep bank, cries of alarm and pain from them as they went. Oshere came to an abrupt halt at the bottom of the hill landing in a rocky stream bed. He dragged himself to his knees,

Fenrir coming alongside pushing his nose into his face and licking him. Gasping for breath, he patted Fenrir. The big man cursed and groaned as he struggled to his feet. "Find Hakon, Fenrir, find him!"

The dog padded off sniffing at the ground, Oshere stumbling along behind him. The pair combed the bankside until a slight whimper from Fenrir announced he'd found Hakon.

"Hakon … Hakon!" Oshere called huskily.

Pushing Fenrir to one side and groping tentatively over the body he found it bent around an old tree stump that jutted out from the bankside. Lifting Hakon gently he eased him clear of it. Working his way to Hakon's head, he drew no response to his frantic urgings. Undoing the helmet straps and removing it, he loosened the coif laces and pushed it back from his head. He felt hot blood on his hands and what felt like the broken bones from the sword stroke sticking up beneath the mail shirt at his shoulder. The cold air around his head brought Hakon around. He groaned softly and coughed, blood and froth sprayed over his chin. His hand slipped down his body to his chest.

"My ribs … I can't breathe …"

"What?" Oshere ran his hands down Hakon's chest and drew a whimper as he felt a spongey softness beneath the mail, the impact of hitting the stump had broken his ribs and going by the blood and gasps punctured his lungs.

"I can't breathe, I …"

"Shush, lad." Oshere whispered. "Here, I'll help you. I'll sit you up the bank that should help you breathe.

Hakon groaned horribly and coughed more blood as Oshere eased him up the bank. Sensing his discomfort, Fenrir pushed in again, whimpering and licking at

Hakon. Oshere moved the dog and offered a drink to Hakon's lips. Hakon drank, then coughed and sprayed blood and water, his head falling back.

"Hakon!"

Hakon's hand groped for Oshere's and locked onto it with a fierce grip.

"I've got you, lad."

"Thank … thank you." Hakon's other hand patted Oshere's shoulder a pained smile showing on his now ghostly face. "Remember … remember to tell …" He coughed again, his body jerking with the effort and more blood running from his mouth. "Remember to tell of my brother on the bridge." The words came out in a rush before he collapsed back onto the bank.

"I'll not forget Hakon, don't worry. Now save your breath … Hakon! … Hakon?" Oshere shook him gently. "Hakon!"

Pushing his face near to Hakon's he tried to feel his breath on his cheek. Feeling nothing, he reached for the large vein on the uninjured side of Hakon's neck.

"God, damn it!" He cursed when his fingers found no pulse of the vein.

Fenrir pushed in close, nudging Hakon's face he whimpered then lay down as best he could on the bank alongside his body. Oshere ran his fingers over Hakon's still open eyes closing them. Reaching beneath his hauberk, he pulled the crucifix from his neck pushing it into Hakon's hand and wrapping the broken chain around his fingers.

"God bless and keep you lad." He struggled to his feet then slackened his helmet strap and took a drink from his water skin.

"Farewell, Hakon Orrifostersson, son of Eysteinn and brother to Bjarke. I'll not forget you lad or you brother ... I'm sorry I can't bury you or raise a marker but you'll be in my thoughts and prayers. I'll carry the tale of your brother home and take Fenrir with me; one of you deserves some peace."

The big man tugged on Fenrir's collar encouraging him to his feet then stepped cautiously down the bank. At the bottom of the bank Fenrir stopped and looked back.

"Come on boy, we've some ground to cover before we reach *Dunholm*."

Historical note

The *Anglo Saxon Chronicle* tells of a giant Norse warrior that blocked the bridge at Stamford and held up the Saxon army's advance. He fought with a long-axe and is said to have slain between twenty and forty Saxons single handed, until he was speared in the groin from below the bridge. There is no record of his name.

King Harald Sigurdsson, (Hardrada) Tostig Godwinson and Eysteinn Orri all perished at Stamford. Harald to an arrow in his throat, Tostig 'possibly' slain by his brother Harold in the fighting and Eysteinn as he counter attacked (Orri's storm as it is recorded) with his men from the ships at *Richale*.

King Harold Godwinson allowed the surrendering Norsemen to go, of the three hundred ships that arrived full of warriors, only thirty was required to take the survivors home, such was the cost in lives at the battles at Fulford and Stamford.

Hastings or *Santlache Hill* was fought from nine in the morning until dark, making it one of the longest and bloodiest battles fought on English soil. There is much conjecture over the battle in regard to the Normans retreating and then turning on the charging Saxons, was it a pre-planned tactic or was it just luck that they rallied? My own thoughts are that the first retreat was genuine being brought on by fright and fear on the part of the Bretons, when they could not break the Saxon shieldwall. The second retreat I think could have been orchestrated by William, as a means of dislodging the Saxons off the ridge, as blunt force from numerous attacks was clearly not going to work.

William did have two horses killed under him and did have to rally his men by removing his helmet and coif to show himself as still alive.

Did King Harold die from an arrow in the eye? The Bayeux tapestry appears to show that or is the falling figure shown in the same picture, going down to an attack by a Norman horsemen, Harold? Alternatively, is Harold shown twice, wounded first in the eye and then hacked down by the Norman Knight? What is known; is that Harold's body was so badly mutilated, that his mistress had to be brought to identify his body by his tattoos that only she would have been privy to.

Harold's *Huscarls* are recorded as dying to a man about their King; such was the bonds of service and warrior brotherhood.

So ended a tumultuous period of bloodshed and violence in English History.

William was crowned King of England on Christmas day 1066, King he may have become but the conquest was far from over. Rebellion, on and off from the Saxons, invasion from the Danes and even rebellion from some of his own Norman Lords would keep William busy in England and Normandy up until his death in 1087.

Of Fenrir, Bjarke's faithful dog and Oshere, *Thane* of *Dunholm*, that is another story.

Poem

Stamford Bridge September 25th 1066

At ease and resting by Stamford bridge on this glorious, early
autumn day
Helmet, coif and hauberk, left on ship at Richale, safely stowed
away
Listless, mead-taken and careless the victorious Norsemen lay.

Drunk on the sweetness of victory, the Saxon dead beneath the sod
Odin and Thor to be thanked for defeat of the Christians and their
God
With bountiful England laid before them, the richness soon to be
endowed
When men's eyes turned suddenly southward to see a rising, dark,
dust cloud.

Horns blew wailingly over the meadow, summoning this Viking
host
Driving men from their sleep and their apathy the Saxon was upon
them almost
The dust cloud promised slaughter and death to those whom had
come to raid
Men looked grimly about them as they took up helmet, axe and
sword blade.

A war hedge sprung up like spring flowers as the Norsemen formed
line and file
A runner was dispatched to Richale for help, a distance of some
fifteen mile
To bring comrades and brothers, helmets, weapons, mail and shields
To arm us and bolster our ranks ere we die here in these English
fields.

*The Saxons came on quickly, King Harold's fighting man banner
to the fore
The shieldwall songs started in earnest as the Saxons advanced to
even the score
For the slaughter given at Gate Fulford the Norsemen must now
surely pay
We'll suffer you Northmen here in England no longer, not even one
more day.*

*Saxon speed and ferocity brought slaughter and saw the Norsemen
undone
Surprised, outnumbered, not ready, all that was left was to run
Crossing the bridge though they regrouped standing defensively
around their King
With axes, swords, shield and spears they formed a metal ring.*

*The Land waster's raven banner fluttered in the wind where
Hardrada stood giant and tall
As onto the bridge strode a lone Norseman, urging Saxons, 'Come,
I will fight you all!'
Hefting a two handed long-axe in great circles that hummed like a
winter gale
He slew warriors by the bloodied handful rending helmet, shield,
leather and mail.*

*As the Saxon dead piled up before him, he traded blow for blow
Sending heads, limbs and bodies tumbling down to the river below
The bridgeboards became slippery with blood and gore from the
vanquished dead
While beneath the bridge, the once clear Derwent water coloured a
darkest red.*

*As the axeman finally fell to tiredness and a spear thrust up from
the bank below
The Saxons rushed across the bridge once more to fiercely attack
their foe*

*The time bought by the brave axeman however, had seen the
Norsemen band
Standing shoulder to shoulder again about their King, they made a
final stand.*

*In this lull of battle Earl Tostig and King Hardrada called for
terms and quarter
We have no terms to offer you said the Saxons, except steel, slavery
or slaughter
There is one thing we will grant you, Hardrada and we swear it
now before God
That's an extra foot of good English earth when we lay you beneath
the sod.*

*The battle started up once more and a Saxon arrow transfixed
Hardrada's throat
The giant went down amidst his Hearth-weru, bright blood spraying
his metal coat
The Norsemen groaned as they saw their King fall while the Saxons
raised a shout
Death is coming to all you Norsemen, they cried, you are fighting
your last bout.*

*The Norsemen closed their shields tighter and grimly beckoned the
Saxons on to die
We still have steel and slaughter to trade they said, we'll leave your
widows to cry
Then battle joined again as the Saxons clashed anew with the
Norsemen's wall
Axe and sword blade beat on wooden shield and then did the Earl
Tostig fall.*

*The Norsemen roared their defiance still as their last leader fell to
the bloodied earth
The Saxons stopped fighting and looked to King Harold and
brothers, Leofwine and Gyrth*

*The Godwinson's rogue brother was gone now, dead along with his
Viking King
Would King Harold offer the Norsemen quarter now for the battle
was his to win?*

*But Harold had no terms to offer, the Viking will die right here
where they stand
They will pay in blood for what they have dome to our beloved kin
and England
The shieldwalls clashed once more then as the Saxons forced the
fight
Then from the east, a war horn was suddenly blowing and more
Vikings came in sight.*

*From Richale, Eysteinn Orri's men had ran in answer to King
Hardrada's call
Breathless and exhausted though they were they swelled the
Norsemen's wall
The Saxons though smelled victory and they would not now be
denied
Your numbers matter nothing they said, you will die where your
brothers died.*

*But Orri's men were grim and staunch and rushed onto the fight
The Saxons forced to give up ground to the new coming Norsemen's
might
But the Saxons bolstered their courage and weathered 'Orri's storm'
Their ranks did stiffen up once more, the shieldwall again to form.*

*More slaughter and death of both nations remained the currency of
the day
The Huscarls and Fyrd of England determined to make the
Norsemen pay
Then Eysteinn too fell to the slaughter, like his King and the Earl
Tostig before
The Saxon pushed forward to victory leaving his body behind in the
gore.*

From noon until dusk the battle had raged, the fields dunged with offal and blood
The Saxons forced the Norsemen steadily back, but together, boldly, they still stood
Ready for Valhalla and the feasting hall the brave would seek Odin's warrior band
Then just before darkness fell the fighting ceased as King Harold held up his hand.

Enough! He said, I say enough! Your King and my brother are fallen, both dead
Put down your axes and blades and get you gone else swear to serve me instead
We Saxons have battled you bloody this day, your brothers lay dead all around
No more blood needs to be spilled now upon our English ground.

So join me now or get you gone from England this is my one and final command
Else, you die you here in these fields as you make your final stand
Some Norsemen turned away towards their ships, thankful to be homeward bound
Others remained where they stood and collected their weapons from the ground.

Falling in with the Saxon rank and file then, King Harold led them all apace
As he retraced his footsteps southward once more in another headlong race
For William the Bastard had landed on England's southern beach
Another would be invader the Saxons would need a lesson to teach.

Also by Garrett Pearson

The Lions and the Wolf Series
The Orphan Cub
In Hannibal's Shadow

Printed in Great Britain
by Amazon